KYN KRONICLES BOOK 6

SHADOW'S FALL

JAMI GRAY

Cover Art: Deranged Doctor Design, www.derangeddoctordesign.com
Publisher: Celtic Moon Press First edition, 2022
ISBN: 978-1-948884-62-4 (ebook) ISBN: 978-1-948884-63-1 (print)

SIGN UP FOR FREE READS FROM JAMI!

Join Jami's newsletter to be the first to hear about new releases, free books, special prices and other nifty events.

Sign up at: https://www.subscribepage.com/jami-gray-books

WHAT READERS SAY...

About Arcane Transporter:

"Taking a refreshing approach to fantasy magic, this fast-paced, economical thriller is told from a highly likable perspective." — Red Adept Editing

About PSY-IV Teams:

"This story is an emotional roller coaster, from betrayal, anger, fear, love..." —InD'tale Magazine

About the Kyn Kronicles:

"...a fantastic paranormal action novel is quite possibly the best book I've read this year. I could not put it down, and had to exercise serious self-control to keep from staying up all night to finish it." —The Romance Reviews

About Fate's Vultures:

"...if you like your characters with a bit more bite, with secrets, with hidden agendas, and all those sorts of things, and your worlds are a far more deadlier place, then this is for you." — Archaeolibrarian

Also by Jami Gray

ARCANE WONDERLAND

Last Call

Bitter Spirits

Rune & Tonic

ARCANE TRANSPORTER

Ignition Point (*Prequel Novella*)

Grave Cargo

Risky Goods

Lethal Contents

Collision Course

Blind Spot

Terminal Drift

THE KYN KRONICLES

Shadow's Edge

Shadow's Soul

Shadow's Moon

Shadow's Curse

Shadow's Dream

Shadow's Fall

Tangled in Shadows (*Short Story Collection*)

FATE'S VULTURES

Lying in Ruins

Beg for Mercy

Caught in the Aftermath

Fear the Reaper

PSY-IV TEAMS

Hunted by the Past

Touched by Fate

Marked by Obsession

Fractured by Deceit

Linked by Deception

BOX SETS

PSY-IV Teams Box Set I (Books 1-3)

The Collapse: Fate's Vultures (Books 1-4)

The Kyn Kronicles Box Set (Books 1-6)

Arcane Transporter Box Set I (Books 1-3)

Arcane Transporter Box Set II (Books 4-6)

"What is madness but nobility of soul at odds with circumstance."

~ Theodore Roethke

Acknowledgments

While this is the end (for now) for Raine and Gavin, I want to thank you all for sticking around for the ride. This series wouldn't have be written without your continued support and gentle nudges to get back to it. So thank you (hugs).

Don't worry, this is not the last of the Kyn. I have many other stories with some of our favorite characters. So long as I can get time at the keyboard, I'll be sure to share.

To my eternal support team (Camille, Dave, Nana, Mona, DeAnna, Kim, and Angie), my personal cheer squad (my beloved Prankster Duo, my Knight and my mom and dad) thank you for believing from the first word. Endless love to you all.

CHAPTER 1

Raine stood in the spill of late-afternoon light, untouched by its faint warmth as it dusted over the gold threads that crisscrossed the medallion design in the thick rug. A tapestry of magic rode the air around her, and she carefully worked a thread of blue-tinted silver power into the existing weave of the subdued earth-tone colors that clung like ivy to the library walls. Her late uncle's warding spell was holding strong, but the time had come for her to claim it as her own. She raised her hands to direct a thread around a particularly dense knot of magic, only to be brought up short by Gavin's tightening grip on her hips.

"Wait!"

She stilled, both on the magical and physical plane. It wasn't easy, holding her place as she straddled the mortal and magical realm, but to rework the wards, it was necessary. "What?"

His hands left her hips, and his arms rose around either side of her. "Hang on," the whiskey-haired man muttered. He curled his fingers around her wrists and gently shifted the position of her hands and the magic she held.

In the colorful tapestry, the undulating lines hovering between her raised palms thrummed but held steady. Normally, the pretty light show would be visible only to her, but to reset her uncle's wards, she needed Gavin's help. That meant utilizing the soul-deep bond that tied them together so he could see what she saw, and that required dropping her mental barriers and being exposed on all levels. It wasn't just a mental and magical drain; it was emotional too. So, when he said nothing more, she warned, "I can't hold this forever, Gavin."

"Well," he said distractedly, "if you don't want to end up a Rorschach painting, give me a second."

He leaned in, and the heat of him pressed along her spine as his chin brushed against her hair. He traced a pattern in the air above her hands, his movements smooth and precise. The hovering magic gained weight and another black-flecked steel-blue thread appeared. It coiled around the existing silvery-blue line and darkened it to a lightning-streaked indigo. "Okay, now, bring it in slowly."

She heeded his advice, and the magical hum in her skull hit a bone-jarring, lower note. She held her breath and carefully nudged the shimmering thread closer to the bronze-streaked earth-tone knot of the existing wards. Inch by inch, she mimicked the knot's pattern until the two colors were a hair apart. On a barely there breath, she said, "Ready."

Behind her, Gavin's murmur rose and fell in a soft cadence as they tightened the threads that bound the warding spell and their magic together. A small, bright burst erupted as soon as the two powers touched.

Blinded by the unexpected reaction, Raine jerked, her head hitting Gavin's chest as she almost lost her hold on the magical threads and blinked rapidly to clear her vision. "What the hell was that?"

She didn't catch his answer as she suddenly came face-to-face with her dead uncle. Dark hair, dark eyes, and built like a long-distance runner, he could be any other successful forty-something professional, if not for the aura of lethal intensity that hovered around him. Her heart thudded painfully.

"Mulcahy?" His name emerged on an undignified squeak, and she reached out.

The image in front of her didn't react.

Gavin caught her arm and pressed it down. "Don't, Raine."

A vaguely familiar stylistic rune hung in the air near Mulcahy, the lines of which appeared to be shaped out of bronzed fire. Now that her shock was ebbing, she could see whatever spell had called the apparition of Ryan Mulcahy into being was tenuous at best. The rune's brightness fluctuated and dimmed. As unusual as that was, it wasn't enough to hold her attention because that was firmly caught by the achingly familiar features of the former leader of the Northwest Kyn, who now stood next to the library shelves. Mulcahy's image wasn't doing much of anything except hanging there like a mirage.

She swallowed against her tight throat and asked the man at her back, "What is this?"

"It's an engrammatic casting." He adjusted his hand until his fingers were tangled with hers, giving her something physical to hold on to. "It's old, old magic based on family lines."

Since her uncle had been around for a couple of centuries, that made sense. "Okay, and what exactly does it do?"

Gavin's tone was dry. "Think of it like a Kyn's version of the original voice memo."

She shifted her weight to the side and turned her head enough to see Gavin's face. "Seriously?"

He glanced down at her, and humor lit his jade eyes. "Seriously."

"Huh." She straightened, stayed in Gavin's hold, and studied the wavering image in front of them. Vague details behind her uncle's image made her think it had been recorded in the exact spot it was replaying. *Weird, but cool.* "So where do we press play?"

"Good question," he said. "Since it triggered when we reset the wards and you were the last of Mulcahy's family, let's try this."

He raised his free hand and made a motion that tugged on their shared magic. In an instinctive response, she loosened her hold on the silvery-blue threads as his voice swept along their telepathic bond and into her mind like a cool, clear breeze. *"I need you to weave this with me."*

"Casting isn't my thing," she warned.

"I know." His humor seeped through their bond. *"But this should be fairly straightforward."*

"You sure about that?" She wouldn't put it past her uncle to have left a few booby traps behind because, well, that was his world, and it was one she was becoming intimately familiar with. Lately, every time she turned around, she got slapped with another one of her uncle's well-kept secrets, like leaving a magical voicemail behind in his library.

"As sure I can be." Then Gavin's attention shifted.

The tapestry rippled, then the silvery-blue threads twisted and turned to mirror the stylized rune. It wasn't easy wielding both her and Gavin's intertwined magic, not even after months of trial and error to discover what they could and couldn't do. However, it didn't take her long to catch on to his plan. She let him lead since thanks to his witch heritage, he was the stronger caster.

"When I say," he warned, *"you'll have to work fast and braid the two casts together."* He began to murmur a spell aloud, and the black-flecked indigo wove between the rune and its reflection, knitting them closer and closer together. When the last line fell into place, his voice echoed on both mortal and magical planes. "Now."

Raine stretched the newly evolved piece of herself that lent her an edge over other Kyn by allowing her to actually see and manipulate magic, and she bound Gavin's cast to the bronze lines powering the rune. It was like forcing two magnets together. After an initial resistance, she made a minute tweak, and the mirrored magics slid together, the lines tightening until the threads appeared to meld. The magic fueling the rune gained strength and depth until it reverberated in her bones and teeth. The bronze lines shifted to a burnished copper streaked with blue.

"Cincinno clavem," Gavin commanded.

Deep inside Raine, where her magic lived, something shifted into place, and the image of her uncle sharpened into crystal clarity. Gavin's strengthening illusion ability turned it so real, she swore if she'd reached out, she would have been able to feel flesh and blood. Staring into her uncle's coffee-dark eyes lit with keen intelligence, she clutched Gavin's hand.

With a breath, the static image came to life then spoke. "Hello, Raine."

Hearing her name in the deep voice she'd thought she would never hear again hurt.

"I could start this with the typical 'If you're watching this...' but since I've yet to see something that hasn't come true, I'll skip the unnecessary parts and move forward on the premise that I didn't escape the assassination attempt." Ryan Mulcahy's smile was as wry as his tone and carried a depth of knowledge gained from dealing with the pesky visions that plagued a seer of his caliber. He tucked his hands in the pockets of his tailored black slacks. "And I'm sure you have an opinion you'd like to share, but luckily, this is a one-way message, so you'll just have to bite your tongue. I assure you, I did everything I could to avoid this particular outcome, but Fate is not one to be denied."

His brief glint of humor faded, and the normally harsh lines of his face softened. "It also makes it easier for me to tell you how proud I am of the woman you've chosen to be without us getting into an argument." He waved a hand as if she had spoken. "I know we've had our differences..."

That was one way of putting it.

"... but from the moment Catriona brought you into this world until I took my last breath, I have loved you."

Her throat tightened. She blinked hard to relieve the pressure behind her eyes and bore down on Gavin's hand.

Her uncle's image set his hand on a nearby shelf and shook his head. "I know you may not believe that, but love is far from simple, and sometimes, to protect those who hold your heart, you have to be heartless." His gaze sharpened, and despite his lack of physical presence, he still managed to pin Raine in place. "That's not an apology, girl, just a fact of life."

He looked away, brushed his fingers along the spines that lined a shelf, then fisted his hand and dropped it to his side. When he turned back, all the messy emotions were tucked behind his normal arrogance. "I'm not sure how long it will take you to find this, so I'll address the most important business first."

He folded his arms over his chest and settled in, his voice all business. "You won't want to hear this, but I need you to find your way past your issues with Natasha. She's going to need you, and the Wraiths at her side, especially considering that with my death, she'll have no choice but to take on the Kyn Council. Cheveyo and Warrick will both back her, and once Carys takes my place as the head of the Fey House, she'll stand at Natasha's side as well. Nat will need their support because she's never been one to tread lightly." He grimaced. "Hopefully, between the other three, they can counter her temper, but it won't be easy."

Nat? The nickname held an unsettling familiarity, but as Raine had learned just after Ryan's death, there was a shared history between the Demon Queen and her uncle. Despite her curiosity, there was a part of her, albeit a juvenile part, that thought, *"Ick!"*

As it often was in life, her uncle wasn't done issuing orders. "I suggest you and Gavin approach Darius Abazi, but fair warning—it won't be an easy conversation. You can, however, trust his information." Something dark moved across Mulcahy's face. "Some advice—be wary. Even an ally can unintentionally betray you."

A depth of hard-won knowledge layered his statement, and she wished he were there so she could ask for details, so much so that her chest ached. And that wasn't the only question she desperately wished to pursue.

His voice regained its previous cool composure. "With what lies ahead, the Wraiths need to remain strong because their skills will be crucial in protecting the Northwest Kyn. My hope is that they will be wise in their choice of leader. Nat will try to manipulate her way into the captaincy, but I trust you to ensure she doesn't succeed."

Her uncle knew Natasha well because she had schemed

and lost. The outcome didn't surprise Raine, not considering Natasha's target—the Wraiths, an elite group of Kyn hunters and assassins who lurked in the shadows of the Kyn world. Their existence was an urban legend to most Kyn, but they were very, very real. In an effort not to become Natasha's pet killers, Raine and the other nine Wraiths had chosen Gavin as their captain. His ruthlessly strategic mindset would play a critical role in the Wraiths' continued existence and hopefully turn the tide in the upcoming confrontation with the Northwest Kyn's most dangerous threat—the biggest, baddest, and oldest of the Kyn, their Council.

In front of her, the image of her uncle appeared to struggle with whatever he was going to say next. Finally, he straightened his narrow shoulders. "There is a unique bit of clarity given when you know your end is close, and I know I'll soon be answering to my sister for, as she would often accuse me of, playing games, but I promise, Raine, I never considered this a game. I know you have questions, about your mother, about your father, about your magic, but I have learned that sometimes providing the answers is more detrimental than allowing you the opportunity to find those answers on your own."

Hearing that, she felt old frustrations struggle to rise, but with no real target, ignoring them didn't take much. What good would it do her to rail against Mulcahy's obstinacy? Even in death, he'd managed to get the last damn word.

"Once Catriona told me about you, I started to shift the pieces of the Northwest Kyn into position. I wanted to ensure when you finally found your answers, you would be able to move the new generation of Kyn forward. We are old..." His voice faded, and for the first time she could remember, his age was apparent in the shadows that drifted over his face.

"Too old." He shook his head, and the haunting darkness broke apart and drifted away. His voice returned to its usual unforgiving hardness. "Too many of us are stuck in traditions and old beliefs, but those will not see us through the coming years. We can't hide from the humans forever, and their curiosity and technology are pushing the curtain aside faster than expected. Not only are we racing the clock, but we are on the verge of extinction, and our survival requires an evolution, not just in attitudes, but in what makes us Kyn. Our magic is shifting, not just in you and Gavin, but whether they want to admit it or not, in others as well."

Hearing Mulcahy voice a possibility Raine and Gavin had barely started to acknowledge, she looked over her shoulder at Gavin. His face was as grim as she felt. Together, they turned back to the magical recording that continued to speak.

"Those changes frighten the Council and others who consider themselves to be powers in our world. They are not ready to accept a new generation of Kyn or the magic they bring because it will change the Kyn forever. And what they fear, they will try to destroy." His dark eyes burned with intensity. "You and Gavin must become the shield for those who will craft our future. I believe the two of you will master the power you share, and when you do, you will become the example others will follow. As Wraiths, you are in a position of strength, so I give you one last assignment —find those like you and protect them, from both human and Kyn, from the Council's machinations, and from themselves. They are our only chance at a future for the Kyn."

CHAPTER 2

Raine stared at the spot where the image of her uncle had dissipated, leaving behind a glittering shimmer of dust motes. A heavy silence settled over the library, broken only by the sound of her and Gavin breathing. Emotions battered her, and her ability to hold open the door between the magic and mundane slipped. The natural barriers Kyn kept between them and the mortal realm snapped back in place. The tapestry winked out, and the world lost its brightness.

She struggled to process everything Mulcahy had said but couldn't get beyond the most painful and obvious point. "He knew." Anger inched out her ever-present grief, and she jerked free of Gavin's arms to pace away. "He knew he was going to die."

"Raine."

She ignored him as the emotional storm churned through her. It was like losing her uncle all over again, wiping away months of grieving and exposing the lingering wounds of his passing. Even hearing the three words her uncle never voiced until it was too late didn't help. Instead of grappling with that unexpected revelation, she fell back on old habits and held tightly to her anger. "He should've told me."

Hard hands caught her and held her still. "Why?"

Gavin's question pulled her up short, and she fisted her hands in his shirt as she narrowed her eyes and glared at him. "Because I could've stopped it."

"Don't be so arrogant." His tone was sharp, spiking her temper, but before she could let loose, he continued. "He said it himself: Fate won't be denied."

"Fuck Fate," she snarled.

His hands left her arms and cradled her face, his palms hot against her skin, his gaze knowing. "Mulcahy didn't tell you because he was doing what's he's always done—protecting you."

The ghost of the orphaned teen she once was railed in denial. She didn't want protection; she wanted her uncle back. Childish though the reaction was, it didn't make what she felt any less painful or real. It also reopened the hollow ache in her chest from the wound left by pulling Mulcahy's body out from the rubble of his magically bombed office. That same ache had never truly closed in the ensuing months.

This is what it means to truly be orphaned. Losing her mother to the brutality of human experimentation had shattered her world and left her struggling to find her footing in a changed reality under the ruthless eye of her uncle. But he was still there. This time when her world quaked, she had no one to hold on to.

That's not true. Gentle reprimand rode Gavin's mental voice.

She winced and angled to brush an apologetic kiss to Gavin's palm in mute apology. Tied together as they were, shielding one another from stronger emotions was difficult. He was right—she might not have blood family left, but she did have him. She drew in a deep breath and used his touch to ground herself as she admitted, "It was still a dick thing to do."

That earned her a dry chuckle, then he tugged her forward until he could press a kiss to her forehead. "It was, but it's done." He searched her face. "You going to be okay?"

She nodded, pulled free of his hold, and let him go. "He was a little late on the heads-up about Darius."

Gavin leaned back against the desk. "Guess it's a good thing I didn't take him out when he showed up, then."

It was her turn to give him a look. "Was that even an option?"

He arched an eyebrow. "What do you think?"

What she thought was that very little intimidated Gavin, including the imposing presence that was Darius Abazi, a member of the Sarielian Order, the Council level's equivalent of the Wraiths. Yes, Darius was a hell of a threat and not just because he belonged to the demon contingent of the Kyn.

Still, she had to agree with Gavin. If Darius had made a play against them instead of helping them uncover the conspiracy in their midst, then she would've been standing at Gavin's side to eliminate the threat. Maybe it was arrogance on their part, but an innate aspect of who they were was based on their inherent confidence in their lethal abilities. Not that they were invulnerable, but so far, the odds had favored them as they faced threat after threat. Although they were still breathing and those who were determined to take them down weren't, their continual survival had come at a cost.

Recalling some of those damages, she murmured, "So we'll continue to keep an eye on him."

"You still don't trust him?"

She couldn't shake the dark look that had crossed her uncle's face when he'd warned about unintentional betrayals. "I think he means well, but you know what they say."

Gavin followed her logic easily. "The road to hell is paved with good intentions."

She nodded and hoped it wasn't Darius who had taught her uncle that lesson because they needed the intimidating demon warrior. He was their inside source on what lurked in the depths of the Council. Then there was his relationship with Natasha, which Raine still wasn't sure she understood. The two scarily powerful demons definitely had something going on, but Raine tried very hard not to think about it. Hell, just imagining the deviously ruthless scheme-queen being involved with anyone left Raine uncomfortable.

She moved to Gavin's side and mimicked his pose, their shoulders brushing. "I have a feeling if he screws up, Natasha will take care of him before we even get a chance." Natasha would take the "woman scorned" thing to unimaginable levels.

Gavin made a muted scoffing noise. "You're likely right, but between Talbot and the Council, Natasha's already got her hands full."

"And whether she admits it or not, frat boy from hell's betrayal cut deep."

Jamie Ryder had been Natasha's trusted right hand and one of the Wraiths. That was until Natasha delivered his head to Leopold Di Marcco, a Kyn council member and the one who had manipulated Ryder into betraying Natasha and the Northwest Kyn.

"It did," Gavin said. "Which means we need to do our job and ensure the head of the Northwest Kyn doesn't get played by a Council asset." His *again* was left unspoken.

There it was—more proof as to why he was the leader of the Wraiths and not her. Raine was more inclined to focus on the immediate threats and leave Darius to Natasha. It made her glad that of all Mulcahy's legacies, she hadn't inherited this one. She slid a look at the man beside her. "I don't think Darius was Mulcahy's only ally within the Council."

His dark-green eyes met hers. "I'm sure he wasn't. Your uncle was a master at the long game. I'm sure we've barely scraped the tip of the secrets he was keeping."

That was exactly what she was afraid of. "So how do we find out who was working with him?"

"Natasha might know."

Raine snorted. "She might, but you and I both know that she's swimming in ugly waters, so if she gets bit, so do we."

For a moment, they quietly considered the situation, then Gavin said, "We need to confirm allies on our own."

She leaned a little deeper into his side and rested her head against his shoulder. "Yeah, we do."

He unfolded his arms and curled one around her waist. "We need to meet with the others."

"How much do we tell them?"

"Everything."

She raised her head and raised an eyebrow.

He grimaced. "All right, almost everything."

She stepped out of his hold and moved over to one of the leather chairs. "Yeah, I don't think telling a group of highly skilled assassins that you and I can play around with their magic will go over well," she commented drily.

That wasn't the only reason she stood apart from the other Kyn. There was also the fact that she, a non-shifter, could choose to shift into the body and mind of a black leopard thanks to the twisted genius of a mad human scientist.

She dropped into the chair, stretched her legs out in front of her, and laced her fingers over her stomach. "Not unless we want to go from hunters to hunted, especially after the shit Ryder pulled."

Gavin sighed, walked over to the chair next to her, and sat down. "With both Ryder and Sullivan dead, we're already down two Wraiths. Plus, Axel is still recovering, and I'm not sure how long it will be before he gets back on his feet."

Gavin's mention of the injured wolf shifter reminded her. "Did Xander tell you about the latest?" Xander, a wolf shifter in the Northwest Motoki pack, was another Wraith. She was mated to Warrick Vidis, the leader of the Northwest Lycos House. More importantly, Raine called her a friend.

Gavin shook his head.

She dropped her head back and told the ceiling, "Axel's been getting into fights." Not normal behavior for the highly controlled Wraith. But since the wolf was still recovering from a demon-casted spell that had almost destroyed him and his wolf, perhaps it should have been expected. "She thinks if we put him back in rotation with a partner, he and his wolf will start to calm."

"I'll talk to him," Gavin said.

They both fell quiet, and Raine could no longer keep her emotions at bay. After months of being tied up with settling her uncle's estate and hiding behind revenge-filled fantasies directed at those involved in Mulcahy's murder, a confusing mix of relief and grief was settling in. Did it mean the open wound of her uncle's death would start to scab over now? Did she want it to?

"What the hell are we doing, Gavin?" The question escaped before she could call it back.

He shifted in his seat until he was studying her. "We're doing what needs to be done."

She choked off a short, bitter laugh and pushed to her feet. "That's not what it feels like." She paced over to the masculine desk that dominated the room. "I know Natasha's got some grand plan to expose Leo's games, but it's taking too damn long." She nudged the leather chair until it spun around slowly. "It's been over six months. How much longer does she need?" It wasn't his question to answer, but he was the only one she trusted enough to ask.

"Taking on a member of the Kyn Council is no easy task, especially when Natasha is forced to work behind the scenes with unknown players."

And confronting Leo DiMarcco wasn't the Demon Queen's only challenge. After Mulcahy's death, Natasha had been left with no choice but to step into his shoes and lead the Northwest Kyn. That included keeping up the day-to-day business of the legitimate front of Taliesin Security, a multi-million-dollar security firm, and juggling the four Kyn Houses of the Northwest.

"What's really bothering you, babe?"

Watching the chair spin, she shrugged but didn't answer.

Gavin sighed and came over to lean against the desk's edge as she continued to avoid his gaze. "You know, if you don't tell me, I could cheat and sneak a peek."

Her eyes snapped to his, and she glared. "You promised."

His lips twitched at her admittedly childish response. "I did, but so did you."

Since she didn't want him utilizing the emotional bond they shared that tied them tighter than tight, she admitted reluctantly, "I didn't understand."

Clearly not following her, he frowned. "Understand what?"

She swallowed and met his gaze. "Why he left this." She waved a hand around. "All of this, to me."

"You're the last of his family. Why wouldn't he?"

Raine folded her arms and just looked at him. Her relationship with her uncle had been filled with resentment, pain, and self-loathing. The last being shared on both sides, a truth she was slowly coming to accept. Years ago, when Raine and her mother had been kidnapped and experimented on by a human scientist, Mulcahy had been the one to find them. But he'd been too late to save his sister's life or his niece from the horrific experimentation that had changed her on a fundamental level. And that had haunted him in ways Raine was only beginning to understand. It was disconcerting to realize that she wasn't the only one struggling.

Gavin caught her at her hips and pulled her close. "He loved you, Raine."

Hearing it said aloud hurt, and the hot pressure behind her eyes blurred Gavin's features. Her voice was rough. "I know."

"And he left you all this because he knew you were going to need it."

Yeah, she realized that, too, after Mulcahy issued his last order. She hadn't initially planned on giving up her home and the isolated land it sat on, but Mulcahy had been the last of her family. So, she'd made the choice to take what he offered. But she got the reason why now after he all but ordered her and Gavin to create a safe haven. Between the spectacular custom home on a private island nestled in Lake Oswego and the substantial financial portfolio she hadn't even looked at, it would be difficult to reject his last wish. So here she was, tying up the last of a life that held more secrets than she could comprehend.

She unfolded her arms and held on to Gavin. "We," she corrected. When he looked at her questioningly, she elaborated, "We need this."

She had already asked him to move in with her and not just because rambling around this place alone would depress the hell out of her.

A spark of humor slipped under his somber mask. "Okay, we need this."

She worried her lip and snuck a look at the man who held her heart. "Are you sure you're okay with this?" She hated to ask and normally would slap herself silly for being so unsure around him, but she wasn't the only one to upend her life.

"This being…"

"Moving in here… with me."

He slid his hands from her hips to the small of her back, holding her in a loose hug. "Raine, if I didn't want to do it, I would have never agreed."

There was no way to miss his sincerity. She dropped her head to his chest and admitted softly, "I miss him."

Gavin tightened his hold, brushed his lips over her hair, and rested his cheek against the top of her head. "Yeah, me too."

She closed her eyes and let the momentary reprieve settle around them. It didn't last long.

Gavin's phone vibrated in his pocket, demanding attention. She shifted so he could pull it out. With all that was happening, they couldn't afford to ignore it.

He looked at the screen and frowned.

"What?"

"Local number," he said then answered. "Hello?"

"Gavin?" A faint voice came through.

Gavin's arm fell away from Raine, and he stepped back, a frown carving deep lines across his forehead. "Mom?"

Mom? Shock rocked Raine, and she missed the response. Gavin went to turn away, but she grabbed his hand and held him in place.

Gavin turned to look at her, his phone at his ear, his attention clearly on his caller. "Why?" Any trace of his softer side was lost under the cool, dismissive tone.

That wasn't a surprise, considering his strained relationship with his mother. He hadn't shared more than the bare essentials with Raine, and with all that had happened, she hadn't pushed for details.

Gavin pulled the phone from his ear, thumbed the screen, and held it out so Raine could hear.

"... in town for a meeting." The feminine voice was on the lower end, with a warm, husky overtone.

Gavin glared at his phone. "A meeting?"

"Yes." His mother's tone made it clear she wasn't about to be questioned. "Since I'm here, I thought we could meet, for drinks and dinner."

His jaw tightened, and he gritted out, "I don't think that's going to work."

"Gavin"—there was a heavy unspoken reprimand in his name only a parent could achieve—"we need to talk."

"No, we don't."

Raine squeezed his wrist, and when he looked at her, she cocked her head. In the depths of his eyes, an emotional storm raged, and she recognized it for what it was—a mix of guilt, resentment, and hurt. Surrounded by the evidence of how fast things could change and the regret it could bring, she brushed a careful *"Gavin"* along their bond. She didn't dare encroach any deeper because this was his, and when he was ready, he would share. It was the deal they made when they realized just how connected they'd become.

There was a weighted silence on the other end, then as if the word was wrenched from her, his mother added, "Please."

Gavin looked away and stared unseeingly at the windows behind Raine, emotions chasing across his face. The quiet ticked by as he struggled, his body stiff, his tension palpable. Raine felt the moment he made his decision, and the humming tension disappeared. "Fine. What time?"

"Thank you." There was no missing her relief and sincerity. "I... we..." She struggled before regaining her composure. "There's things I need to explain."

"Mother..." Gavin's patience was waning. "What time?"

"Seven? There's a restaurant downstairs. The Porter's Club, I believe it's called. I'll reserve a table for us."

He looked at Raine and told his mother, "Add a seat. I'll be bringing someone."

This time, it was his mother's turn to pause. "You're bringing someone?"

"Yes, and since I have no plans of keeping things from her, whatever you have to say can be said to both of us."

Her voice was agitated when she said, "I'm not sure tha—"

A muffled pop sounded, one Raine couldn't place, followed by a startled exclamation. Then there was a clamor of noise that indicated the phone had been dropped, followed by a muffled exchange.

"Mom?" Gavin called, his demeanor switching from pissed to worried in a blink. "Mom? What's going on?"

His only answer was dead air as the phone disconnected.

CHAPTER 3
GAVIN

Gavin followed the GPS's directions to the downtown hotel called High Pointe and made the twenty-minute drive in record time. The entire way, he did his best to not think. Not to dwell on what was behind his mother's aborted conversation. Not to obsess over whatever mess she had once again dragged to his door. But it was pointless. It never failed—any time Nyla Durand made an appearance, trouble followed.

Like I don't have enough shit to handle right now.

He was just beginning to find his footing with the Wraiths. The initial twelve-member group was down to ten, and two of those weren't fully operational. Axel was dealing with nearly losing his inner wolf, and Chayton was filling in for Cheveyo the head of the Northwest Magi House. In an attempt to discover how deep Leo's rot had spread, Cheveyo and Tala Whiteriver, the head of the Southwest Magi, were meeting with the other Magi houses.

Although he'd been elected by the majority to lead the Wraiths, most were still waiting to see if he could. Hell, he was sure the only reason he'd ended up with the captaincy was the Wraiths' mutual need to spite Natasha. Normally, juggling the various personalities wasn't an issue, but lately, it left him gritting his teeth.

In fact, ever since that bitch Lawson had shot Talbot's trippy-ass drug into his veins, his hold on his temper and magic was slippery as shit. His temper was just a matter of discipline, but his magic was a different story. No matter how disciplined he was, the power that churned inside him was stronger, wilder, and highly unpredictable, which spawned insidious doubts that tore him to shreds. Whatever the demented scientist had unlocked wouldn't be stuffed back into a cage, and if he didn't learn how to rein in his altered magic...

Before that thought could finish, he wiped it from his mind so the silent woman sitting in the passenger seat wouldn't catch it.

He slid a glance her way, taking in the fine-bone jaw and the cat-like tilt of her gray eyes. Her raven-dark hair was pulled back in its usual braid. The thin, scattered streaks of white were visual reminders of their ordeal in Arizona. Unlike most with Fey blood, her beauty wasn't the otherworldly type. Instead, it reflected the lethally mesmerizing soul she carried. From the beginning, that core inner strength had fascinated him, but now, he counted on it as he fought to reclaim what Lawson had stripped from him.

She turned those quicksilver eyes his way, and whatever she saw had her reaching out to cover his hand that was fisted on the console between them—an unspoken declaration from a woman who rarely exposed her softer side. He aimed his attention back to the road but brought their joined hands up and rubbed her knuckles over his jaw, taking comfort in her touch. He was becoming more and more comfortable with her mental touch, even as it brushed against his soul. If anyone had told him a year ago that he would voluntarily tie himself to a woman at a soul-deep level, he would have laughed his ass off. If they had told him that woman would be Raine McCord, the surly, temperamental, sexy, stubborn, mysterious, and undeniably feminine Wraith, he would have questioned their mental faculties. But that was exactly what had happened, and fuck him if he wasn't thanking all the gods that it had.

He continued to hold her hand as he turned into the maze of downtown streets and used her touch to curb his growing worry. In minutes, he was pulling into High Pointe's valet lane. He got out, tossed the keys of Raine's SUV to the young valet, and hit the lobby doors, Raine on his heels. He beelined to the reception desk, where the twenty-something clerk stared wide-eyed at his approach. Urgency rode his ass and left him too impatient to be polite. He barked, "Nyla Durand's room."

The young woman's professional smile dimmed, and her mouth opened and closed, but no sound came out.

"Nyla Durand's room," he repeated as he loomed at the counter.

Raine put a restraining hand on his arm and leaned in to gain the girl's attention. "You have a guest, Nyla Durand. She's his mother. They were on the phone, and the call was dropped. We're concerned about her."

The receptionist's gaze bounced between the two of them, and her smile grew strained. Gavin knew the next words out of her mouth would be something along the lines of privacy. Before he could react, he felt Raine's magic uncoil. He may not have her ability to see magic unless she shared it with him, but there was no mistaking the skin-ruffling brush of Fey-based magic as it swept by him to wrap around the clerk. The strained smile eased into something more genuine, and the woman's focus homed in on Raine. Humans called it glamor. Gavin called it expediency, and so did Raine, apparently.

Raine gentled her tone as the magic settled in. "Could you please verify her room number for us?"

The receptionist nodded eagerly and turned to her computer. Gavin fought the urge to snap at her to hurry the hell up as they waited.

Lines formed on the woman's forehead as she hit a couple more keys. Then she looked up. "I'm sorry. My computer's having an issue. I'll just…" She indicated another terminal farther down the counter. Without waiting for Raine's response, she scurried over to it.

Raine winced, stepped back from the counter, and muttered, "Sorry, forgot."

"You're good," he murmured back. Raine had a love-hate relationship with all things electronic. She'd told him once she loved to hate it, and it returned the favor. Some part of her magic did not play well with technology. At least she was thinking straight enough to use it, even if it interfered with the computer.

"Ma'am," the receptionist called as she headed back toward them, her gaze on Raine, Gavin all but forgotten. "It's 591. Do you want me to call up?"

"No, thanks," Raine said.

Gavin turned and headed toward the elevator. He hit the call button. Raine came up to his side as the doors opened, and she followed him inside. Instead of hitting the button for the fifth floor, he hit Four. He wasn't about to walk into an ambush blindly. He caught Raine's look and gave her a one-word explanation: "Stairs."

She nodded, shifted closer to him, and put her hand on his shoulder. He looked back to see her lift her boot and fiddle with it. He angled his body to block her movements from any watching electronic eyes. When she dropped her foot back to the floor, he caught the glint of metal along the inside of her wrist. His lips quirked as he turned to watch the light over the door. His woman tended to tuck blades everywhere, and she had just palmed one of them. Neither one of them carried guns because Kyn and guns didn't always work together. They preferred edged weapons that wouldn't falter.

With no easy way to hide retrieving his blade, he drew his magic close, grateful when it obeyed.

There was a minuscule bump in the magic he held as Raine did the same, then her voice filled their bond. *"You'll need to take care of the cameras in the hall."*

"I've got it." He called up a concealment spell that would hide their presence from the hotel's security and held it at the ready. It was an easy enough cast for a witch, even more so for a Fey-blooded witch like him. There was a slight chance that those holding his mother weren't Magi or Fey, and if that was the case, they might get lucky with the hotel's security footage. He made a mental note to get someone from Taliesin on the security footage just in case.

The elevator stopped with a soft ding, then the doors slid open. He held his position in front of Raine, keeping her back as he used one hand to keep the elevator doors open. From inside the metal cage, he scanned the hall. The air felt heavy, and it was too quiet. *"Active magic?"*

"Not now, but recently," she confirmed. *"I'm guessing a silencing spell?"*

That made sense. He released the concealment spell and sent it down the hall like an invisible wind, taking care of the cameras. With a speed gained from years of offensive and defensive casting, he snapped a counter spell to release the unnatural quiet. Like a switch had been thrown, the normal sounds rushed back in, replacing the oppressive silence with the indecipherable murmur of a TV, the hum of the air conditioner, and the soft chords of music. If whoever had left the silencing spell was still here, they would know they weren't alone.

He took point as they strode down the hall toward room 591. It was the last room on the end and nearest the stairwell. Although the door wasn't latched, but propped open by the security bolt, there were no signs of disturbances. He stopped just to the side of the door and motioned Raine toward the emergency exit that guarded the stairwell.

She glided past him in silence and stopped at the heavy door. With the bond open, he felt her test for unseen threats, but he couldn't read the response. He tensed when she depressed the bar, pushed open the door, and stepped into the stairwell for a quick scan. That tension remained until she reappeared and shook her head. The stairwell was empty.

He stretched his senses, trying to identify potential threats that might be lying in wait, and found nothing. He reached out to Raine. *"Can you tell if anyone is inside?"*

She gave him a nod, and with the next breath, the world slipped sideways. When it leveled, it was wrapped in a vibrant tapestry. Gods, he loved this unique bent of her magic. Being able to see magical signatures gave them an unexpected advantage when hunting other Kyn. And with his mother involved, he needed every advantage he could get. Fading threads of virulent green and ugly brown, the remnants of spent magic, curled around the door and slipped through the opening.

Gavin drew back from the bond and let Raine lead. This was her magic. He was just along for a ride. He felt the tug and stretch as she sent it farther inside, searching cautiously, but he didn't sink into it. One of them had to stay in the mortal world in case something or someone came at them, and he didn't dare leave her back unprotected.

She shifted her gaze to his, her gray eyes now a glowing silver as she followed her magic. *"What am I looking for?"*

"Anything." It was a sucky answer, but all he had.

Her frustration drifted through their bond, but she didn't comment, just kept searching. The moment stretched, then she was back, sounding slightly distracted. *"Whatever happened left seriously murky echoes."*

That left his stomach in knots. *"Heavy magic, then?"*

She canted her head in agreement.

That didn't surprise him. His mother was a hell of a powerhouse. That was what made her a renowned witch in her own right.

But Raine wasn't done. *"Found traces of an Amanusa. Not many, and they're fading fast."*

A demon? What the hell was Mother doing with a demon?

There was only one way to find out. He used one hand to push the door open far enough for Raine to enter first. He followed, letting the door close as he stepped out of the small entry and stopped next to a frozen Raine.

The living room space was plush, and a partially open door on the right led to a bedroom. Clearly, his mother had opted for the top-level suite, but here were the signs they'd searched for in the hall.

The TV on the wall hung at an awkward angle. One of the chairs was overturned, the cushion nearby. At the window that overlooked a narrow ledge, a curtain rod was partially yanked from its anchor, spilling the blackout curtain onto the floor. Under the TV, a heavy lamp lay on its side on top of a dark-stained dresser. Fresh divots marred the surface, along with slivers of the shattered bulb that lay among more fragments on top of a crushed light-linen lampshade.

He went to step around Raine, but she grabbed his arm, pulling him up short. "Wait."

Fighting back the itch to move, even though clearly his mother wasn't here, he snapped, "What?"

She studied the scene, her eyebrows drawn into a V as she searched the traces of magic. "I don't know," she murmured. "There's something here, but I'm not seeing it."

He twisted his arm under her hand until he could thread his fingers through hers. "Show me."

She did as requested and used the strange quirk of their soul-deep bond to allow him to view the room through her eyes. Like every time they did this, it took a second for him to adjust to the undulating tapestry of magical echoes as it lay over the inert hotel room. The nauseating mix of green and brown sharpened into a tangled knot that hovered between the overturned chair and the window. The colors were fading even as he watched, but he studied that knot and realized it was a complicated cast. Tiny glints like flickers of fireflies teased the edge of his vision, making it hard to concentrate. He turned to follow one of those flickers, but it winked out.

He turned back to the knot, determined to unravel the spell, but a flash of stunning aqua interspersed with gold caught his attention. It licked along the knot's edges before disappearing into the ether. That thread drew him, called to him, and he realized it belonged to his mother. That wasn't enough to determine what kind of spell she had used, though. Whatever it was, it was definitely defensive, considering the knot was all but choking it out. He peered closer at the lingering magic, concentrating on the strangely mesmerizing pattern of green and brown. Something about that tangle bothered him, but he couldn't pinpoint why. The knotted mess made it challenging to identify, but he recognized part of the spell.

Raine went to take a step forward. "What is that?"

He curled his hand on her wrist, holding her in place. "Best guess? A retrieval spell."

Obviously reading his hesitation, she asked, "But?"

"But not like any I've ever seen before," he admitted reluctantly.

"Because it's fading or…"

He shot her a look. "That's probably part of it, but there's something more at work there."

She reached out a metaphysical hand and poked at it.

His gut clenched in warning. "Don't play with it."

She glared at him. "I was trying to figure it out."

"Well, stop before you do something that can't be taken back." The knot in his gut eased when she stopped playing with the threads. To ensure that curiosity didn't kill his cat, he raised his hand, and with a single command, the lingering remnants of the spell blinked out. With that weird knot gone, the traces of magic drifted away.

"Dammit, Gavin," she groused and released him from their shared vision.

Unapologetic, he let her go. "Curiosity will bite you in the ass, babe."

"And how will we figure out what it was?" she asked as

she bent to slip her blade back into its hiding spot in her boot.

"We'll ask Cassandra, later." With Cheveyo out on the road, Cassandra Miwa, one of the Northwest's oldest Magi and healers, was their next best bet for all things witchy.

Raine straightened, narrowed her eyes, and crossed her arms over her chest. "How much later?"

"After we find my mother." He wanted answers as much as she did, but one thing at a time. He crossed the space between the overturned chair and the window where his mother was probably taken and tried to piece together what few clues they had.

He turned in a slow circle. A hairline crack snaked from the bottom corner of the thick-paned window, but there was no impact pattern to indicate the cause. He ran his fingers along the crack and hissed when a brief sting nipped his skin. He yanked his hand back and searched his fingers for the minor cut, but the skin was unbroken. He shrugged it off and wiped his hands against his thigh. He righted the overturned chair, picked up the cushion, and found a cellphone. "I'll be damned."

"What?" Raine asked from the other side of the room. She set a silvery shawl that shimmered like a finely spun spiderweb back on the arm of the couch.

He held up the cellphone in answer. He swiped the cracked screen, and it lit up. Unsurprisingly, it was locked. He tried a couple of codes with no success.

Raine stayed back, probably not wanting to chance frying the phone. "Your mom's, I'm guessing?"

"Yep." Gavin fiddled with it. If his mother was like the majority of the population, Kyn or not, there had to be something on it. He tried a couple more combinations without success.

"I'm going to check out the bedroom," Raine said.

He nodded without looking up. Instead, he pulled out his phone and opened a custom app developed by the IT gurus at Taliesin. His mother wasn't one for complex technology and tended to gravitate toward simple codes. The app should be able to break the security fairly quickly. The drive to uncover his mother's secrets was gaining teeth. As always, when she tore into his life, she was going to leave it in shambles.

"Gavin?" Raine called from the bedroom.

He moved to the doorway and peered into a room dominated by a king-sized bed covered in deep jewel tones. Another one of those chairs that hotels provided as an alternative to curling up in bed sat on the far side. Two nightstands jutted out from either side of the wall art that doubled as a headboard. "Yeah?"

She was crouched next to a pair of matching roller bags —one larger, one smaller—that sat on the side closest to the door. The logos peppering the gray material of the cases gave them a feminine vibe. She flicked the lock on the larger bag. "How good are you with unraveling your mom's castings?"

"Decent. Why?"

She looked back at him. "Because these are locked, and I want to see if there's anything inside that will help us understand what's going on here."

He eyed the luggage, his frustration mounting. She spelled her luggage? Did she think that TSA was going to riffle through her underwear? He moved back to the nearby wet bar just outside the bedroom door, set his and his mother's phones next to the opened gift basket, and went back into the bedroom, where Raine waited. "I can tell you what's going on."

Raine raise her eyebrows and waited.

"She's playing games." It came out bitter, but then past experiences with his mother would do that to anyone. Why had he come? This wasn't his mess, and gods knew he'd barely survived the last time his mother decided to drag him into one of her schemes.

"With who, and why?"

He shrugged and tried to freeze out the simmering anger that threatened to erupt. "Don't know. Not sure I care."

"Okay." Raine drew out the word carefully. She studied him, clearly concerned. "I get you two don't get along, but she's missing, and it's not a she-went-out-for-a-walk type situation here." She cocked her head to the side, and her voice softened. "What's going on with you, babe?"

A muted ding from the elevator drifted down the hallway, but it barely registered as the resentment and pain that always rose when dealing with this mother wormed its way deeper. The threat of it triggered a whisper of warning, and he snapped closed his end of their bond. Raine didn't need to witness his lack of control. "She's a game player, and since one of her games killed my father, I'm not in a rush to get hooked into whatever mess she's got going now."

Understanding swept across Raine's face. "Okay, but still, it might be—" She stopped midsentence and used their more intimate form of communication to warn, *"Incoming."*

He turned toward the bedroom door. *"Who or what?"*

She came up behind him. *"Shifter."*

He strode into the front room with Raine at his back as the front door swung open.

Ryuu Kern, the Motoki Pack's Second and Taliesin's IT

Security Chief, walked in. His dark gaze took in Gavin and Raine's presence. He came to a stop and frowned. "What happened?" His attention went to the ransacked room behind Raine then back to Gavin. His whipcord frame went wired, and his voice took on a suspicious edge. "Where's Nyla?"

CHAPTER 4

Testosterone filled the air as the two men faced off. Before Raine could say a word, Gavin snapped, "That's what we'd like to know."

"Hey, Ryuu." Raine put a restraining hand on Gavin's back and tried not to flinch when he shrugged it off and moved toward the dresser, trapping Ryuu between them. "Fancy meeting you here."

The wolf didn't look away from Gavin, which didn't bode well. Stare downs with shifters generally didn't end well, especially if that shifter happened to be second to the top dog in the Northwest. Sure enough, an amber sheen rolled through Ryuu's dark eyes, indicating that his wolf was prowling just under the surface.

"Gavin." Raine sent the warning down their telepathic bond but got nothing in return. She frowned at Gavin's unusually aggressive behavior because it was completely unlike him. Something had happened earlier to set him off, and she had a feeling it wasn't just whatever history lay between Gavin and his mother.

"It was a last-minute thing," Ryuu told her without

taking his attention from Gavin. His body was loose under the black slacks and green dress shirt, but she had no doubt he was ready for any move Gavin would make. "Vidis got stuck with another meeting. He asked me to take this one."

The tension emanating from Gavin licked along Raine's skin, and she inched closer, her instincts whispering a warning. She tried once more. *"Gavin, what the hell?"*

This time, Gavin blinked, breaking his visual lock on Ryuu, but the tension remained. Gavin moved back near the chair and shook his head as if trying to shake something loose.

Clearly, he was agitated, but she couldn't figure out why. She kept up the conversation. "Can you share what the meeting was about?" It was strange to realize she and Gavin had switched roles. Instead of her being the one to start an argument or make things worse, it appeared this would be his turn. That just proved when it came to family, no one was immune to the drama those relationships created.

"I'm not exactly sure." Ryuu finally tore his gaze from Gavin, looked at her, and shrugged. "It's my understanding a meet was requested yesterday regarding a situation that might have spread into our territory."

Raine frowned. "And Vidis agreed?" That didn't sound like him. The Northwest Alpha wasn't exactly a people person and tended to like to know what he was walking into.

"He didn't have much choice. The initial request came from above him, and Nyla's name was shared as a contact this morning." As he answered, Ryuu's attention once more went to Gavin. "Are we going to have a problem, Durand?" There was an unmistakable growl in his question. If he had been wearing his fur, it would've been standing on end.

Raine turned and saw Gavin was now standing still. His head was lowered, but his eyes were locked on Ryuu. The muscles in his arms flexed as his hands curled and uncurled at his side. The rare show of temper was unusual enough, but it was the banked fury burning in his gaze that gave her pause. "Gavin?" She slid in front of Ryuu, deliberately putting herself between the shifter and the witch. "Hey, what's wrong?"

He gave a jerky shake of his head as a muscle worked in his jaw, and his body remained stiff.

She opened her end of the bond, but frustratingly, he kept his closed. It was times like this that she wished she had a better understanding of their connection. But soul-bonded Kyn were few and far between, and the closest example she had to pull from was Xander and Vidis, neither of whom were chatty Kathys. So she and Gavin were winging it. Not a comforting thought at that moment.

Ryuu moved up behind her, and Gavin's eyes snapped to the movement, like a predator sighting prey.

Yeah, something was definitely off with Gavin. She waved Ryuu back without looking away from Gavin's too-still form.

"Gavin..." She kept her voice soft and tried once more to find her way around the lock he had on their bond. "Look at me."

His gaze flicked to her, to Ryuu, and back to her.

Anxiety tried to take hold, but she fought it back. "You need to let me in."

He grimaced. *"Trapped."* The word whispered through her mind before he once again snapped shut his end of the bond.

Understanding hit.

Gavin was caught in a spell, and he was doing

everything he could so it wouldn't use their bond to trap her as well. Clearly, Gavin's earlier attempt to eliminate the spell's remnants hadn't worked. Casting might not be her thing, but she understood enough to know a trap needed an anchor.

Where in the hell would it be?

She throttled her urge to rush in and let her vision shift so she could study the area around him. When they'd first entered the room, the ugly green-brown knot had captured her attention, but there had been something else... something that bothered her. What was it?

The feline predator that was the other half of her woke to join the hunt, unhappy their mate was being threatened. Together, woman and cat studied the room on both planes. Unfortunately, there was nothing obvious. The floor and walls near Gavin remained empty, so she widened her mind's eye until she found it. A barely there pulse of ugly green-brown winked from the crack in the window. Even worse, a thin tendril coiled around Gavin's wrist was slowly winding its way up his torso.

The leopard deep in her soul crouched and gave a soft warning hiss. With no time for subtlety, Raine let her cat rise under her skin and partially shifted her hands until lethal, curving claws appeared. She ignored the growl from the wolf behind her. "Ryuu."

"Yeah."

"Don't hurt him."

Using the speed and dexterity of her cat, Raine lunged at Gavin and targeted that ugly magical vine. Her man was no fool, but thinking he was the target, he spun out of the way. By the time he realized what her true target was and went to stop her, Ryuu was there. He swept out his leg to hook it around Gavin's. The move threw Gavin off balance, and he crashed back into the dresser. No longer concerned with Raine, Gavin pushed off the dresser and rushed Ryuu.

Ignoring the two grappling men, Raine sank her claws into the magical tendril and proceeded to rip it apart. The thread disintegrated under her attack, but to make sure it could do further damage, she reared back and smashed her booted heel into the window. The impact reverberated up her leg, but the crack remained unchanged. With a feline snarl, she fisted her human-shaped hands and slammed her foot into the window again, this time fueled by desperation and determination.

A burst of ugly color flared then disappeared as the initial crack widened. Another wisp of color escaped as the spell dissipated and fractures spiderwebbed from the lower corner of the window. Determined to destroy the lingering magic, she hauled back for a third strike.

Her wrist was caught in a familiar grip. "Enough, Raine."

She stared at the now-shattered window, her chest rising and falling as she sucked in air to level off her adrenaline rush. She dragged in one more steadying breath and finally looked at Gavin. "You sure?"

"Yeah." He tugged her back from the window then let her go.

She was relieved to see his earlier anger and belligerence had been replaced by a steely-eyed focus. His shoulder-length hair was no longer held back in its usual tie but spilled around his face, and a red mark slashed along his cheekbone where Ryuu landed a hit.

Ryuu moved out from behind Gavin and retucked his shirt, his normally dark eyes a feral amber. "Someone want to tell me what's going on here?" There was a rough bite to his voice as his wolf clearly wasn't appeased by his tussle with Gavin.

"Whoever took my mother left behind a trap." Gavin ran his hands through his hair, pulling it back. His gaze swept over the floor, and he frowned, clearly disgruntled. "I thought I cleared the room."

"You did." Raine spotted his hair tie over by the dresser. "There wasn't anything left behind when you did your thing, remember?"

"But you sensed something," he pointed out.

"Yeah, but…" She picked up the hair tie and handed it to him. "It was well hidden."

He took it and quickly wrapped it around his hair, his eyes going to the fractured window. "A delaying tactic, then?"

Raine flexed her stiff fingers. "Probably." When Ryuu brushed past her and moved to the window, she couldn't help but warn him. "Careful."

Ryuu shot her a cool look then bent his head closer to the window and inhaled. When he straightened, a frown creased his forehead. "Witch and…"

"Demon," Raine added. "I'm not as familiar with their magic, which might explain why we didn't catch whatever it was they set in the window." She met Gavin's considering gaze. "The witch Ryuu's picking up would be Nyla, which leaves us with a mystery demon."

He looked beyond her at the window. "We need to talk to Natasha."

"I doubt it's one of hers," Ryuu said.

Raine had to agree. After a series of challenges that ended with Jamie's betrayal, Natasha had reeducated her people on why it wasn't smart to piss off the Demon Queen. That lesson had been taken to heart. "Probably not, but even so, she would want to know someone's playing in her sandbox." *Again.*

Ryuu studied the room with narrowed eyes. He stalked to the front door and stood there for a moment with his head canted as he scented the air. He turned and walked slowly back to them, his nose twitching. He slid around Gavin and came to a stop in the area where Raine was beginning to believe Nyla had been standing when she called her son. "They didn't use the door, but the scents are concentrated here."

"If they didn't use the door..." A Kyn could enter a locked room by Shadow Walking, but the ability to travel between the waking and magical worlds tended to be limited to those with Fey blood. Since that was something both she and Gavin could do, she had to ask Gavin. "Could your mom—"

He was shaking his head before she could finish. "No, my father was Fey, not her. The Shadowed paths are closed to her."

That left one other option. "The demon?" she wondered aloud. "Maybe whoever our demon is decided to use the Side"—a place she only recently learned about—"to pop in and snag Nyla, and then returned the same way?"

If that were the case, it might not mean good things for Gavin's mom because the Side was a demon realm and did not play nice with any Kyn. Not to mention it was a mind-breaking nightmare for humans. The closest Raine had ever gotten to the Amanusa realm was when Natasha dragged the traitorous Ryder into it to deliver her brutal brand of justice. Just catching a glimpse of Natasha's true form had haunted Raine's dreams for months. Not that she would ever admit that tidbit to the Demon Queen.

"If that's the case, we're screwed." Ryuu propped his

hands on his hips. "There's no way to follow them through the Side."

"No, but maybe Natasha can," Gavin said.

The room's AC kicked in, and cool air swept through the room. Ryuu's nose wrinkled, and he went wired. Raine opened her mouth to ask what was wrong, then he moved with the liquid grace only a shifter could achieve and rushed out of the room.

Raine and Gavin shared a look then followed him to the hall. Ryuu was halfway to the elevator when he pivoted and came back.

Gavin waited until he got closer to ask, "What?"

"Shifter." Ryuu kept his voice low, but there was no disguising the growl underneath. "The scent trail was already dispersing, so I missed it when I arrived."

Raine blinked. "The AC?"

Ryuu nodded. "It stirred up traces, but nothing trackable, which means it's been a bit since they were here."

That meant the shifter might have jack all to do with their situation. She sighed. A burst of canned laughter escaped from a nearby room. Not keen on continuing the discussion in the hall, where anyone could listen in, she caught Ryuu's eye, tilted her head back toward the room, and nabbed Gavin's hand. All three went back inside Nyla's room.

Once they were back behind a closed door, Gavin headed toward the wet bar. He picked up the two phones and grimaced.

Seeing that, Raine asked, "Did it work?"

He shook his head and turned to Ryuu. "We need to find out why my mother was here."

"I'll see if Vidis can get more details from whoever contacted him." Ryuu shot Gavin a sharp look. "I'm not trying to be rude, but before I bring my alpha into this, is there any other reason that someone would target your mother?"

"Probably," Gavin admitted grimly. "But I wouldn't know."

Ryuu's brows rose, but he wisely sidestepped Gavin's answer. "I'll see if I can get ahold of the security footage here before I head back into talk to Vidis."

"Before you go." Gavin handed over Nyla's damaged phone. "Any chance you can get into this? I tried the app. It didn't work."

Ryuu took the phone from him and thumbed the screen. "It's still in a testing phase, so I'm not surprised." He moved to the dresser and set the phone on top, then he pulled his phone out of his pocket. His fingers danced over the screen. "Let's see…" He paused and did some more finger dancing. "Yeah… okay, good." Another longer pause ensued as he did something with both phones. Raine was starting to get impatient when he said, "Got it." He picked up Nyla's phone and handed it to Gavin. "Here."

Gavin took it and looked at the screen then at Ryuu. "How'd you reset the security so fast?"

Ryuu's grin was fast, with a hint of mischief. "I could bore you with a long, involved explanation, or we can leave it at 'I'm just that good.'"

As Gavin scrolled through the phone, Raine rolled her eyes. "Ego much?"

Ryuu brushed his knuckles under his collar. "Hey, when you're good, you're good."

"Got something," Gavin interrupted their byplay. "A couple of local numbers called just before she called me, time blocked on her calendar for tomorrow morning marked private, and a text string from an unknown number."

Ryuu got serious. "Let me see."

Gavin handed over the phone, and Ryuu got to work, downloading the digital breadcrumbs. "I'll send this information back to Taliesin, have them start identifying what belongs to who, and have them let you know as soon they get that."

"How long will it take?" Gavin's impatience was clear.

Ryuu flicked him a glance then went back to the phone. "Hopefully, not long."

Raine figured that since he was Taliesin's IT security chief, he would know. However, there was no way she and Gavin could sit idly by while the electronic trail was traced. "While we're waiting on that, Gavin and I will go see if we can get a face-to-face with Natasha. Find out if she knows about any visitors." It was a lame attempt at keeping Gavin busy and not her first choice, but it was all she could come up with on short notice.

"Good luck." Ryuu handed the phone back to Gavin. "I'll let you know what I find out from Vidis."

CHAPTER 5

After Ryuu left, Raine and Gavin stuck around long enough to do a quick, but thorough search of Nyla's luggage, which turned up nothing of interest. Raine kept a close eye on Gavin as she zipped up the bigger case. "Do we take these or leave them?"

He avoided her gaze and stared at the bags for a moment. "Leave 'em." He went to turn away but caught her look and sighed. "If we take her luggage or check her out, it'll clue in whoever's involved that we know something's up. We leave it, and hopefully, they'll think we're still unaware."

She wondered if that cat wasn't already out of the bag. "Didn't tripping that spell already give the game away?"

He grimaced. "Like I said earlier, I think it was a delaying tactic to buy time."

Maybe, maybe not. Something about the spell worried her. She followed him out of the bedroom and toward the front door. "What was it, anyway?"

"I don't know." His admission was reluctant. He stopped with his hand on the door and looked back at her.

"The casting wasn't something I recognize, but whatever it was ramped up what I was feeling." He pulled open the door and waved her through.

She slipped past him into the hall and waited while he pulled the door closed. "Stairs or lobby?"

"Lobby." He tested the door to ensure it was locked. "Less suspicious."

She stifled her sigh because ducking out via the emergency exit would have been her preference, but he was right. The receptionist would be more likely to call in security if they didn't show back up. She followed Gavin's rigid shoulders down the hall and realized his earlier anger wasn't gone, just tempered. Once they were in the elevator with the doors closed, she asked, "How likely is it that they set it specifically for you?"

He braced his hands on the handrail and leaned back, his eyes aimed at the digital screen counting down the floors. "That would imply they knew we were related."

It struck her that he was trying too hard to keep his emotions from her. The realization stung, but she understood his reaction. Unfortunately, she couldn't leave it alone. "I didn't think you kept it a secret, considering you two share the same last name."

Silence followed them down a couple of floors before he admitted, "I don't, but I also don't go out of my way to acknowledge it."

"So you don't think it's a possibility."

"I think," he said as the elevator slid to a stop. "Even if it is, we don't have enough information to understand what that means."

She had to agree, but it didn't mean it wasn't something to consider. The doors slid open, and she walked at his side through the lobby. There was a young family checking in, but the reception clerk spotted them. Without slowing, Raine managed a polite smile, raised a hand, then followed Gavin out the main lobby door. They headed to valet, and the attendant didn't make them wait. After reassuring them he would only be a minute, he dashed off to get the SUV.

As soon as he disappeared, Raine pointed out in a low voice, "Eventually, someone somewhere is going to get worried about her."

Gavin settled his sunglasses in place. "Maybe, but until then, we let this play out."

She studied him carefully and recognized that he was done with this conversation. "Okay, let's see what Natasha can tell us."

Her SUV pulled to stop in front of them, the valet jumped out, and before he could hand the keys to Gavin, Raine snatched them out of his hand and aimed for the driver's side door. "Thank you." When Gavin's brows rose above the rim of his sunglasses, she called back, "My car."

She slid into the driver's seat as Gavin handed over a tip and got in on the other side. Once he closed the door and strapped in, she got them on the road to Taliesin's offices in Tigard. "You should probably call Rachel and see if she can make room on Natasha's schedule."

When she got a distracted hum from Gavin, she shot him a look. He was thumbing through his mom's phone.

"Gavin?" she called as she turned her attention back to the road.

"Yeah?"

"You going to call Rachel?"

"Not yet."

When he didn't elaborate, she stifled an irritated sigh and held on to her waning patience. She swallowed a snarky comment that would do nothing but aggravate him. *See, I can adult, sometimes.* "Why?"

"Because we've got another stop to make first."

She braked at a light and looked at him. "Excuse me."

His earlier grim look was gone, replaced by one she recognized—the satisfied look of a hunter who'd just caught the scent of his prey. "Found an address in her browsing history. Time stamp coincides with an unfinished, deleted email. Address is local, no name on the email, but the draft was dated yesterday."

That would be before his mom landed in Portland, presumably.

"Take 26 east," he directed without looking up from the phone. "Looks like it's Noble Fir Park."

The light turned green, and Raine made a right, heading for Highway 26. "What would she be doing at a park?"

"Hell if I know." His phone spoke up and told them it would take them twenty-four minutes with current traffic. "But if the email is to be believed, she was supposed to meet someone there today."

"So, we what? Hang out at the park and hope someone shows?"

"Got a better idea?"

Honestly? No. "What if the meet already happened?"

"It didn't." There was no doubt in his answer.

"How are you so sure?"

"Time stamp on the luggage claim ticket puts her flight coming in shortly before she called me."

"And since she was calling from her room—"

"Means she went straight from PDX to the hotel." He typed something out on his phone, and a swoosh sounded.

Since she couldn't recall any rental keys lying around

Nyla's room, it lent Gavin's decision added weight. She maneuvered around a slow-moving VW. "And Natasha?"

"I asked Ryuu to loop her in." He shifted in his seat, angling toward her. "If we're lucky, we'll be able to add more information to the discussion."

His logic was sound, but there was something in his tone she couldn't read. Add that to the fact he was still holding himself apart from her, she was uneasy. "What am I missing here, Gavin?"

A heavy silence filled the car before he reluctantly admitted, "I don't know what my mom's involved in, but I do know, whatever it is, we can't trust the initial picture."

His serious tone had her reaching along their bond, but since he was still shut up tighter than a drum, she found nothing useful. She offered cautiously, "There's a story there."

"There is."

"You want to share it?"

A long moment stretched by before he spoke, and she wasn't expecting where he started. "You're aware that there are other organizations like Taliesin?"

Where is he going with this? "You mean respectable fronts that Kyn can hide behind without frightening the humans? Yeah."

"My father worked on a contract basis for one overseas." Before she could ask which one or where exactly, he said, "Don't. Where isn't important here."

Since Gavin never shared about his family, and she found she was more curious than she realized, she snapped her mouth closed and listened. If nothing else, it would make the drive go faster.

"He met my mother while on assignment. He told me

later he knew when he saw her that she would be his. Unfortunately, he loved her more than she loved him."

Used to being the more jaded of the two of them, she was taken aback by the cynical edge in his voice. Clearly, his parents' relationship was an emotional minefield, and without a clue on how to avoid making a wrong step, she skirted around it. "Can I ask what his assignment was?"

His answer took the long way around. "Back in the mid-1900s, right around the same time the second Industrial Revolution was gaining steam, my father was hired by two powerful Kyn families, the Byrnes and the Seatons, as a mediator in a trade agreement negotiation. They shared a bad history that made the negotiations a tricky proposition. But my father was very, very good at maintaining the peace."

If he was anything like Gavin—who could alternately maneuver hard cases like herself to where he wanted them and charm the coldest of souls, like Natasha, into his plans —then she could see that. "And your mom's role in this?"

"She was the Byrne's eldest daughter and presumed heir to her family's business."

She wrinkled her nose. "Please tell me this isn't some Kyn version of *Romeo and Juliet*."

That earned a dry chuckle. "No, it was more like a twisted version of *The Winter's Tale*."

She knew enough about that play to know it rivaled a modern-day cross between a soap opera and a reality show, complete with jealous assumptions and vengeful regrets. In other words, it was a complete shitshow. "So once upon a time, the two families were friendly?"

"Yep, right up until Old Man Seaton accused his pregnant wife of sleeping with Grandpa Byrne."

"In Shakespeare's version, the wife was innocent, and

her jealous ass of a husband was the father of her unborn child."

"Not this time. Old Man Seaton's wife did have an affair, but it wasn't with Grandpa Byrne, but one of Seaton's buddies, who died in a challenge circle just after she gave birth to her second child, a son."

"A challenge circle?" She wasn't familiar with the term.

"Think of it like a Kyn's version of a duel."

She blinked. "Like pistols at dawn?"

"More like spells at dawn, but yeah, you get the point. Anyway, as the boy grew up, his connection to Seaton's buddy was obvious, proving Grandpa Byrne innocent, but the friendship between the Byrnes and the Seatons was understandably strained."

She figured that was a polite understatement, considering the Kyn could hold world-class grudges. "So, you're dad ended up playing referee with..."

"Old Man Seaton and my grandfather."

"Not the son?"

Gavin shook his head. "The Seatons had a streak of bad luck. The oldest died in the Crimean War, the wife died a few years later, and the youngest never made it past his twenties, leaving Old Man Seaton a widower with no direct heirs at the time."

The Kyn were long-lived, so it was no surprise events could stretch over timelines and family connections could rival Gordian knots. "Wow, yeah, okay, I can see why negotiations would be tricky."

"'Tricky' is the nicest way to describe it," Gavin said. "According to my dad, it was like walking both deaf and blind through a minefield while juggling cats."

The imagery caused an unexpected snort of humor, and

she waved away her response. "Sorry, it's just that was… Your dad had a way with words."

For the first time in the last couple of hours, Gavin lost his grim demeanor, and a genuine smile broke free. "Yeah, he did, but he was always spot on."

"What happened with this cluster?"

"Negotiations dragged on for weeks, and during that time, my parents started a relationship."

There was a note in his voice that had her asking, "And that was a bad thing because?"

"As the Byrne heir, she was supposed to marry into another prominent family."

"She was engaged?"

"Not officially, but it was all but considered a done deal."

Raine considered the timeframe they were talking about and gave Nyla silent props for choosing her own path despite her family's expectations. "Since she hooked up with your dad, bet that was a fun conversation."

Gavin shifted in his seat and readjusted his legs in the limited space. "I don't know about fun, and neither of my parents ever went into detail about it, but she chose not to tell her parents until after the agreement was reached. When the dust settled, my dad was looking for a new position in America with a brand-new wife."

"I'm guessing he and your mom wanted distance from her family?"

"He did," Gavin said. "Her, not so much, but the Byrnes' influence made it uncomfortable for my dad to continue his work in Europe, so she followed him to America, where their reach didn't extend. It didn't take him long to gain a reputation that put him and his skills in high demand."

"What about your mom? Did her family cut her off?"

He snorted. "They tried, but she was their only daughter, and she knew how to get what she wanted. It took years, but eventually, when my grandfather finally passed, she was named heir."

His bitter undertone made her proceed with caution. "That makes for a great romance story, but it doesn't explain why you think your mom didn't love your dad or why you two aren't close." She snuck a glance at him to see him staring out at the window, his jaw hard.

"It's not that she didn't love him," he grudgingly admitted. "It was more like she has a healthy sense of self-preservation."

"That's not always a bad thing," she pointed out carefully. "Especially in our world." When living among beings that considered power and knowledge keys to survival, self-preservation was a must.

"I agree, but if taken too far, it can be." He pulled in a deep breath, and when he continued, his voice was empty. "My father disappeared when I was in my teens. He went out on a job and never came home. My mother is no pushover, and she's a highly respected and powerful witch. Initially, both of us were determined to find out what happened to him. It took a couple of years, but when we finally confirmed he was dead, we started to work out the who and why behind his murder." He stopped, and a heavy silence filled the car.

Raine waited, giving him time.

When he spoke again, his voice was harder than granite. "We got the why, and we were ready to confront the who when she chose to walk away and forced me to do the same."

Oh, Gavin. She didn't need their bond to feel the depth of his fury buried under layers of ice. She tightened her grip on the steering wheel so she wouldn't reach out. From the vibes he gave off, her comfort wouldn't be appreciated. "Did she have a reason why?"

His bark of laughter was harsh with old rage. "The man who betrayed my father held strong ties to a demon-blooded sorcerer clan who threatened to financially wipe out the Byrnes."

It didn't take much for her to put together the pieces, not with what she knew of Gavin. In one of their very first confrontations, Gavin discovered that she had defied her uncle's edicts and hunted and killed those who'd targeted her and her mother. When he cornered her on why she'd stopped shy of completing her personal hit list, she admitted that killing them was becoming addictive. It was a lie she'd told herself to hide the fear of what and who she was becoming. He was quick to call her on her bullshit, and now she knew why. Like her, he was a Wraith, and bloody retaliation and justice lay at the core of who they were. "You went after him anyway."

His lips curved with a merciless sort of satisfaction. "I didn't give two shits about the Byrnes. But for her, I made sure there was no blowback for that family."

But Nyla wouldn't hold the respect she did if she wasn't as sharp as her son. "But she found out."

"She did, and after she shared her opinion, I left. Eventually, I ended up in Portland, and once Mulcahy approached me..."

"The rest was history?" Her tone was casual when she was feeling anything but. Despite Gavin's tight hold on his emotions, things were seeping through. Not much, but enough to know that despite his icy indifference, his relationship with his mother had left a lasting mark. When he didn't say anything, she cleared her throat. "At least you two still talk."

He gave another one of those snorts. "If you can call it that. She finds an excuse to call every few months. Last time, she was in town on a layover and wanted to meet to discuss a situation she was dealing with. Since you and I were busy, I turned her down."

Raine put two and two together, remembering the call he'd received the first time she was at his place. "Wasn't that, like, seven or eight months ago?"

"Yep." Before she could figure out what to do with that information, Gavin said, "We want the next exit."

She made her way across the lanes to the exit and followed his directions to the park. She pulled past the little empty hut and into the lot, where a handful of other vehicles were parked. There was an RV camper, a couple of compact four-doors with empty bike racks, a mini-van, a mud-caked Jeep, and a couple of the electric sedans that were starting to show up everywhere.

A couple of joggers were doing stretches near the trailhead. A biker zipped through the parking lot toward one of the cars with a bike rack, and an older gentleman was walking what looked like two cotton balls. Nothing and no one stood out as Nyla's contact.

Raine backed into a spot that gave them an unobstructed view of the entrance, turned off the SUV, and checked the clock. It was closing in on four o'clock. "Was there a time in that email you found?"

"Nope."

She folded her arms over the steering wheel and stared out the window. "We hang out here for too long, someone's going to get spooked."

"Yep." He undid his seatbelt and opened his door. "Which is why you and I are going for a walk."

She blinked at him and looked down at her black jeans, heavy-soled boots, and T-shirt then back to him. "Not exactly dressed for a hike."

He stood in the door, dressed much like her, bracing his arms on the doorframe and roof as he half bent so he could see her. "Don't think anyone's going to care."

He was probably right. She heaved a sigh and threw open her door, hearing him shut his. She got out, set her sunglasses in place, and met him at the hood of the SUV. They weren't exactly inconspicuous. "If her contact sees us, they're going to bolt."

He grabbed her hand and grinned. "Then I guess we'll get a workout."

She curled her fingers with his, shook her head, and followed him to the park.

CHAPTER 6

Raine and Gavin strode along the trail, occasionally moving aside when they met a runner or biker. They stayed on the path that circled the lot, doing their best to be just another couple enjoying the spring afternoon. Sunlight spilled through the trees, and a soft breeze made its presence known every now and again. As they walked through the muted calm of the afternoon, Raine's tension eased, and so did her fierce hold on her magic. It stretched awake, sniffed around, and checked for any other nearby Kyn.

Gavin's voice slipped into her mind. *"Feel anything?"*

"Not yet." She let her inner cat rise to help take in the surrounding scents. While her ability to see magic often came in handy, where Mother Nature ruled, she was better served by her cat's sensitivity. Besides, lowering her mental walls without knowing who or what lay in wait could be dangerous.

They turned down the path that rounded the far end of the lot. Behind the protection of her lenses, she scanned their surroundings and spotted a ratty tent tucked under a cluster of trees, half-hidden by the shadows. A few yards farther up the path was a bench and judging by the wide berth the dog walker was giving it, the man lying on the bench was the tent's owner. As they got closer, she took note of the stained baseball cap that was pulled low and hid all but the white-streaked-brown-bearded jaw of the man resting on a makeshift pillow of bundled, faded flannel. Tan skin was stretched over a wiry frame clothed in a dingy T-shirt, dirt-stained jeans, and grimy sneakers propped on the armrest.

But what caught Raine's attention was the lack of distinctive odors that generally accompanied those without access to facilities. In fact, when the part of her that was testing the air brushed up against fur and magic, the cat inside her bared its teeth with a low warning growl. *Shifter.*

She squeezed Gavin's hand in warning as they closed in on the occupant of the bench. *"Gavin."*

"I see him." He squeezed back and didn't change their pace. *"Let's see if he follows."*

They strode past the bench and continued along the path. Her spine crawled, but she didn't look back. *"He's watching."*

"I know. We need to take this out of view."

She tightened her grip on his hand to combat the itch to draw her blade and scanned the path ahead. *"There, there's a footpath over to the left."*

Unlike Raine, coiled and ready, Gavin was calm and focused. *"I see it."*

They turned onto the smaller, less used path and walked deeper into the surrounding foliage. The sensation of being stalked returned with a vengeance, but with each step, they pulled farther away from curious eyes. They wound around a particularly thick tree, and a small clearing with a lone picnic table came into view.

"Lead him there," Gavin sent through their bond, then he let go of her hand, slipped off the path, and disappeared into the shadows.

"Wait, wha—"

Gavin's magic flared, cutting her short, and at her side, an image of him popped out of thin air. Understanding came in a flash, Gavin wanted her to play bait. As the illusion moved forward, she fell back to walk behind it and groused, *"A little warning next time."*

His amusement seeped through their bond. *"It should be enough to draw him in, but you'll have to do the talking."*

"Got it." As she trailed behind the image, she couldn't help but admire Gavin's masterful ability to weave realistic illusions. If she hadn't known better, she would have believed Gavin was still trudging along toward the clearing. *Here's hoping the shifter won't figure it out until it's too late.*

She followed the doppelgänger to the picnic table. It took a seat with its back to the stalking shifter, leaving Raine the other side. She wasn't about to get tangled up with the table, so instead of sitting across from the illusion, she hitched a hip on the table's top, crossed her arms, and waited. She did her best not to stare at the image facing her. Gavin's illusion had always been good, but after he was dosed with a new-and-improved version of the same serum that had been used on Raine, his creations had gained a disconcerting depth.

The shifter glided into the shade that edged the clearing. He stayed near the trees, his movements stiff and cautious, likely because he sensed the unseen trap. Gavin was very, very good at staying invisible, though. Seconds passed before the unknown Kyn decided to make his move.

He crept around the clearing's edge but didn't move out of the trees, and his gaze skittered over the area before finally focusing on Raine.

He stopped and called out, "You having a picnic?"

Raine held her position and pushed her sunglasses up to the top of her head. "Supposed to meet a friend here."

The shifter rocked back and forth on his toes. "Looks like you already got one of those."

"Had another one who was planning on coming." Raine kept her attention on the shifter as Gavin's illusion turned his head to the side without turning around. "But something came up, so she told to me go ahead without her."

The shifter shuffled another foot closer, edging away from the trees and into the glen. "Is that so?"

Gavin dropped from a branch above and landed silently behind him. The shifter spun around, sinking into a defensive crouch. The illusion disappeared, and Raine straightened from her perch, a hidden throwing knife at the ready. Caught between Gavin and Raine, the shifter spun sideways and tried to keep them from his back. His head jerked between the two as Gavin slowly straightened and crossed his arms over his chest.

"Not looking for trouble." The rough edge to the shifter's voice warned he was hovering on the verge of a shift.

"Neither are we," Raine assured him, her voice low and calm.

The shifter angled his head and sniffed the air. He frowned and tried to inch out from between them, but Gavin moved with him. Realizing he was caught, the shifter froze. "Whatcha want?"

"You got a name?" Raine asked.

He held her gaze for a second then said, "Mike."

Gavin adjusted his weight, and Mike tensed. Raine used the distraction to inch closer. "Nice to meet you, Mike."

Mike turned back to her.

"I'm Raine." She raised her chin toward Gavin. "That's Gavin. Were you the one that was going to meet my friend?" Raine decided to chance it and added, "Nyla. That's who was going to meet me."

Mike's nod was hesitant at first, and he kept trying to hold her gaze. When he couldn't, he continued to bob his head in a nervous tell. "Heard she was looking for a couple friends of mine. They hadn't been around for a while. She asked to meet. I agreed, but..." His head nods switched to jerky shakes, and under the brim of his hat, the whites of his eyes flashed. "Now I'm thinking it's best if I just get. They're probably just on a walkabout, and I don't want to make waves."

Behind him, Gavin inched forward, forcing Mike to do the same to stay out of reach.

Before Mike could balk at Gavin's move, Raine eased back to bracing her hip against the table and tucked her knife away. "We could really use your help, Mike." She put the few clues he revealed together and thought fast. "Nyla wanted to be here, but her flight was delayed. She asked us to come in her place and find out when you last saw your friends..." She trailed off, and just as she hoped, Mike did what most do when prompted—he shared.

"About a month ago," he said. "The three of us—me, Sam, and Dani—we had a sweet setup down by the river, but you know they did that sweep. And we had to move, you know?"

When he paused, Raine nodded. Portland routinely swept through the homeless camps that popped up downtown and spilled into the riverfront areas, trying to clear them out. The displacement camps would disappear for a few months then creep back in, in a never-ending cycle. "Did you three find a new place?"

The jumpy shifter shuffled back in an obvious attempt to get Gavin out from behind him, but he was smart enough not to discount Raine, and his eyes bounced between the two. "Well, Sam and Dani, they were scouting some new spots, but they never made it back."

Raine braced one palm on the table by her hip and flicked her fingers on the other hand in a silent signal to Gavin to hold. She really didn't want to have to chase Mike down. "Sam and Dani, are they like you?"

Mike stiffened, and he stopped eyeing Gavin to focus on Raine. His tone was belligerent when he spat, "Whatcha mean?"

At the unmistakable challenge, Raine's inner cat rose and padded forward. As it brushed under her skin, Raine stared at Mike, her attention focused as she flexed her fingers in an unconscious mimic of her cat's claws. Magic coiled around her, wanting to play, but she locked it down. She wasn't trying to make Mike piss himself, just answer her question.

A full-body shiver wracked his frame, and he dropped into a crouch, his eyes sliding away. His voice was rough when he asked, "You mean shifters?" He tried to meet her gaze and failed.

Without blinking, she nodded.

This time, Mike's eyes stayed on the ground. "Yeah."

A tense moment passed as she nudged her cat back. Appeased by Mike's submission, it gave a disdainful sniff, followed by the flick of its tail then retreated. Raine cleared her throat. "So you're Motoki?"

Mike gave a hoarse bark of noise, part laugh, part guffaw. He shook his head, his lip curled in distaste. "Nope, we're travelers. Ones like us aren't real popular with packs."

Well, that sucks. If he had been part of the Northwest pack, she could've gone to Ryuu and Xander, maybe even Vidis, for reliable information about Mike and his friends. But since it sounded as if they weren't part of a formal pack, finding out why Nyla was interested in them would be a challenge.

"What do you mean 'like us'?" Gavin's question cut into her thoughts and brought Mike up out of his crouch as he skittered back so he could see Gavin.

He opened and closed his hands as his shoulders jerked. "This... I..." He shook his head, obviously struggling to answer. He snatched his hat off, revealing an unkempt tangle of dull-brown hair, and twisted it with his hands. He sucked in a big breath, raised his head, glared at Gavin, and raised his chin. "I wasn't always like this." He yanked up his dingy T-shirt.

Gavin's gaze narrowed, and Raine straightened from her perch.

Mike's torso was crisscrossed by scars, the kind that came from claws and teeth. Not the typical marks left by dominance fights but something much more vicious and much crueler.

"You're Bitten." Raine's voice was soft with unmistakable sympathy. Human survivors of a near-death attack by a shifter were few and far between because mortals tended not to survive the initial physical transformation. If they made it through the horrifying first shift and lethal wounds, then they had to learn how to live with a highly intelligent predator filled with primal rage. That was never an easy endeavor, especially when those human victims could barely comprehend that the monster they feared had set up shop in their souls. Xander had once explained that the lack of control was one of the main reasons Bitten tended to rank near the bottom of most packs. That, and they were limited to shifting at the will of the moon.

Stubborn pride flashed over Mike's face as he dropped his T-shirt and faced her. "Yeah."

Mindful of the wolf's dignity, she buried her sympathy. "Does Vidis know you're in town?"

There was no way to miss Mike's flash of fear when she said the alpha's name, but he swallowed hard and managed a jerky nod. "Yep, we cleared it with that Kern guy."

"Sam and Dani," Gavin said, forcing Mike's attention to him. "Were they both Bitten as well?"

Mike cocked his head. "Yeah, we stick together."

Raine made a mental note to touch base with Ryuu. Maybe he would have something about the trio's history since the pack tended to execute those who turned humans and keep an eye on their victims.

Mike shuffled his feet and muttered, "Well, we stuck together until they took off on me."

"They do that a lot?" she asked before Gavin could. When Mike turned to her, she added, "Take off on you? Without letting you know?"

Mike shrugged. "Sometimes, but never this long." He looked between them. "That's why when your lady friend was asking about any recent disappearances, I mentioned them. I wasn't real worried at first, but now, well..." He painstakingly straightened out his hat and put it back on. "No one's seen them, not since they were over near Washington Square checking out some spots we heard about."

Why would Nyla, an out-of-town—hell, out-of-country—witch, be interested in missing shifters? Raine added the question to her growing list. "Do you have photos of Sam and Dani?"

Mike shook his head.

"You have last names for them?" Gavin pressed.

Mike snorted and shuffled closer to Raine. "No need for those." He scratched his neck. "Think Sam's was something like Ferris or Harris, something 'iss.' Don't think Dani ever said hers, though."

A dog barked nearby, and Mike's head swung in that direction. So did Raine's, but Gavin stayed on target. "What did they look like?"

When Mike continued to stare off where the dog sounded from, Gavin called, "Mike."

Mike blinked and turned to Gavin. "Sam's younger than me, stands about"—he held his hand an inch or two above his head—"yay high. Dani's older, maybe closer to fifty?" He shook his head. "Not real sure on that, but she's a little thing." He moved his hand to mid-chest. "Only hits about here."

"Anything about either of them that sticks out?" Raine asked since those descriptions were far from helpful. "Something you'd remember if you met them?"

Another bark sounded. This time, another answered it, and a canine conversation started up. Before long, human tones joined the din, trying to quiet it down.

Mike's attention went back toward the trail. "I need to go back. Don't want them messing with my stuff."

Raine knew they were going to lose him. She glided forward until she was close enough to grab him if he darted. "We just have a couple more questions, then you can go."

Flicking her a glance, he rocked on his toes, and his muscles tensed. "Don't know anything more."

She moved her hands out, palms forward, and softened her voice like she would with a wary animal. "Easy, Mike, easy." She caught his muddy-brown eyes with hers and recognized the amber sheen from when she dealt with Xander and Ryuu. Yep, Mike was about done. "We just want to make sure Sam and Dani are okay. To do that, we just need a way to recognize them. Can you give us that much?"

He nearly vibrated with tension, and it was clear he was fighting his nature. "Sam's bald and has a scar, here." He brushed a finger from the edge of his nose to the top of his lips. "Surgery from when he was a kid, makes it hard for him to talk sometimes."

Tall, bald, and with a cleft-lip scar. Okay, we can work with that, maybe. "And Dani?"

His eyes flickered, and his agitation increased until he was rocking back and forth. "She likes colors, does her hair in all sorts of rainbows, but doesn't always turn out so good. Not even when she spikes it up. Told her she looks like she was electrocuted by a unicorn." He brushed his hand over his right eye. "She wears an eye patch, 'cause the one that turned her went for her face and left his mark."

Sounded like Dani would be the easier of the two to identify.

"I gotta go." Mike inched away from Raine, his gaze darting between her and Gavin. "I gotta go."

Raine eased back and felt Gavin do the same, both of them giving the antsy shifter room. The last thing they needed was a Bitten losing it at a public park. "We'll let you go, but want you to know we appreciate your help, Mike."

He stilled and stared at her, clearly stunned that they were really going to let him leave. "That's it?"

"That's it," Gavin said. "Unless there's more you can tell us?"

Mike shook his head, spun, and without another word, dashed away.

Raine watched him disappear into the trees as Gavin came to stand at her side. "Why is your mom asking about missing homeless people in Portland?"

"Your guess is as good as mine," he said, tone absent, his attention clearly somewhere else.

She studied his hard jaw. She didn't need their bond to see he was struggling. She'd been there, torn between not wanting to care about the storm swirling around a loved one and trying to stay free of their drama. Unfortunately, this time, Gavin wasn't going to be given much choice, not when someone had clearly targeted his mom.

"Maybe we should start with the obvious." When he gave her a puzzled frown, she clarified, "What exactly does your mom do that would earn this type of attention?"

He shook off whatever was bothering him and refocused on Raine. "Honestly, outside of dealing with the Byrne family holdings, I don't really know."

She grabbed his hand and started back out of the clearing and toward the SUV. "Then I guess we should probably go find out."

CHAPTER 7

As Raine and Gavin headed back to the offices at Taliesin, Ryuu called, and when he discovered they were on their way to meet with Natasha, he told them he would be joining them. Fifteen minutes later, they pulled into Taliesin Security. This late in the afternoon, the office was quiet, but as they stepped onto the elevator, a pair of females followed. They were caught up in their conversation about project deadlines and didn't register their surroundings until after the door slid shut.

When one of them caught sight of Raine and Gavin, her eyes widened, revealing the telltale red ring of an Amanusa around her irises. She turned away immediately and nudged her friend, who stopped midsentence and looked behind her. The second woman's gaze landed on Gavin, who leaned against the back wall, arms crossed, gaze aimed at the door, and made an audible gasp.

Yeah, sister, I feel you on that. Raine fought back her amusement, used to similar reactions when females got anywhere near Gavin. She'd recently decided to find it amusing instead of infuriating. Otherwise, she would spend all her time trying to get bloodstains out of her clothes. He wasn't the kind of man, mortal or Kyn, to fade into the background, but what soothed her green-eyed monster over the last handful of months was the knowledge he was all hers.

As a unit, the two women shuffled into the front corner. The elevator stopped on the fifth floor, which housed the marketing department, and Gavin's admiring duo got off. Just before the door drifted shut, Raine heard one of them say, "Oh my god," which was followed by the other saying, "I know, right?"

At Gavin's beleaguered sigh, Raine dropped her head to hide her grin, but she couldn't help but tease, "It's so hard to be you."

"Shut it," he muttered, clearly exasperated.

They reached the top floor, and the elevator doors opened to the recently reconstructed reception area of Taliesin Security. Redone in an elegant mix of stone, wood, and glass, it held very few similarities to its previous incarnation, but its newly cultivated elegance did match Taliesin's current CEO, Natasha Bertoi.

Standing guard at the reception desk that divided the offices was the impeccably dressed and coolly classy Rachel, her red hair in its typical complicated updo, her modelesque form draped in tailored lines that Raine would never bother to attempt. Outfits like Rachel's would never last a day in her line of work. The redhead had served as Mulcahy's guard dog for years before taking up the same position for Natasha, and to this day, Raine still wasn't sure what Kyn blood flowed in her veins.

Rachel greeted Raine and Gavin with a genuine smile, the welcome warming her angular face. "Ms. McCord, Mr. Durand, lovely to see you two."

"You too," Raine returned, not bothering to tell her to drop the formality. It never did any good. "Natasha's expecting us."

She nodded. "Yes, of course. They're in the conference room. Mr. Kern just arrived as well." Rachel hit something on the console in front of her. "If you two go on back, I'll let them know you're here."

With murmured thanks, Raine took the lead as they rounded the desk and headed back. Months ago, after the explosion that killed Mulcahy, she'd purposely avoided this area like the plague. Too many memories haunted the space. Strangely, it was the reconstruction that made it so she could walk through without her heart hurting. Although Natasha had decided to keep her old office, she had altered the space that had once housed Mulcahy's office into a glass-enclosed conference room. Currently, the interior glass was shaded for privacy, but the double door remained open.

Raine stepped inside to find not just Ryuu and Natasha, but another unexpected visitor. She rocked to a halt and felt Gavin do the same behind her as she met the red-ringed, ice-cold blue eyes of Darius Abazi. "Aren't you supposed to be somewhere in Europe?"

"I was," Darius answered, unperturbed by her less-than-welcoming tone. "Now I'm here."

Gavin shifted from behind her to stand at her side. *"Something's up."*

"You think?" She couldn't stop her sarcastic rejoinder. She eyed the petite blonde standing at Darius's side. "Who's after you?"

The Demon Queen's ever-present smirk deepened, and a hard light entered her unusual red-ringed periwinkle-blue eyes. "Not everyone has it in for me like you, dear."

As ever, Natasha managed to wiggle her way under Raine's skin. To share her disbelief, she raised her brows. "Wanna make a bet?"

"I'm playing escort," Darius cut in before the two women could get into their normal barbed exchange, and his gaze went to Gavin.

Gavin made the connection immediately in a clipped tone. "For my mother."

Although it wasn't a question, Darius inclined his head.

"You did a shitacular job there, Abazi." Anger and accusation rode Gavin's voice.

The demon that resided inside Darius roused, darkening the air around him. The faint hint of sulfur curled through the room, and a primal fear coiled in Raine, drying her mouth. Pissing off an Amanusa was never wise. Pissing off one like Darius was suicidal. He was part of the Order for a reason, and he hadn't become a premier predator in the Kyn world by happenstance.

She reached back and grabbed Gavin's hand in warning. His fingers tangled with hers in a painful grip. Deciding it would be best if the two didn't get a chance to come to blows, Raine asked, "Why?"

Darius's jaw flexed under his neatly trimmed goatee. "Corwin requested it."

Gavin stiffened, and although his face remained blank, shock echoed through their bond.

Raine looked at Natasha. "As in Councilman Corwin Westbrooke, the liaison for the European Kyn and one of the names we were looking into after Mulcahy's death?"

Eyes cold, face even colder and no sneer in sight, Natasha dipped her chin in agreement.

Completely thrown by this development, Raine

frowned, but she wasn't the only confused person in the room.

Anger and disbelief boiled around Gavin. "Why in the hell would Corwin request you accompany my mother?"

"That's why we're meeting." Natasha waved to the nearby chairs. "Now, if you're done posturing, let's take a seat and see if we can find out what's going on before this blows up in our faces." She took the seat Darius pulled out for her, and once she was settled, he took the one to her right.

"Too late," Raine muttered.

Gavin shot her a look, then he stepped back, pulled out a nearby chair, and held it for her. He waited until she was seated before claiming the seat to her left. Ryuu got stuck sitting smack-dab in the middle of the two couples. Shaking his head, he took his seat and set his tablet on the table in front of him.

Once everyone was settled, Darius answered Gavin's earlier question. "Nyla and Westbrooke share a close friend, Giles Drake. His daughter, River, failed to check in during her US walkabout, so he asked them to help track her down. The last time he spoke to her, she had just arrived in Portland. He's been trying to reach her, with no success."

Gavin shifted his chair and stretched out his legs. "For how long?"

"Two weeks." Darius's reply was grim.

Gavin's gaze sharpened. "Why go to Westbrooke and my mother? Why not get one of the Trackers and have them hunt the girl down?"

"River is Westbrooke's goddaughter," Darius answered.

"That wouldn't stop a Tracker from hunting down a missing Kyn," Gavin pointed out. "If anything, I think they'll be all over that."

"Not if the local alpha is not your biggest fan," Ryuu said. When everyone's attention shifted to him, he grimaced and looked up from his tablet. "The London Alpha is a bit of a blowhard, with an admitted prejudice against what he calls 'watered-down shifters.'" He looked at Darius. "I'm assuming Drake and his daughter qualify?"

Darius dipped his chin. "Giles belongs to a Greek family of shifters who can trace their line back before the Razing."

Raine blinked. That was a hell of a long stretch, considering the Razing was the first known instance where the humans rose up to erase the magical races. Their crowning achievement? Burning down the Library of Alexandria. The tremendous loss of recorded Kyn history and how the Kyn were all but wiped out was one of the main reasons the Kyn did their best to stay under the human radar. Unfortunately, the rise of technology and modern man's curiosity was dangerously close to exposing the last of the monsters hiding in the dark.

"And power wise?" Gavin asked.

Darius shrugged. "Unconfirmed."

Not an unusual circumstance. Raine had met plenty of Kyn who weren't keen on sharing how much or how little magic they wielded. "So, they could go either way, then?"

Darius studied her for a moment then reluctantly admitted, "They could, but while Giles and River admitted to being shifters, his wife was an unknown."

The former Mrs. Drake's reticence wasn't unexpected. As Kyn bloodlines became more and more convoluted with each passing generation, the older Kyn turned into unbearable snobs, which in turn left the younger Kyn a little hesitant to share. But one word snagged Raine's attention. "What do you mean 'was'?"

Darius and Natasha shared a look, then Natasha gave

the barest tilt of her head in a silent go ahead. Darius turned those eerie blue eyes their way. "Giles has been a widower for the last decade, maybe a little more. Not many remember his wife, and it appears that Giles prefers that, not just for him but for his daughter."

Curious and curiouser, and Raine didn't share her soul with a big cat for nothing. "There's a story there."

"There is," Darius admitted. "But it's well-hidden."

"Even from you?"

His smile was grim, and his tone even grimmer. "Even from me."

So whatever story it was, it would be a doozy, but something whispered Darius knew more than he admitted. His reluctance to share left Raine wary, but she couldn't force him to spill. She hadn't forgotten just how lethal the demon could be.

"Leave it." Gavin's mental warning was enough to keep Raine's mouth shut. Out loud, he said, "That doesn't explain why my mother's involved."

This time, Natasha answered. "Your mother works for Corwin. Or perhaps *with* is a better word choice." Some of the ice in her expression melted, and her voice took on a careful note that had Raine bracing. "For the last few years, she's been a constant at his side, both romantically and professionally."

There was a moment of pained shock, quickly followed by anger before Gavin brutally locked down their connection. Raine dropped her head to hide her wince and shifted in her seat. Next to her, Gavin repositioned so he was closer to Raine's chair, and under the cover of the table, he reached out and caught her hand in his. He didn't loosen his mental hold, though. She held tight, offering comfort the only way he would allow.

"If she's sleeping with him"—Gavin's voice was bland, but his eyes burned—"then she's getting something in return."

"Well, I should hope so," Natasha purred.

Gavin glared at her, but Darius looked as if he were fighting a laugh. He cleared his throat and said, "I can't attest to the basis of their relationship, but when Giles reached out, Nyla agreed to come here to follow River's trail."

"But why her?" Gavin asked. "My mother's expertise is warding, not tracking. "

Darius met his gaze. "Because she's been tracking a series of Kyn disappearances for the last year."

CHAPTER 8
GAVIN

Gavin stiffened in shock at Darius's pronouncement, but before he could process it, a wave of bitter fury seeped down the bond.

Raine's grip on his hand tightened, her nails digging into his skin. "General Cawley." She spat the name at Natasha. "I warned Mulcahy that if we left him alive, it would come back to bite us in the ass."

Only Raine could put two and two together and come up with seven, but it wasn't difficult to follow her logic. She'd spent years hunting down those behind her captivity and torture because that was what those experiments were—torture. Something he had first-hand experience with after his time with Talbot's renegade scientist. The last time Kyn went missing, the general's and the Talbot Foundation's fingerprints were all over the mess. He had no doubt those same nasty-ass prints would end up smeared over this too.

Completely unruffled by Raine's agitation, Natasha said, "We have no proof it's the general."

Raine opened her mouth to argue.

Clearly anticipating the next accusation, Natasha raised her hand, palm forward. "Nor is there any proof of Talbot's involvement."

The caustic mix of frustration, anger, and fear roiled down the bond from Raine as she snapped, "They're not exactly going to be obvious about it." She glared at Natasha. "Tell me you still have eyes on him."

This was not a subject Raine could be objective about, not after she'd tried warning her uncle about Jonah Talbot, only to have her concerns blown off until it was too late, and Gavin paid the price. He tried to caution Raine to back off, but she wasn't listening. He wasn't trying too hard, though, because deep down, he shared her sentiments. The last thing they needed was another Kyn leader too arrogant to listen.

Natasha's eyes flashed, and she raised her pointed chin. "I don't answer to you, girl."

"Don't you?" Raine shot back. "You're the leader of the Northwest Kyn, Natasha. It's your job to protect us from all threats, even human ones."

Gavin grimaced as red flashed through Natasha's eyes. *"Dammit, Raine."*

"No, Gavin." Raine glared at Natasha. *"This isn't going to happen again. This time, I'll damn well make her listen to me."*

The red rimming Natasha's eyes brightened, and her voice gained an unnatural depth. "I know exactly what my responsibilities are, and it doesn't include explaining myself to you."

Gavin wanted to snarl at both women to take a fucking breath, but he didn't get a chance.

Raine ripped her hand free of his hold and slapped the table. "Tell me you're watching that bastard!"

Natasha's lips curled, and the air around her

shimmered. For a heart-stopping moment, a monstrous shape rose above her. Gavin shoved his chair back, but Darius murmured her name, and the mirage faded into nothing. A tense silence swam through the room as the two women continued their stare down.

It wasn't easy, but Gavin shoved aside his own volatile emotions and rising resentment at Natasha's seeming arrogance. Too often, the Kyn leaders underestimated the humans and their capacity to harm the Kyn, but this was not the way to get the Demon Queen to listen. *"Raine, stand down."*

This time, his warning made it through. The turmoil filling the bond pulled back, but she didn't look at Gavin. Instead, in an unspoken concession to Natasha's position, she dropped her gaze. He knew it was the closest Raine would get to an apology.

Strangely, Natasha recognized that, and her voice was somewhat conciliatory when she said, "I have eyes in his company."

That took Gavin by surprise. He wasn't the only one. Next to him, Raine stiffened and raised her head.

A flash of what could've been understanding was there and gone as Natasha finished. "There's been nothing to indicate Talbot or the general are up to their old tricks. However, I will admit to being a smidge distracted lately, what with Leo's meddling in our affairs."

The storm of emotion pulled back even more as Raine said, "With everything that's happened in the last few months, I'm sure he's not the only one taking advantage of our distraction."

"No, he's not," Natasha confirmed without elaborating.

Gavin shot Natasha a sharp look, not liking what her answer indicated. If she was worried about someone or something that matched Talbot's level, it had yet to make its way to his ear as the Wraith's captain. He made a mental note to press for more later. First, though, he had to find his mother and fix whatever mess she'd dragged to his door.

The Demon Queen tucked her horns and claws behind her composed façade. "The last thing I want is the attention of another council member, so I need you and Gavin to focus on finding Nyla."

Since he was all for that, he kept his mouth shut and nodded.

Ryuu cleared his throat to gain everyone's attention. "And there's my cue." He looked at Gavin. "Since you and Raine took the long way home, I'm assuming you found something else?"

Before Gavin could respond, Natasha asked sharply, "What do you mean 'something else'?"

Ryuu winced and mouthed, "Sorry."

Gavin sighed and answered Natasha, "Whoever kidnapped my mother left behind a distraction."

She leaned forward, her gaze sharp. "What kind of distraction?"

"A spell that amplified the emotions of whoever tripped it."

She looked between him and Raine, her delicate features gaining a calculated edge. "Who tripped it?"

He ignored Raine's snort and admitted, "I did."

Darius raised a dark brow in question. "Did it work?"

Gavin shared a wry look with Ryuu, who snorted. "Close enough to count, in my opinion," the shifter said.

Natasha drummed her polished nails against the table. "That doesn't seem like a serious-enough spell to make a difference."

"Serious enough," Gavin said. "The only reason Ryuu

and I didn't tear each other, and that room, apart was because Raine was there. She was able to pinpoint the anchor and destroy it."

Darius studied Raine. "The anchor was…"

"Hidden in the crack of the window," Raine finished.

Natasha made a soft hum, her focus on Gavin. "Could your mother have left it behind?"

Her question made it clear she knew all about Raine's ability to see magic since most spells could only be identified if blood was used or if the caster had a unique style. "There was nothing of her in the spell."

Before she could push for more, Ryuu spoke up. "We know a demon was involved in the abduction."

That caught Natasha's attention, and her head whipped around. "A demon?"

Ryuu nodded. "And maybe a shifter."

Darius leaned in, his gaze focused. "But you couldn't track either?"

Ryuu shook his head. "Like I told those two"—he waved a hand at Gavin and Raine—"the shifter's scent was already dispersing. I caught a hint in the hall and again in the room when the AC kicked in, but it could just as easily belong to a previous guest. The demon's scent, however, was concentrated only in the room, not at any of the exits."

"Which makes us believe"—Gavin studied the demonic couple across from him—"the demon took my mother through the Side."

Darius tipped his head, and Natasha gave a small shrug as the two appeared to have a silent conversation.

"Want to share with the class?" Raine's question was dry.

Natasha turned back to them and tapped one blood-red nail absently on the table's top. "Considering who Nyla is and the power she wields, a demon would want her incapacitated if he took her through the Side. Otherwise, it would be debatable if either of them would survive."

Something eased in his chest. "But she would survive?"

The two demons shared another one of the indecipherable looks, then Darius said, "Yes, but it would take a skilled hand to hold a Magi in the Side."

"He would know," Raine's voice slipped into his mind.

"Yeah, I remember. Demon wizard." He'd made that discovery while working with Darius to undo a convoluted death spell. Running into an Amanusa who was also a formidable wizard had thrown him, but then again, considering who Darius was and the woman he'd ended up claiming, he probably shouldn't have been surprised. No matter the situation, demons loved to toss in their wrenches.

Of the four Kyn Houses, the Amanusa were the most volatile and tended to be touchy as shit about their abilities. They were the results of couplings between the twelve Watchers, or Fallen Angels, and Kyn and human women. While the children with human mothers rarely survived into adulthood, those with Kyn mothers did, and when they did, no one knew how weak or strong they were until it was too late.

Even though it might rile Darius, Gavin asked point-blank, "That mean we're looking for someone like you?"

"I appreciate the compliment." Darius bared his teeth in a predatory smile even as Natasha's eyes narrowed. "But if it was my handiwork, we wouldn't be having this discussion."

Yeah, that's what Gavin thought, too, but still... "Why is it every time you show up, things go to shit?"

Darius didn't lose his amusement. "Luck?"

He didn't think luck had anything to do with this. He looked at Natasha, who had pulled out her phone and was typing into it. "So, any ideas of who in your house would be able to carry it off?"

She glanced up. "Not off the top of my head, but I'll start putting together a list of possible troublemakers."

He didn't have a lot of confidence that Natasha's list would be all that helpful. This situation wasn't like the one with Jamie—it wasn't solely aimed at the Northwest Kyn. This was more like an unlucky twist of fate thanks to his mother playing outside her league and stirring shit up. The fact she'd hooked up with a powerhouse like Corwin Westbrooke didn't surprise him because it was in line with his mother's normal schemes. But tracking missing Kyn as a favor? He wasn't buying that shit. That wasn't her style. If it didn't help her bottom line or her reputation, she wouldn't waste her time. *So, what in the hell is Nyla Durand getting out of this?*

He turned to Ryuu. "Did Vidis confirm it was Westbrooke who requested the meet?"

"He did," Ryuu said. "The call came in late yesterday, and when Vidis explained his schedule was booked, Westbrooke pushed the issue. Said his representative would be flying in today with questions regarding a missing shifter visiting from London, who may or may not have to pass through our territory. Vidis was under the impression it was a simple meet, so he asked me to take it."

"Visiting shifters have to get permission from the regional alpha, right?" There were various protocols when dealing with visiting Kyn, most of which depended on which of the four Houses the visitor belonged to. He wasn't solid on the Lycos House protocols.

Ryuu nodded. "Knowing who's here helps if something

happens. Generally, a visiting shifter will notify the pack of the dates they're in town for and where or who they're staying with. That way, we know who to talk to if trouble pops up. There's a site that tracks all that data."

"Sounds like a pain in the ass," Raine muttered.

Ryuu grimaced. "It can be, but it's a form of CYA."

Since even the mildest misunderstanding could escalate quickly when teeth and claws got involved, shifters had covering their asses down pat.

"But," Ryuu continued, "I already checked, and we didn't receive any such notifications. So I reached out to nearby packs and got a handful of names. I'm still waiting on a couple of callbacks to verify where the visitors were coming from, but we should know more by morning. I'll run information as it comes in, see if anything ties to Nyla or Westbrooke, but without knowing who I'm looking for, this could be a crapshoot."

Gavin shared a look with Raine then turned to Ryuu. "Might have something to help you narrow that search down. Two Bitten wolves that are MIA. A male—tall, bald, with a cleft lip—and a female—short, fifty-something punk with an eyepatch."

"That's oddly specific and doesn't match anyone local." Ryuu cocked his head a glint of gold in his dark eyes. "Where did you get your information?"

It was Raine's turn to speak up. "A homeless shifter that goes by Mike and currently calls Noble Woods home."

Recognition flickered in Ryuu's face. "Mike Stearns out of California, hit town about four months ago and was supposed to be working down at the docks." He recited the information from memory, then he frowned. "How did you connect with him?"

"He was our long way home," Gavin said. "Found an

unfinished email on my mom's phone with an address and time, and since we're in hurry-up-and-wait mode, I—"

"We," Raine corrected.

Her quick correction ignited a spurt of amusement, and Gavin glanced at her before turning back to the others. "*We* decided to go check it out and see who showed up."

"And this Mike person," Natasha cut in when Ryuu went back to his tablet. "Why was he meeting your mother?"

If I knew that... He dropped his hands to his lap and, under the cover of the tabletop, fisted them. As he opened his hands, he breathed away his frustration so he could keep his voice level. "According to Mike, she was looking for a couple of his friends, Sam, the guy, and Dani, the woman, who recently disappeared when the city swept through the riverfront and cleared out the camps."

Out of sight of the others, Raine patted his thigh, offering comfort. To the others, she said, "Which leaves us with three missing shifters with no ties to the local pack."

"We did trace one of the numbers from your mother's phone." Ryuu didn't look up from his tablet, his fingers flashing over the screen. "One of the calls made this morning belongs to a downtown hostel, The Claim Jumper."

Ding, ding, ding. "Hostels tend to cater to young travelers, right?"

"Yeah," Ryuu answered absently without looking up. "I recognize it because Taliesin uses it for out-of-town interns."

Halle-fucking-lujah, something solid. At least he wouldn't spend the night pacing the floors. "Send me the address. Raine and I can swing by tonight."

Ryuu's fingers flew over the screen, and at his hip, Gavin

felt his phone buzz. "Done." He met Gavin's gaze. "I'll also see if Xander's available. Maybe she can get something from your mother's room that I missed."

"Thank you." His voice was rough, but he couldn't help it. Ryuu's offer eased another knot in his gut. Putting the Northwest's best tracker on the room might gain them another trail to follow. No matter how messy his relationship with his mother was, he couldn't help but worry.

"Was there anything on the other numbers?" Raine asked.

Ryuu shook his head. "One turned up private, so we have to dig down to find the owner. We're still coming up empty on the text string."

Gavin turned to Darius. "Any chance you can get me a photo of River?"

"Tonight?"

"Would be best." He wanted to make sure when they hit the hostel, they had something more than a name to verify. He pushed back his chair and rose. Raine did the same at his side.

"I'll reach out to Westbrooke." The dark-haired man stood and offered Natasha a hand.

"If he comes through, send it to my cell." When Darius nodded, Gavin put his hand to the base of Raine's spine and nudged her toward the door. He went to follow but stopped and looked back. "Can you get information on the other missing Kyn from Westbrooke?"

Darius raised a dark brow. "I can try."

"Send it to me," Ryuu said without taking his attention from his screen. When no one responded, he looked up. "The more information we have, the more data points I have to access. Maybe we'll get lucky and tie some of this together."

Gavin hoped Ryuu's optimism proved true, but experience made him doubtful. His neck was crawling with anxiety. It felt like they were dealing with a puzzle that not only had missing pieces but was mixed with another one. It drove him nuts.

"And maybe we'll be able to take care of Talbot once and for all." Raine's bloodthirsty sentiment echoed through their bond.

"Only if we can do so without exposing ourselves to the humans," he reminded her. Despite their personal feelings, they both understood that they couldn't take matters into their own hands when it came to Talbot. Not when doing so might tip the scales of how accepting humans would be when, not *if*, the Kyn came out of the shadows. And that momentous event crept closer and closer every day.

He turned back and headed to Raine, who waited at the door, only to be pulled up when Natasha called their names.

The Demon Queen raked them with an assessing gaze. "I want your word that neither of you will go off half-cocked after Talbot."

He didn't dare look to Raine, but he kept his determination to hunt Talbot from his face.

"It's good to want things," Raine said.

Natasha studied them both for a long moment, then she let out a resigned sigh and gave them one last order. "If you can't give me that, can you keep me informed so I can handle the fallout?"

Gavin exchanged a look with Raine. "That, we can do."

"Good."

With that, he and Raine left to hunt.

CHAPTER 9

The hostel wasn't quite what Raine expected. Situated a few blocks from the downtown riverfront, The Claim Jumper had started life in the 1800s as a sailors' hotel. At some point in recent years, though, it was reclaimed as an "upscale boutique hostel," a phrase Raine had found on their website. A quick scroll showed rooms that started just under the hundred-dollar mark and topped out at a hundred fifty. Not a bad price considering the location. If the pictures held true, the rooms could rival some of the higher-end hotels.

"Upscale hostel?" She looked up from the phone with a frown. "Aren't hostels supposed to be all about economy and budget?"

As Gavin navigated the tight streets of downtown, his shoulders moved in an offhand shrug. "Guess they figured they needed to up their game to compete with all the Airbnbs floating around."

"Uh." Raine looked back down at the screen and scrolled through the images. "Looks like they have dog-friendly rooms."

Gavin stopped at a light and shot her a look as people spilled into the crosswalk. "Seriously?"

Raine kept her attention on her phone and buried her grin deep, where he couldn't see or sense it. "What?" she asked innocently.

"I dare you to share that comment with Xander." Gavin turned back to the road as the last pedestrian darted across and the light turned green. He added drily, "And when you do, I want to watch."

Yeah, Xander might look like a curvy, blonde goth fairy princess, but as a fellow Wraith, she could easily give Raine a run for her money should she decide to throw down over that kind of comment. Raine pocketed her phone and smiled. "Yeah, I think I'll skip poking that particular wolf."

"Smart of you." Dry amusement tinged Gavin's voice, and the constant low-level anxiety that seeped from him finally started to back off.

"That's me—all about being smart." She ignored his disbelieving scoff and took what felt like her first easy breath since starting the emotional roller coaster ride of the past few hours. Part of her wanted to reach out and assure him they would find his mother, but there was no missing his unspoken signals to back off. She would give him until tonight, then all bets were off.

She looked out the windows and searched for the four-story olive building pictured online. "Hopefully, Darius will be able to get River's picture."

"I'm sure he'll come through," he said. "In the meantime, we see if River ever checked in and work out from there."

"Chances are any video surveillance is already gone." Especially since businesses didn't tend to keep their security footage for very long and, according to Darius,

River had been missing for at least two weeks. "You have a plan for getting around the pesky privacy policy?"

He drummed a finger on the steering wheel. "We can try asking."

She rolled her eyes. "And when they say no?"

He gave her a look.

She sighed. "Okay, so let me rephrase—when you fail to charm their pants off, then what?"

"Oh ye of little faith," he murmured.

He had reason to be so self-assured. She studied his profile. The setting sun glinted off the deep reds that snaked through his pulled-back dark hair and the scruffy shadow that lined his strong jaw, giving him a roguish vibe. The rust-red T-shirt set off the gold undertones of his skin and didn't completely hide the protection markings most mistook for tattoos that scrolled from shoulder to wrist. From his dark-haired top to his lean-legged toe, his appeal was more than his eye-catching physical package. It was the tiny cracks that his ruthless and dangerous nature slipped through that tipped him from sexy to dangerous bad boy. But sometimes, even that wasn't enough.

"If we can't get anything, we're dead in the water until Taliesin's lawyers can come through with a subpoena."

In the cup holder between them, his phone buzzed with an incoming text. She grabbed it, held it up to Gavin's face to unlock the screen, then went to his texts. Darius hadn't wasted time getting in touch with Westbrooke. Not only had he sent a picture of River Drake, but there was a short list of names with a single letter in parentheses after it. That was followed by *"R's working these now."*

Raine pulled up River's picture and took in the laughing visage of a twenty-something female with short, gold-streaked brown hair in a cute, but edgy style. She was standing on some street lined with brick buildings, grinning for all she was worth, her brown eyes with a hint of gold aimed at the photographer. It could have been any day-in-the-life-of-happy-young-woman image on social media.

"Pretty girl." She scanned the attached list as the phone buzzed with more incoming texts. Darius had sent over a couple of other photos to accompany the other names on the list. She turned to Gavin with a frown. "Darius sent the other names that your mother was looking into, mainly shifters, a couple of Magi. No Fey, no Amanusa."

"Did he give you anything else?"

"A couple of pictures of some of them, and then indicated that Ryuu's working on them now." She put the phone back in the cup holder, and when Gavin slowed, she peered through the windshield. "Is that it?"

"Yep." He hit his blinker and turned onto the street alongside the hostel. They went another block before they found a public parking lot across from a Chinese restaurant. They walked down the sidewalk through the stomach-rumbling scents of peanut oil, scallions, soy sauce, and ginger. Couples and singles meandered in and out of the restaurant as evening shadows stretched along the street.

They strolled past the boarded-up windows of an empty shop and the narrow brick façade of a comedy club. The club's patrons were starting to gather, and the ticket window was open, but the main doors remained closed. As they walked along the side of The Claim Jumper, where arched windows lined the floors, Raine noted the sturdy metal fire escape that zigzagged up the side of the building. Faint laughter drifted down from the roof, and Gavin looked up.

"Rooftop terrace," Raine murmured. When he turned to her, she added, "It was on the website."

He shook his head as they came up on the large windows that looked into the small café that dominated the corner where The Claim Jumper stood. Clearly, it was the place to be. Patrons filled the small tables inside and milled out onto the sidewalk.

Gavin slowed then stopped near an empty bench just outside the café. "Change of plans," he said in a low voice and tilted his head toward the windows framing the café. He took a seat, tugged her down next to him, wrapped an arm around her shoulders, and pulled her close. The door leading to the café opened, the soft ring of a bell escaping as two laughing couples tumbled out and headed farther down the street.

Raine rested her head on his shoulder. They were just another couple out for the evening. Mindful of the many eyes and ears, she used their mental bond to ask, *"What are we doing?"*

He bent his head over hers and rubbed his chin over her hair. *"Ryuu said Taliesin uses this place to house interns, so let's check to see how many are Kyn."*

Considering the Kyn were drastically outnumbered by humans and tended to stick to their own, Raine wasn't going to hold her breath. Behind her shields that kept the world at bay, she found the beautiful, mesmerizing ties of blue and silver that bound her to Gavin and to the natural magic that was so essential to the Kyn. She drew it close and felt the moment Gavin finally eased his side of the bond open.

As the magical connection settled into her soul, it was hard to describe the sense of belonging that followed. For so long, she'd been isolated by the wild and unpredictable nature of her magic. Surviving the twisted experiments of the elder Talbot had stripped her of her identity as Kyn and twisted her magic in unrecognizable ways, leaving her a misfit. When she'd emerged from the lab, she was no longer Fey, but something, someone else. She, who had no known shifter blood, shared her body and soul with a leopard, and she could do things no Fey should be able to do. It left her unwilling to explore her abilities, and instead, she focused on using her enhanced predatory nature to become the ultimate hunter, a Wraith.

When she and Gavin teamed up to save Cheveyo from a Soul Stealer, they created a bond not seen outside Bonded shifters. Her connection to Gavin served as a reassuring anchor that allowed her to explore the unknown depths of her magic. Together they discovered just how unique her ability to "see" magic truly was, but it wasn't without its costs. They'd spent months testing their boundaries, only to realize that while they might have the basics down, they had barely scratched the surface of what they could accomplish.

But this, scanning a small group in an enclosed space, should be easy. Raine closed her eyes and pulled the familiar hum of magic close. She brushed the silvery-blue bond that connected her to Gavin. *"Ready?"*

His arm tightened around her shoulders. *"Go."*

She lowered the barrier she held against the world, and her magic swept out like a living net visible only to her and Gavin. When she opened her eyes, she let out a small gasp. Here, in the heart of the city, where technology dominated, the tapestry was a chaotic web of muted threads interspersed with small bursts of brilliant colors. Colors that indicated Kyn. *"Holy crap."*

Correctly reading her shock, Gavin said, *"This hostel is definitely Kyn friendly."*

It was easy to pick out the humans—they were the blurry smudges—but over at the corner table was the gold-glinted chocolate of a witch with strong earth magic. Another table held the reddish glow of a lower-level Amanusa next to the icy ethereal blue of a Fey.

A jolt of satisfaction from Gavin had her asking, *"What?"*

"The desk clerk."

It took a second for her to realize that although the door they sat outside of led directly into the café, the café itself shared space with the front desk and lobby. Sure enough, the male behind that counter radiated a grass-green glow. *"Witch?"*

"That or a Fey," Gavin confirmed.

Either way, it meant they might not have to deal with the normal reticence about privacy. The clerk wasn't alone though. There was a huddle of bodies in front of the counter, one of which was Kyn, but the rest? She thought they were human, but there was something there, something she couldn't pinpoint. *"Huh."*

"What?"

The strange phenomena disappeared, and Raine shook her head. *"Nothing."*

He took her at her word. *"Ready to go chat with the clerk?"*

"Let's do it." She started to draw back but paused when something brushed against the edge of her awareness.

Gavin didn't miss her sudden stillness. *"What is it?"*

"I don't know..." She turned in the direction of the disturbance and scanned the nearby intersection. Other than the typical evening activity of pedestrians and cars, nothing and no one stood out.

"Raine?"

Instead of answering, she widened their magical net until it filled the intersection, hoping for a repeat of whatever was tripping her up. Out in the open, unencumbered by barriers, the magic lapped at inanimate objects like cars and buildings, only to slide around them like water around rocks. It swept over those walking or standing nearby but trying to cover such an open expanse thinned the power to nearly transparent levels. The only things she could pick up were the dark colors of what she was betting was a wizard standing outside a small bookshop across the street and a couple more witches or Fey—she couldn't tell which—going into the small grocers on the opposite corner.

"Raine?" Gavin called aloud.

"Sorry," she murmured. She took a deep breath and tugged the mental shield back in place. When she opened her eyes, the world appeared dimmer and darker, and a dull throb had set up shop at her temples. "I thought I felt something, but there's nothing there." She rubbed her cheek against Gavin's shoulder. "Ready to get this show on the road?"

He tilted her chin up with a finger and studied her face for a moment before finally responding. "All right, let's do this."

CHAPTER 10

Raine and Gavin bypassed the café's entrance to hit the second door that led into the hostel itself. Gavin pulled open the door and stepped aside.

"Oh." The startled exclamation came from the petite, dark-haired woman who looked up from her phone and pulled up short on the other side. Dressed in business casual, she wasn't the type Raine expected to see at a hostel, but then again, what did she know? Globe-trotting wasn't her thing.

"Please." Gavin waved his free hand, indicating for her to pass through.

"Thank you." Her smile was warm and polite, but her brown eyes were sharp as she took in him and Raine.

Something in her perusal made Raine pause as she returned the smile with a nod. The woman turned to the left and strode away, but Raine continued to watch for a few moments longer.

"Raine, you okay?"

"Yeah." She shook off her momentary distraction and stepped into the narrow confines of the hostel's lobby. It wasn't what she expected. With pops of color and eclectic decorations, it clearly catered to the young-adult crowd but without the dorm vibe. Instead, it was like walking into a boutique hotel.

With Gavin at her back, she crossed the brick floor toward the front desk as the scent of cinnamon and spice tickled her nose. Greenery was everywhere, tucked into the exposed rafters and piping of the old architecture, giving the enclosed dimensions a sense of space. An old key rack hung just to the right of the door, protected by glass and filled with white paper coffee coasters decorated with personalized comments, drawings, and photos. A few café tables were tucked into the bay windows overlooking the sidewalk. The cushy bench decorated with a couple of throw pillows offered another spot for those indulging in caffeine and sweets.

"Evening," the young man behind the counter called out. "I'll be with you in just a few." He turned back to the trio of backpack-and-duffel-bag-laden men huddled in front of the curved counter bordered with old ironworks.

Raine and Gavin drew closer and stopped a polite distance away as the desk clerk finished explaining the curfew and dining options. Clearly recognizing them as Kyn, the shifter casually repositioned so he could unobtrusively watch Raine and Gavin even as he listened to the clerk's spiel. It was an instinctive move, driven by a Kyn's innate ability to pick up on the unspoken "otherness" that set them apart from the humans. It also doubled as a subtle warning to back off.

"The café is open until midnight, but if you're looking for something a little more substantial, I would highly suggest the Tap Room just down the street." The clerk's gaze darted between Gavin and Rain and his three check-ins, but his polite smile didn't waver.

"Is there room service available?" the shorter of the two humans asked with a distinct German accent.

"No, but we will happily accept deliveries for you."

There was a quick spate of German, then the shifter picked up his duffel, and his key card. "Thanks."

His companions followed suit. Gavin and Raine stepped back as the trio walked past on their way to the elevator. The shifter brought up the rear and kept sneaking glances at Raine and Gavin as he guarded his friends' backs.

Raine followed Gavin to the desk. The clerk watched them approach, and his smile went from open and friendly to cautious and strained. "Evening."

She glanced at the clerk's name tag helpfully pinned to his shirt and did her best to appear non-threatening. "Hi, Dawson."

She clearly failed because his Adam's apple bobbed, and he took a small step back before catching himself. "H-Hi." His voice gained an octave, and his gaze skittered nervously between the two of them. He cleared his throat and managed a more professional, "What can I do for you?"

Gavin leaned an arm on the counter, his expression serious but polite, his version of intimidating charm. "We're hoping you can help us. Earlier this afternoon, a woman by the name of Nyla Durand called. She may have left a message for one of your guests."

The young man's Adam's apple did another bob, and his eyes darted away nervously. "We respect our clients' privacy and can't sh—"

"Dawson." The kid's name came out on a dangerous purr as Raine let a little bit of her power free, knowing it added an unsettling light to her gaze. When his eyes widened in panic and his breathing turned choppy, she continued, "If you want us to contact Chayton before you spill, feel free to stick to your company's policy."

Invoking the name of the intimidating Magi who was ruling in Cheveyo's absence was as effective as a compulsion spell. He kept his voice low, but the words tumbled over themselves. "She tried to leave a message, but the guest wasn't here."

Gavin pounced. "As in they'd checked out?"

He shook his head, his hands fluttering over the counter in a nervous tell. "No... I mean, I don't know."

The air around Gavin roiled with frustration, and Raine put a restraining hand on his arm. *"Easy,"* she warned through their bond. If they reduced Dawson to a gibbering pile, they would get nowhere. In a rare reversal of roles, she took over as Gavin pulled back both physically and emotionally, giving the trembling clerk a chance to breathe. "Could you explain that for us?"

Dawson gave a jerky nod and started to talk. "The woman who called this morning—" His eyes flicked to Gavin and back to Raine. "Ms. Durand, she tried the room, but there was no answer. She asked us to see if the guest was in, said the message was important. Avery, my manager, had me run up, but there was no answer, so she told Ms. Durand, asked if she wanted to leave a message, but she said she'd call back." He rocked nervously and managed an uncomfortable shrug. "Afterward, Avery had housekeeping check on the room, and they reported that it was empty, like no luggage, no sign of anyone being there. She had them go back on their records, and they said the room's been like that for almost a week, so Avery had me close out the account a couple hours ago."

Gavin pulled out his phone, swiped the screen, then

turned it toward Dawson. "Is this the guest you're referring to?"

The young man leaned in and looked at the photo. When he raised his head, his earlier nervousness was replaced by relief. "Yeah, that's her. River. River Drake."

"Do you know when River checked in?" Raine asked because the timeline wasn't adding up. According to Westbrooke, River had been missing for almost two weeks, not a handful of days.

"Yeah, it was a couple weeks ago. I remember because she paid for the first week at check-in, and well, we just charged another week to her card." Dawson frowned. "Hey, is she all right? Is she in some kind of trouble?"

There was something in the way he asked that had Raine and Gavin exchanging a look. Gavin pulled his phone back. "What makes you think River's in trouble?"

Dawson started to roll his eyes, caught himself, and said with clear youthful disdain, "Well, she and her boyfriend ghosted on her room, and all sorts of people are coming around asking questions. Altogether, it kind of has the makings of a true crime episode, you know?"

No, Raine didn't know, but she got his point. However, she was much more curious about the other thing Dawson had mentioned. "Boyfriend?"

Clearly following her train of thought, Gavin started thumbing his screen.

Dawson's gaze jumped between the two of them. "Yeah, kind of a new thing, I think, because initially, they had separate rooms, but a couple days after River checked in, they asked about switching to a single room."

Gavin held out his phone to Dawson. "Any chance one of these was her boyfriend?"

Dawson took the phone and scrolled through the

images from Ryuu. He paused, frowned, and slowed as he ran through the photos. "No, none of those were the guy, but a couple look familiar."

Could we have caught a real-live break? Excitement sparked, and Raine turned back to Dawson. "Any chance you can get us their names and when they were here?"

Dawson shrugged. "I can try." He handed the phone back to Gavin and lowered his voice. "But, um, I don't think the boyfriend was Kyn."

That comment brought Raine's attention on point. That kind of sensitivity meant the kid had to be a mid-level witch because most Magi couldn't pinpoint another Kyn unless something specific gave them away—such as the sense of standing next to a live wire that belonged to shifters or the skin-crawling uncomfortableness that emerged around the chaos-loving demons. "He was human?"

Dawson nodded. "One with money, though he tried to downplay that fact, but he had that kind of entitled attitude, you know?" He rolled his eyes then realized what he'd done, and his cheeks reddened. He cleared his throat. "Anyway, like I told the woman who was asking about him, I got the impression they were fairly new as a couple."

That pulled Raine up short. "What woman?"

"She just left. Said she was with the FBI, had a badge and everything." Dawson paled.

The face of the dark-haired woman from earlier popped into Raine's head. *"Well, shit."* She kept her attention on the clerk and didn't look at Gavin. *"What the hell is the FBI doing poking around in this?"*

"Hell if I know, but it sounds like their focus is the guy, not River."

"I hope you're right. Otherwise, this situation got a whole lot trickier."

Neither one of them wanted to deal with a government agency, especially if they could avoid it. She needed to see if she could track their mysterious agent. *"You stay here, see what else you can get from the kid."*

"And where are you going?"

"I'm going to follow little Ms. Agent, see if she's up for a chat." She pushed off the desk and aimed for the door, hoping they weren't too late.

"Keep the bond open, Raine." There was no missing the command in Gavin's order.

She gave him a nod and pulled open the door.

Behind her, she heard Gavin tell Dawson, "Let's rewind. First, tell me about your chat with the agent."

She headed for the door, knowing five minutes was more than enough for a solid head start. *"She's probably already gone."*

"Probably. But watch your back anyway and be polite."

She pushed through the lobby door and left him to it. *"Yes, dear."*

As the sun began its retreat and shadows stretched between the structured paths of the urban jungle, leaving pools of shadows in its wake, Raine wound her way through the early evening crowd. Under her skin, her leopard padded forward, scenting the evening breeze. With the ease of practice, she filtered through the tangled mix of food, perfume, sweat, exhaust, and dozens of other odors that wafted from the various openings lining the street. She tried to pinpoint the one she needed but failed. It was a long shot, especially when trying to track in the heart of the city, but she wasn't about to give up.

Unlike Xander, whose wolf could track a scent through the most difficult terrain, Raine and her cat were still working out their balance. Raine had only recently been able to accept the feline predator that lived in her soul. Once she did, she discovered just how crucial the cat was to her ability to hunt. Not only was she faster and quieter than Gavin when stalking their prey, but her ability to see in the dark and her sensitivity to scent was eerily similar to that of her leopard. Add that to her ability to visually track magic, and there was a reason being a Wraith suited her so well. All in all, despite the occasional bouts of temper, which may or may not have to do with her feline half, she finally had to admit her unplanned upgrades weren't a bad trade-off.

She studied the passing faces, trying to locate the dark-haired woman as she wended her way down the block. She stopped to wait for a light and felt that strange barely there brush from earlier, just before she and Gavin entered the hostel. Somewhere nearby, magic was being worked. She did a three-hundred-sixty-degree scan and found nothing.

Time for option two.

She cracked open the barrier that kept the modern world at bay and the strange, illuminated tapestry flickered to life as the world around her resolved into a magical weave that sat above the physical world like a half-imagined tattered quilt. In this place between worlds, it was obvious that magic and technology did not play nice. The rough, dark lines of man's fervent devotion to technology dominated the fluid threads of natural magic, and the tangled mess left her with a massive headache.

The sounds of traffic and conversations faded into the

background as she focused on identifying the traits carried by the four Kyn Houses in the metaphysical weft and warp. The easiest to pinpoint would be the Amanusa's knotted threads, a reflection of their chaotic natures. The shifters had smoother lines that mimicked the close alignment of their dual aspects. Then there were the brilliant starbursts that belonged to the Magi, who instinctively straddled the magical and mundane. The more elusive, ethereal threads that were few and far between belonged to the Fey.

Working on two levels wasn't easy. Someone brushed by her as the light changed, and bodies began to walk across the street, carrying her with them. She managed to dodge dog walkers and strollers while trying to pin down the flutter brushing the edges of her consciousness. It was so faint as to be nearly nonexistent and scared of losing it when she hit the sidewalk, she stepped out of the flow of foot traffic and put her back to a brick building. Only then did she narrow her concentration.

"What is it?"

She gave Gavin's question a mental hiss then said, *"Give me a second."*

She sifted through the threads until she uncovered an opaque knot that wavered in and out of focus. *"What in the hell is that?"*

"Where are you?"

"About a block south, just pass the ATM, east side of the street."

"Show me," he demanded.

She sent the image, and tension sang through their bond.

"Can you get a lock on it?"

"Maybe." She lowered her barrier a little more, and the clash of man and magic slammed into her. Stuck in the

heart of urban sprawl, the disconcerting psychic noise of the two was bone jarring. She sucked in a breath, gritted her teeth, and kept her mental eye on the unusual knot that kept flickering in and out of focus. *"It's a slippery little bugger."*

Not about to lose sight of it, she pushed off the wall and followed her instincts as they led her around the corner and away from the busier street.

"What are you doing?"

"My job." She stalked down the street and followed the tug into a small alley tucked between two buildings. The strange little knot gained definition, even as it flickered and faded, but it didn't disappear completely. Obviously, distance was a factor in what she saw.

"Whatever you do, don't play with it."

She rolled her eyes, even though he couldn't see her, and moved toward the back of the narrow space, where curious eyes couldn't see her. The weird tangle of lines hovered in the far corner next to a dumpster. *"I wasn't planning on it."*

"Then why am I getting the impression you're about to do something stupid?"

Probably because she was. *"I wouldn't call it stupid."* She inched closer, and the knot did its flicker-and-fade act again.

"Really?"

"More like necessary." The knot reappeared, and she realized that with every flicker, it was fading even more. *"Remember Flagstaff? When we retraced what happened with the Soul Stealer?"* She cupped her magical hands around the unknown signature, close but not touching, not yet.

There was a moment of silence. *"You want to read the magic's echo."*

Since it wasn't a question, she didn't treat it as one. Revisiting the past was tricky as all get out, especially when it required connecting with an unknown magic. There was something about this that wasn't right, though, and she couldn't let it go.

"Your damn curiosity is going to get you killed." Clearly, he had picked up her thoughts and wasn't happy about it. *"Give me a second."* His presence pulled back before she could respond.

She understood his concern. The last time she'd attempted something like this, the lingering magic fueling the echo contained a spell that had almost killed her. It would have succeeded if Gavin hadn't broken the cast before it finished. She counted her heartbeats and studied the fading knot.

Gavin's grim acceptance filled her mind. *"All right, if you're determined to do this, let's get it done."*

She took a big breath and braced. *"Don't let go."*

"You know I won't."

With that, she erased the hair's breadth of distance and wrapped her metaphysical hands around the knot. The world took a sickening tilt. When it steadied, she was sharing the space with a man who stood a good three to four inches shorter than Gavin. It was disconcerting to view the happenings of the past, and if she hadn't been tied so tightly to Gavin, she would have easily lost herself in the memory. Tethered as she was, she cataloged details for later, knowing Gavin was doing the same.

The mystery man wore a blue flannel, dark jeans, and a baseball cap. He stood with his back to her and carried a couple of white plastic bags. His image was faint, fading in and out, just like the magic she'd trailed. Raine didn't dare move, afraid of losing hold of the tenuous thread, but whatever happened here was recent enough to leave traces.

Puzzled, she watched as he threw the bags with red lettering into the nearby dumpster, ripped off his cap, and tossed that in as well. He stripped off flannel to reveal a black T-shirt, wadded it up, and tossed it into the dumpster. Then he turned to face Raine.

Brown hair, dark eyes, broad forehead, square jaw, no distinctive marks on his face or arms bared by the T-shirt—he could have been any average joe walking down the street, if not for the discordant way the magic fluctuated around him. He looked down the alley toward the street as if ensuring he wasn't being watched. Confident he was alone, he straightened, and a strange shimmer hovered around him like a mirage.

His face rippled as if something under his skin were trying to tear free. Her stomach lurched, but then he dropped his head as the magic around him flared sharply. When he suddenly gained a good three inches in height and thirty pounds in muscle, Raine worried she was losing her grip. Then he raised his head, which now sported a darker color, and revealed a totally different profile.

Shock rocked through her. *"Illusion."*

"A damn good one."

She had to agree. The hair was not only darker, but shaggier, the cut not so neat. The jaw was more angled and carried a bit of a shadow, and the nose was more sculpted. It was his eyes that had Raine sucking in a breath, though. In the brief moment the man turned her way, she caught the hint of red that ringed his iris. *"Tell me I'm seeing things."*

"You're not."

She went to follow the demon as he strode past her, his longer legs making quick work of the alley.

"Raine, stop!"

Gavin's sharp warning pulled her up short. *"What?"*

"Look at the weave."

She turned back to the knot still cupped between her palms. Not only had it doubled in size, but some of the threads keeping it connected to the overall tapestry were torn, their ends ragged and seeming to disappear into nothing. Those torn ends were coiling around her fingers and making their way up her wrists, winding around her magic like ugly gray worms. *"What is it doing?"*

"I don't know, but you need to let go."

On that, they were in agreement. She yanked her hands back, only to have pain shoot along her nerves as the nasty worm-like threads tightened on her magic. It was an ugly mimicry of what the Soul Stealer had once done, and not about to endure that agonizing experience again, she reached for the power that burned deep inside her and struck out.

White brilliant light filled her vision and seared along the threads, turning the gray worms to ash. When the silent flame died down, her hands were still tangled with the knot, but most were inert, and the mirage-like version of the world had stepped back. With fingers gone clawed, she tore away the last remaining threads, shredding the demon's lingering hold.

She didn't need Gavin's sense of urgency to raise the shield between her and the world, cutting off her connection to the tapestry. Whatever blood that demon called his was something she'd never seen before, and that made him way beyond dangerous.

CHAPTER 11

Raine, half-blinded by the pain in her head, stumbled toward the alley's entrance and braced one hand against the brick. Between the rough texture under her palm and Gavin's mental presence, she managed to stay upright.

"You okay?"

"I will be. Just need a minute." She sucked in air and rubbed at the ache in her chest. They couldn't leave it like this. *"I've got to follow him."*

"You going after him alone isn't smart."

"If I don't, we're going lose any chance we have of tracking him." She couldn't shake the feeling this demon was the same one that had taken Nyla. Why else would he be here? Of course, that begged the question of where he'd stashed Gavin's mother. She sucked in more air, and the throbbing ache ratcheted down a notch.

"He's Amanusa. All he has to do is slip into the Side, and we're screwed," Gavin pointed out roughly.

"All the more reason for me to stay on his heels." Raine straightened, took another bracing breath, and cautiously lowered her barrier once again. The tapestry unfolded

before her, and she cautiously sifted through the threads, searching for breaks in the natural pattern. To her left, it remained placid and undisturbed, but to her right, it rippled with the occasional spark of color and telltale snags of disturbances. She blocked out her physical discomfort, narrowed her focus, and moved out of the alley, headed toward the street she'd turned off from.

Curiosity was a cat's undoing, and she wondered if she had missed something in her rush to track down the agent. Her mind churned as she retraced her steps. She hit the corner and crossed with a quartet of well-dressed young professionals. *"Gavin, does the hostel have security cameras?"*

"You mean inside or outside?"

"Either."

"Let me find out." His presence withdrew.

It was a long shot. But they were chasing a Kyn, and most older Kyn tended to ignore technology, not because they discounted it, but because they didn't truly understand it. She didn't think that kind of back-ass-ward thinking was in play. *But just in case...*

She eased out of the way of two women so busy chatting, they weren't paying attention. The kelly-green lines wrapped around one indicated a witch, and her companion was tethered by loose knots of soft yellow and silver, identifying her as low-level Amanusa. The witch looked up and caught sight of Raine. Her eyes widened. She bumped the shoulder of her friend and altered their path to the outside edge of the sidewalk. Raine gave the two skittish women a polite smile and got small, shaky ones in return as they rushed away.

"No go on video." Gavin's voice filled her head.

She batted aside the flicker of disappointment.

Obviously catching it, he asked, *"What were you expecting?"*

"I'm not sure." She picked through her instincts. *"I feel like we're missing something."*

He paused then proved she wasn't the only uneasy one. *"Or someone?"*

Was that it? Was the demon working with a partner? *"Maybe?"* She knew her uncertainty was clearly evident. *"I'm trying to figure out why he's here. Is he tracking the agent, your mother, or us?"* She continued to make her way down the sidewalk as she searched through the ever-expanding web for signs.

"The only connection between my mother and the hostel was the number in her cell," he pointed out.

That ruled out the agent. *"Did you tag a tail?"*

"No." He didn't sound happy, but she wasn't all that thrilled about missing something so obvious either.

"Me either." She fiddled with the puzzle pieces as she waited for the little white man to give permission to cross the street. *"Could he be the boyfriend?"*

"Dawson said he was human."

"He could be wrong." She shifted aside as an older man talked on his phone while a small dust mop tugged at the leash in his other hand and dared to inch closer to Raine's boots.

"It's a possibility."

She moved her foot, trying to discourage mini-fido from nibbling on her boots. *"But you don't think so."*

"No, but we need to find out who this demon is—"

"Or who he's working for or with," she added, feeling a cautious excitement. The strange, skin-ruffling sensation from earlier made a comeback, stronger than before. She pivoted to follow. *"I think I've got something."*

"I'm almost done. Wait for me." Gavin knew her too well.

A flurry of high-pitched growls and yips erupted at her feet. She glanced down to meet the rabid eyes of the long-haired bit of fluff with a Napoleon complex. She bared her teeth in silent warning, and the mutt lost its courage.

"Dammit, Raine." Gavin's frustrated impatience beat at her. *"I don't like this."*

The signal flashed, and she crossed the street, slipping through the others as she locked on to the faint trace. If she wasn't careful, she would lose them. *"It's heading toward the river."*

His flash of concern was quickly stifled. *"Watch yourself."*

After spending years working solo, she was still getting used to the partner thing, but it didn't take a genius to read between the unspoken lines. *"I've got this."*

"That's not what worries me." His sentiment carried a skeptical pragmatism that nagged her.

"You think he's meeting up with a partner." The minute she put it out there, the logic clicked. *"I'll be careful, Gavin."*

"I'll follow as soon as I can."

Knowing he could use their connection to retrace her path, she said, *"Understood."*

She passed a leather shop and remained vigilant as she crossed the opening of a small, dark parking lot. That elusive thread pulled her deeper toward the riverfront and away from the chatter and activity that buzzed around the restaurants and bars. She veered away from the serene park that curled along the riverbanks and headed toward the metal fencing draped with construction tarps.

The sidewalks emptied, going from clean and well-lit to cracked and shadowed as the sun lost its grip on the encroaching night. The nose-wrinkling odors of the river drifted along the early-evening air and joined the miasma of rot and disrepair that clung to the battered structures behind the fence strewn with signs warning of imminent gentrification. This was not the venue for tourists, but a haven for those society would rather pretend didn't exist, at least until they were kicked out for those with money in their pockets.

Raine continued to track the elusive magical trail even as she noted the huddled figures tucked into dark corners. She turned off the street and down a makeshift boardwalk winding between the fenced-off lots of new construction and the abandoned streets filled with heavy-duty machinery. Her prey was either lucky or smart because this close to all the man-made metal and technology, the magical echoes all but disappeared into the night.

She noted where the trail's fading streaks wound around a cluster of construction dumpsters and disappeared beyond the fence. With the magical trail all but at an end, she let the mortal world take center stage and eyed the wire mesh. Somewhere behind it, in the ramshackle collection of buildings and rusted cranes, was her prey.

She called on her cat and used the graceful coil of muscles to spring up onto the edge of the dumpster, leap over the fence, and land softly on the other side. She remained in a crouch as she checked for cameras, but other than the motorized equipment illuminated by the lone security light, the rest of the area remained dark and shadowed by the heavy machinery standing guard over a pit seeded with the beginnings of new build. Just beyond and to the side of the pit was a pile of cargo containers and a small building that had probably once housed an office area. Scattered farther back were cargo cranes that rose like giant gallows against the light-strewn skyline and dangled over the dark waters of the Columbia.

That uncomfortable sensation whispered against her magic again, a deliberate lure, like a quivering rabbit. Just enough to tempt. Anticipation curled in her veins, and relying on the excellent night vision of her cat, she studied the area around the pile of cargo containers. Stacked in multiples of varying heights, it was a maze of nooks and crannies that would be perfect for a clandestine meet. She slipped a thin, black-hilted blade from her boot-sheath and held it at her side as she straightened. Staying to the deeper pools of shadows, she crossed the yard, her footsteps silent, her focus on her hunt.

Driven by a sense of urgency, she kept her back to the container walls, slipped into the shadowy narrow spaces, and followed the magical rabbit trail deeper into the deadly maze. The sounds of traffic faded, as did the reach of the lights. Tension replaced her wariness as a waiting silence crept in under the cloak of deepening shadows. She approached the edge of a container, stilled, held her blade at the ready, and moved only her eyes, searching the cramped confines around her. There was a small clear area ringed by containers and what looked like a makeshift worktable off on the far side. She didn't dare step out of the relative shelter of the containers because something was out there, doing the same thing she was—hunting.

Her instincts flared, but warned by her cat, she was already spinning around, her blade slashing out as the piece of darkness rushed toward her, forcing her closer to that open space. The blade made contact, and a sibilant hiss sounded. The darkness struck back. Raine took the only option available and leapt backward and into that space, curving her spine to keep her stomach from being opened. A thin line of fire kissed her skin. A warning to move faster.

The shadows boiled out of the narrow passage and spilled into the cleared area, resolving into a man who wielded a thick iron chain. He dragged it along the ground like a beloved pet. He gave a seemingly negligent flick of his wrist and sent the chain snapping in her direction, like a taunt.

Shit, if that hit, she would be in serious trouble. Her immunity to cold iron was higher than most Fey blooded's, but it wouldn't stop her bones from breaking under those thick links. She inched back farther into the open area, hoping to draw him away from the containers.

He followed, but his casual pace left her uneasy. So did the strange, dizzying dance of shadows that coiled around him as he circled to her left. It took her a second to realize he was using his illusion ability to mask his face. To combat the disorienting sensation of the demon's constantly shifting features, she focused on the unearthly glow of his red-ringed irises.

She didn't need her cat's hissed warning that she was being herded, it was obvious. Unfortunately, she didn't dare turn her back to him, so she pivoted with him, knowing there was more here than met her eye. Hair at the back of her neck rose. She darted to the side and slashed out, following the kiss of her blade with the clawed tips of her free hand, tearing through cloth and flesh.

A pained howl was abruptly cut short and replaced by a hair-raisingly deep growl of menace accompanied by the rattle of the chain. She dodged the chain with inhuman speed and years of honed muscle memory, but it was enough to drive her back, putting her prey farther out of reach as she tried to catch sight of her second attacker.

The writing shadows deepened, turning into a hazy fog that played tricks on her eyes. A minute shift in the air to her right had her striking out blindly. There was a grunt, but the bone-bruising grip of the chain wrapped around her blade and smashed into the back of her hand. Her fingers spasmed under the pain, and the blade tumbled from her grip.

A low, chilling chuckle echoed her furious hiss. She tried to pinpoint its direction, but the disorienting fog made it difficult. Shadowy figures were there and gone, seeming to inch closer. Sound was muffled as if her ears were clogged with cotton. Unable to trust her eyes or her ears, she kept her back to a container as anxiety nipped at both her and her cat. She flexed her aching hand, pleased to discover it was badly bruised, not broken. She crouched, coiled, waiting for a moment to strike, and pulled her second blade free from her boot.

Gavin's cool voice cut through her rising confusion, and she could sense him getting closer. *"Don't trust your eyes."*

Heeding his advice, she closed her eyes, gritted her teeth, and dropped the barrier between her and the world. When she opened her eyes, the world had taken on a strange dual-level perspective. Traces of magic licked among the shadows, and she focused on those tethered to the demon she faced. The other that danced around her, seemingly tied to nothing, she ignored.

Illusions. Not real.

She gathered her magic, into a ribbon of white, fluorescent power and let it flow into her blade, setting the metal alight. Then, using the powerful muscles of her cat, she leapt across the space between her and the demon. Her attack was fast and quiet, not giving the demon a chance to use his chain whip. She carved an X pattern through the densest lines of red gold, her magic all but searing through those threads that lay over vulnerable pulse points. The demon's pained howl hurt her ears, but she didn't let up, slashing out and forcing him to retreat.

The demon stumbled back and let go of the chain, but he didn't go down. He managed to smash a fist into her stomach, forcing her back enough to put space between them. He followed up with a vicious kick.

She blocked the kick and struck back with blurring speed. Her claws tore through his shoulder before he knocked her away. Then his figure appeared to break apart as something inhumanly large burst from the fragile human form. Wicked horns flicked in and out of the shadows, and something darker rose from behind him, blocking out the sky. The red glow of his eyes now burned with vengeance, and the almost six-foot-tall human was replaced by an eight-foot-plus pissed-off winged demon.

She stood there, fighting for breath, as panic locked its hands around her chest. "Oh shit."

The demon threw back his head and roared.

"Run, Raine!"

Heeding Gavin's warning, she and her cat turned tail and ran.

CHAPTER 12

Raine darted into the maze of containers, chased by the echo of the demon's roar. For maybe the first time in her life, she got an inkling of what the poor bastards she hunted felt like. And she had to admit, it sucked ass. As she raced between the containers, her initial spurt of instinctive panic faded, allowing her to think. With only one blade left, taking on an Amanusa in its demon form was not her smartest move, but desperate times and all that. She just needed to keep the beast occupied until Gavin caught up, which should be soon. Once he joined the party, between the two of them, they might be able to make the demon lose his head—literally.

Feeling the demon's presence bearing down on her, she didn't stop to look back. She raced around a container and found herself caught in a dead end. She dropped her blade and reached for her cat. Between one breath and the next, she shifted into the more nimble and stealthier feline form. Without waiting around, her cat leapt immediately for the top of the container.

Her claws found purchase on the pitted surface of the corrugated metal. The bruised bones of her hand left one paw weaker than the other, making the scrape of claws against metal overly loud, but she couldn't afford to be trapped. She ignored the ache, climbed to the top, and crouched in the darkness, her gaze on the wavering form of the stalking demon.

Like a nightmarish mirage, the demon's form wavered in the unusually silent night as it was caught somewhere between the Side and the mortal realm. Raine had witnessed the phenomenon twice—once when her ex-best friend tried to kill her and again when Natasha had fought with Ryder. Just like before, it was hard to get her brain to accept what she was seeing because a demon's form defied reason.

She waited for the demon's attention to turn away before she crept along the tops of the containers, away from human eyes and toward the riverfront. She stayed low, taking advantage of the concealing shadows. The tactic wouldn't work for long, but she needed just a little more distance. She didn't get it.

The demon raised his head, his split nose sniffing the air. He jerked his head around and zeroed in on her. The fiery gaze locked on to where she crouched, and the black lips peeled back from serrated fangs.

Deep inside her cat, Raine winced. That was one ugly-ass demon.

"Move, Raine." Gavin snapped and sent her the image of one of the loading docks down by the river.

Using the cat's enormously strong legs, she sprung for the roof of the far container. As soon as her paws hit metal, she was off and racing toward the river, the demon hot on her heels. She locked on to Gavin and the flare of active magic surrounding him. She wanted to ask what the hell he was doing, but there was no time left for anything more than a warning, *"Incoming."*

She was running out of containers. Every inch of fur was standing on end in warning, so instead of jumping to the last metal box, she changed course and hit the ground. An angry snarl erupted behind her, followed by the deafening sound of metal crumpling under something heavy. A tremor ran through the ground under her paws.

Shit was about to get real.

She dug deep and sped up, racing low, her dark fur blending into the shadows as the night around her took on weight. Using the glowing beacon of Gavin's presence, she adjusted her route. The air above her shimmered with heat. She rolled out of the way and narrowly avoided being shredded by the demon's claws. Back on her feet, she raced around construction debris and wished she dared to use the cranes, but going high wasn't smart. The fucker behind her was too freaking tall. A muted flap of heavy wings was her only warning before spikes of agony raked across her back. *Seriously? It can fly too?*

She snarled, swiped out, and felt something tear under her claws.

The demon's answering howl was strangely flat as he swatted her away.

She ignored the burn of fire along her back and down her hips and rolled to her feet. A rough pull on her magic nearly made her stumble. *"What are you doing?"* she hissed along the bond.

"Ensuring our hunt doesn't make the late-night news," Gavin shot back.

Her answering snarl came from both the woman and the cat because that was the least of their worries right now. The air pressure behind her shifted. She dodged to the side and rounded a yellow machine. Metal screamed under tearing claws. Buried in her cat, Raine winced at the ear-shredding noise as she aimed for the man crouched on the dock, his magic dancing wildly around him. He didn't look up from his casting, and she prayed that the demented prick on her ass was too focused on getting to her to click into the power Gavin was channeling.

Heavy metal screeched across the rough cement behind her, and the demon's presence closed in until she swore she could feel the hellish heat of his breath on her neck. Anxiety, terror, and adrenaline tore through her, but she focused on Gavin's spell that was reshaping the tapestry around him. *"Gavin."*

His hands moved, and the final piece of magic snapped into place. He stepped back, and in the tapestry, a circle of power flared to life. *"Bring him to the dock."*

Raine aimed for the circle and felt the moment Gavin transitioned to the Shadowed Paths and out of the demon's sight. She really wanted to follow him, but since her role was bait, she drew the demon closer to the dock. She leapt over the casting, careful not to let any part of it touch her, and landed on the other side. She turned and, with the dark river at her back, faced the demon. She lowered into a crouch and snarled in challenge.

The demon, intent on taking her down, wasn't paying attention to his surroundings and lumbered into the circle of magic that lay in wait. Gavin stepped out of the Shadowed Paths and, with the quickness of a lightning strike, triggered his spell. The answering flare of magic was so bright, it blinded Raine. She blinked rapidly as the demon caught inside screamed, but it was hard to tell if it was in anger or pain. Connected to Gavin as she was, she could feel the spell's tremendous drain. She added her strength to his even as she studied the spell to figure out what Gavin was doing. *"We can't hold him."*

"Not trying to," Gavin bit out, but the spell's power deepened.

Then what in the hell is he—

Realization hit her about the same time the pissed-off demon figured it out. Gavin was forcing the demon to make a choice—shift back to human form or escape through the Side.

The demon fought the spell's grip, his fury and frustration palpable, but faced with certain decapitation if he lost his demon form, his decision was inevitable.

So was the fact that when he made it to the Side, they would lose their ability to track his ass back to Gavin's mother, unless... *"Keep him busy, just for a few more seconds,"* she urged Gavin, knowing what she was about to do was risky, but determined to try.

He didn't answer, and she called up a basic tracking spell while the demon snarled at Gavin. Taking advantage of its distraction, she anchored the spell to one of the pitted red-gold threads attached to the demon. It wasn't easy keeping her touch light. In fact, the demon swung back her way and swiped out. She danced back and prayed to whatever gods were listening that the spell would hold. Tucked under one of those weird wings, it glowed a dull red silver, appearing and disappearing as the wings batted at the air.

Good enough.

She prowled along the circle's edge, her body low to the ground. She bared her teeth and let loose a menacing rumble, hoping to keep the demon focused on her and not the irritating itch of the spell. The demon tried once again to break free of Gavin's hold, but the circle of power held strong. Cleary aggravated by his inability to get to either of them, the demon gave one last vicious snarl. Then he took the easiest route and disappeared into the Side, leaving behind a hint of sulfur.

Twenty minutes later, Raine pulled up the zipper on a faded red hoodie then tugged it over the rolled-over waistband of the oversized sweats that Gavin commandeered from somewhere nearby. Although a bit worn and grimy, they didn't smell, which she counted as a plus. The minus, shifting from cat to woman meant losing her clothes, and she'd rather like those pants.

"Here." Gavin handed over her boots with her blades tucked inside.

"Thanks." She leaned against a stack of boards and slipped her boots over her bare feet. She winced when the move pulled at the long rake marks marring her back and hiss of air escaped.

Gavin put a hand on her shoulder and tugged up the hoodie. "He got you good." His fingers drifted along her side, and when they hit a particularly deep bruise, she flinched. "We need to get you fixed up."

"I'm good." Lying down sounded like a good idea, though. On top of all her aches and pains, her head was throbbing from her prolonged trip with the tapestry. She ignored his snort of disbelief as she straightened.

He let the hoodie fall back into place. "Fine, but I need to stop at the hostel on the way back to the car." He grabbed her hand and gave her a gentle tug. "Dawson was pulling dates and names when I ran out." He led her away from the containers and back toward the river. "You know that tracking spell may not work."

She managed a shrug. "Maybe, maybe not, but it's worth a shot."

He stopped and looked at her.

Since he wasn't moving, she stopped as well. "What?"

He caught her face in his hands, something working behind his eyes, then he gave her a quick, hard kiss. When he pulled back, he said, "Thank you."

A lump set up shop in her throat. She rubbed her cheek against his palm. "You're welcome."

He let her go, reclaimed her hand, and began leading them deeper into the site.

She looked back over her shoulder. "Aren't we going the wrong way?"

"You really want to jump the fence right now?"

"No."

"Then we'll go the long way."

The long way meant slipping through the narrow gap where the fence stopped before the sharp drop-off into the river. They kept to the shadows and made their way back to the park and the familiar lights and noise of the street. As they started back up the street, Raine's outfit garnered a few sidelong glances. She sighed.

Gavin caught it. "What?"

"Maybe you should quiz the clerk on your own while I wait at the car because this"—she waved a hand over her borrowed outfit—"isn't going to work."

Humor flashed through Gavin's face. "Yeah, you might be right."

"Go." She shooed him on. "I'll meet you at the car."

"Watch your back." He increased his pace and stalked off toward the hostel.

As he strode by one of the restaurants, a figure huddled in a darkened doorway held out a cup and rattled it. Gavin dug into his pocket and dropped money inside without breaking stride. The man mumbled his thanks, but stayed vigilant, eyeing Raine as she got closer.

She offered him a small smile as her pockets were empty. "Evening."

"Evening, miss." His gaze darted to Gavin's retreating back and returned to her; his voice was a pleasant baritone that didn't fit with his weather-worn appearance. "You might want to stick close to your man, there," he warned as she walked by. "These streets don't play nice anymore."

She paused and turned back. "They were nice?"

"Once," he admitted in a low voice as if reluctant to be overheard. "Not so much lately. They chased us out of our homes, locked us up." His gaze skittered around as if he worried the same "they" would be lingering nearby. "Gotta stay hidden." With that last ominous comment, he clutched his cup close and hustled off.

But the brief interaction gave Raine an idea. More than video cameras watched the flow of humanity that ran through the streets. Those who called the streets home had a front-row seat to nefarious happenings. It might turn up a big, fat goose egg, but maybe she would get lucky.

She took the next corner and made her way to the lot via the back alleys and empty sidewalks. As she strode into the less-illuminated areas, she shifted her gait, shortening her stride, hunching her shoulders, and running her hands through her hair until it tangled. As a disguise, it wasn't much, but it might be enough combined with her borrowed outfit and the night's concealment to pass as one of the invisible ones.

It took another block before she found what she

searched for huddled near the back door of one of the bars. Two men—one old enough to be marked by life, the other, still young enough to escape it—were crouched in the feeble glow of the light, Styrofoam boxes held close to their chests as they ate with their fingers, their bodies wrapped in a collection of oversized shirts and blankets.

She deliberately scuffed her heel against the ground to gain their attention and inched out of the shadows. "Evening."

The younger one half-turned to hide his dinner, while the older one puffed out his chest and frowned. "Don't got enough for you."

She nodded and did her best not to appear threatening. "'S all right, I'm good." She looked around and rocked back and forth on her heels. "I'm looking for my friends. They were gonna meet me down there." She waved toward the end of the dark, empty street. "Did you see them come by yet?"

"Didn't see nobody," the older man growled.

"You sure?" She added a hint of whine to her tone. "You'd remember her. She's wearing this cool patch, right here." She covered her eye and noted the slight jerk the younger man couldn't hide. "She said she'd meet me here, but she's not around."

The grizzled old man shoved his box to his companion, straightened his shoulders, and stalked forward. He didn't stop until he got right in Raine's face. "She ain't here, is she, girl?"

Keeping to her role, she stumbled back, lowered her head, and cowered. "Sorry, sorry, just worried. She was supposed to be here."

Unmoved, he continued to frown and crossed his arms over his chest. "You need to go on and get."

"I'm getting. I'm getting," she muttered and shuffled away. She stuck close to the buildings and reached for the shadowed paths in the nearby unlit spaces. An icy wind curled around her skin as the walkways between worlds opened. Shadow Walking wasn't something to undertake lightly. The twisted, warped version of reality that made up the in-between was accessible to those with strong Fey blood, but they were easy to get lost in. She stepped inside, and if the two men were watching, she had just faded into the night-shrouded streets. She didn't dare wander too deep along the twisted paths, not without knowing where they led, so she held her position and relied on the sharp hearing of her cat.

The younger man muttered, "Bet she's talking 'bout Dani."

"Then she's gonna be disappointed," the older one said. "And if she keeps it up, she'll be disappearin' just like that daft old woman."

"Dani wasn't crazy, Matt. Sam said they was being followed—"

"Sam was wrong, boy," the older man snapped. "She was convinced men in black was after her, but she ain't someone the government ever be interested in." The sounds of movement came, followed by a gruff "Let's head out."

"But I'm not done yet."

"Finish back at camp. Got a bad feeling', and I ain't sticking around to find out why."

Raine waited for their footsteps to fade before she stepped back into the real world. After the icy winds of the between, the cool night air felt comfortingly warm. She considered following the two men but knew they would either chase her off or clam up tight. Neither reaction would get her any closer to what was going on down here. It wasn't much, but at least it confirmed that Dani and Sam hadn't simply wandered off.

Blowing out a breath, she turned and headed through the frustratingly empty streets and back to the car.

CHAPTER 13

White walls and bright lights blinded Raine as icy agony burned through bone and tissue. Her heart slammed in her chest, a film of red hazed her mind, and try as she might, she couldn't escape from whatever held her ruthlessly in place. There were voices nearby. Cold and clinical, the inhuman drone roused old nightmares.

"Not again." Rage scrambled for a foothold under the rising flood of panic, but it kept slipping and left her buried under the breath-stealing wave of debilitating fear.

"Raine." Gavin's voice sliced like a shark through the numbing depths, tearing into her mind with brutal determination. "Wake up."

She reached for him and came awake on a shuddering breath. Her muscles were wracked with tremors, and a thin clammy sheen of sweat coated her skin. Her eyes opened, and there he was, his hair falling around his face as he held her gaze from inches away. She held tightly to his arms as he leaned over her, blocking out the weak moonlight and leaving them half-hidden in shadows.

His jade-green eyes were steady and his voice calm as

he offered her a much-needed anchor. "You're okay. Take a breath for me."

She tried, but the choking nightmare surged forward. Her lungs refused to work as the panic pounded at her. She shoved her palms against his bare chest, trying to escape.

He trapped her palms against his skin, holding them against his warm flesh. "Shh, it's okay. Just follow me."

She opened her mouth and tried, but the tight bands coiled around her chest wouldn't loosen. Under her palms, she could feel the steady beat of his heart, but it couldn't drag her out of the relentless pull of the lingering nightmare.

In an unexpected move, he rolled over, taking her with him, reversing their positions until she lay on top. He kept one hand over hers, not letting her go, and cupped her face with the other hand. His head came forward, and he gave a sharp nip to her lower lip. Not enough to hurt, just to startle. Then he commanded, "Breathe."

The inconsequential sting was enough to break the vicious cycle's grip, and with a harsh, rasping inhale, her lungs found air.

Gavin watched her from inches away, his gaze a combination of determination and concern. "Take another."

She did, and this time, it was easier.

"Good, keep doing it." He breathed with her. With each exhalation, tension leached from her coiled frame. After a couple of breaths, his hand left her face to pet down her spine in long comforting strokes, easing away the lingering tremors of her nightmare.

She dropped her head until her forehead rested against the hard planes of his chest. As both her breathing and mind calmed, his scent and presence wrapped around her, adding another barrier between her and her nightmare. She turned her head until his heart beat under her ear, drowning out her slowly calming pulse.

He continued to stroke his hands over her spine until the last of her tension slipped away. Only then did he say, "It's been a while." He must have caught her wince because his arms tightened. "Settle, babe. That wasn't a complaint. Just pointing it out."

She rubbed her cheek against him and reluctantly admitted, "I think the conversations about Dani and Sam triggered it."

"Probably." His muscles shifted under her cheek as his hands kept stroking.

She lay in his arms and greedily took comfort from his touch. Part of her continued to be stunned by his presence in her life. She had never once considered she would have someone of her own. Forever changed by the elder Talbot's twisted experiments, she had struggled to find herself and her place in Kyn world. Determined to never again find herself at the mercy of another, she'd embraced the soul-deep anger that fueled her and became the lethal hunter of not just the nightmarish madmen who were her personal demons, but of the monsters even the Kyn feared. It had left no room for things like self-reflection, love, or acceptance because those weren't options for someone who hated what she was and what she'd chosen to be.

Then Gavin had decided to hold up a mirror and show her that who she was and what drove her didn't define her. It wasn't until she'd almost lost him to the same sick science that had changed her forever that she'd let go of that destructive self-hatred and embraced the hunter she was. It wasn't easy, not at first. She had to set aside her self-imposed guilt; find a way to forgive herself, her mother, and her uncle; then accept the truth of who and what she was. Otherwise, she would eventually lose Gavin.

Even after that, they'd struggled to find their way to each other, mainly because she wasn't good at the whole trust thing. She'd been working on it, determined to make her place at his side when he tied them together at an inescapable level. With no other choice, they managed to get out of their own way and come together to save each other. He was more than a lover, a friend, and a partner. He was her other half, just as bent and damaged as her. Still, somehow, together, they were whole. They worked. And that made him her fucking miracle, even if she couldn't admit it out loud.

He brushed a kiss against the top of her head and turned them to their sides until they were face-to-face. "You're mine too."

She closed her eyes to keep back the press of emotion and brushed a soft kiss against his chest. She dropped her head to rest on his arm and licked her lips, tasting the hint of salt and male. Her hands began to roam as a different kind of heat leeched the last tendrils of ice from her skin. She traced the long, lean muscles of his arms with her fingertips, mapping their lines. On the return journey, she continued her barely-there touch over his jaw, feeling the soft rasp of bristles. She shivered but sank her hand into the silky strands that fell around his face and rose to catch his mouth with hers.

Their kiss started out gentle, but it wasn't long before the heat and hunger that simmered between them rose to the surface and demanded to be fed. She licked and teased even as his hand swept over her naked skin. He cupped her breast, his thumb sweeping over her nipple as he rolled her to her back and took over. His mouth left hers to trail a series of teasing nips and hot, open-mouth kisses that ended with him curling his tongue around her aching nipple before sucking it into the heated cavern of his mouth. A rumbled purr escaped as she arched closer, her hands buried in his hair, holding him close.

His mouth wasn't the only thing getting busy. His other hand drifted lower, teasing his way to her aching center, and she could feel him, hot and hard, against her.

Eager for more, she hooked a leg over his hip in silent encouragement. When his fingers continued to tease and he seemed to be perfectly happy at her breast, she managed a breathless warning. "Gavin."

He gave her breast one last carnal kiss before he raised his head and gave her a small, wicked smile. His fingers stilled, and she squirmed under his burning gaze. "Tell me what you want."

After months of intimacy that was far beyond physical, she had no qualms being blunt. "You," she demanded, gripping his shoulders and arching to rub herself against him. "Filling me. Hard and fast."

Red rode under his skin, but he went back to using that damned frustrating featherlight touch, refusing to give in. "What if I want to play for a bit?" He slid his fingers into her dampness, circling, but never touching where she needed it most.

Her spine arched, and her hips surged, desperately trying to follow that elusive caress, but she wasn't a fool. She uncurled one hand, stroked over the dips and lines of his abdomen, and slipped between their bodies to wrap her hand around his hot, thick length and stroke.

His flush deepened, his eyes turning almost luminous in their hunger, and the cords along his neck went taut. A low guttural groan escaped, and she gave a wicked grin of her own.

"Then I guess I'll just have to keep myself occupied." She swept her thumb over his tip and spread the silky drop over his sensitive head. His hips surged as he thrust into her hold in his own version of encouragement, and her answering laugh was husky.

They continued their sensuous play until the night's quiet was replaced by labored breaths, soft gasps, and heated moans. Raine tumbled through the fire only Gavin could create and let it burn away the outside worries as she followed him into a world where only they existed. Taste and touch took on a depth she knew she would find only with him. The depth that echoed in the emotional bond tied them together at a level so deep, it was indescribable.

She was coming out of her skin when he finally decided to give in to her demands and sank into her with a hard thrust that had her spine bowing. He held himself above her as he continued to thrust, slow and deep, until she demanded, "Faster."

He kept his pace frustratingly steady as he took her mouth in another heated kiss. She curled her arms around him, holding him close, and for added incentive wrapped her legs around him and began to ride, determined to drive them both crazy. Safe in both body and heart, she gave him what she would never give another. She put her lips to his ear and whispered, "Please."

His slow, seductive glide hitched, and instead of giving in, he stilled, turning to capture her mouth with his. When he raised his head, her mind was a blur, and her body was all but burning up. Her hips moved restlessly, trying to force him to move.

"Gavin, love, please, move," she begged as she stared

into his eyes. It was a plea she would never give another because there was no one else she trusted to be this vulnerable with, and he knew it.

"Gods, I love you, woman." His voice was rough, but there was no missing the depth of emotion.

She swallowed against the choking emotion and whispered back, "I love you too."

He held her gaze, and she felt the moment he broke, when hunger, love, want, and need all smashed through his tightly held control, shattering it in the most decadent way. He ravaged her mouth as he began to pound in her with a hard, fast pace, pushing her higher and higher, the storm between them wild and hot. When they finally broke free, their mingled cries filled the night.

CHAPTER 14

GAVIN

"There's something off about this demon."

Gavin leaned against the credenza that sat under an elegant painting and watched Raine pace the confines of Natasha's office with her normal fluid grace as she finished with their verbal recap of their riverfront adventures. Thanks to the Kyn's ability to heal quickly, most of her injuries from the previous night's encounter with the demon were all but gone. That hadn't stopped him from indulging in a very up-close-and-personal exam this morning in the shower—partly to check her injuries, partly just because he liked to run his hands over her. Memories crept in, bringing along a now-familiar hunger that roused more than his blood pressure. Raine shot him a look, and he dropped his head to hide a small grin. He folded his arms and adjusted his stance as he yanked his body back in line.

"There's something off about most of us." Natasha's voice was droll. She didn't look up from the papers in front of her. "You need to be a bit more specific."

Wary tension wiped away his amusement. Chances were damn high that Natasha knew exactly what he and

Raine were capable of, but he wasn't about to hand the Demon Queen proof on a silver platter. It was too dangerous. Theirs was an ability that could easily be exploited for all the wrong reasons. *"Be careful,"* he cautioned silently without raising his head. He felt Raine roll her eyes.

Before Raine could expound on her observation, the phone on Natasha's desk buzzed. Natasha's pen stilled, and she looked up with a frown. She used one blood-red nail to hit a button. "Yes?"

"Apologies, Ms. Bertoi." Rachel's tranquil voice came over the speaker. "But Mr. Kern is here with Special Agent Iliana Krychek from PCD. They say it's urgent."

Gavin shared a look with Raine.

Natasha turned her gaze on them, an eyebrow raised in question. "Send them back, please."

"Yes, ma'am."

Natasha set her pen down with a disturbing deliberateness then sat back in her chair, folding her hands in front of her. Her eyes were predatory, her smile sharp, and her voice carried an amused bite. "It appears we're about to find out what your mysterious agent wants."

Raine came over and stood next to him as they waited for Ryuu and the agent to arrive. Under her breath, she muttered, "Guess the boyfriend wasn't human."

He watched Natasha push back from her desk and stand. "Or they've figured out he hooked up with a Kyn."

"Or," Natasha said without looking at either of them as she came around her desk, "there's something more at play."

There was always something more at play, especially if Division was involved. The Preternatural Crimes Division was a specialized unit composed of psychic humans, created specifically to investigate what they called "unexplained" crimes. Nine times out of ten, Kyn were somehow involved. Most of his interactions had been with their sector chief, Victor Osborn, who'd been a good ally to the Kyn through the years. Despite his innate fairness and compassion, he was still a man caught between a rock and a hard place when it came to the political maneuvering of the powers that be.

A sharp knock interrupted Gavin's musing, and he straightened.

Natasha settled back against the front edge of her desk and called out, "Come in."

The door swung open to reveal Ryuu. His gaze bounced from Natasha to Raine to Gavin, then back to the impeccably dressed Kyn leader. "Natasha, I apologize for interrupting, but there's someone who needs to talk to you..." He looked back over his shoulder, stepped inside the office, then moved aside, putting his back to Raine and Gavin.

The dark-haired woman from the hostel stepped into the office, but she stopped in front of Ryuu, her attention clearly on Natasha. Ryuu reached behind the agent to pull the door closed then brushed his hand against her lower back in a subtle nudge. The woman gave a tiny jerk then moved forward.

There was a burst of amused speculation from Raine. *"Huh."*

Gavin kept his amusement to himself. *"Caught that, did you?"*

"Hard to miss."

She was so right. The Motoki Pack's Second appeared to not only know Special Agent Krychek, but also feel somewhat protective of her. Gavin wondered how long that had been going on.

Iliana was taller than Natasha but shorter than Raine and carried herself with an unmistakable confidence. She took in the room's other occupants, and her eyes widened. Genuine amusement lit her chocolate eyes as they zeroed in on Gavin and Raine. "Ahh," she murmured.

He inclined his head, and without moving from his side, Raine waved her fingers.

Iliana's lips twitched, but that glint of humor was tucked under polished professionalism when she turned to Natasha and inclined her head. "Ms. Bertoi, I apologize for interrupting, but thank you for seeing me."

Natasha's attention remained focused, and her polite smile didn't waver. "Of course, Ms. Krychek. Taliesin is always happy to assist Division." She motioned to Raine and Gavin. "It seems you've already met Mr. Gavin Durand and Ms. Raine McCord."

"Not officially." Iliana turned toward them and did another one of those nods. "Mr. Durand, Ms. McCord."

"Gavin," he corrected.

"Raine."

"Iliana," she returned.

"Please," Natasha cut in. "Have a seat." She waved Iliana to one of the chairs. As the agent repositioned the chair and sat, Natasha leaned back against her desk.

Ryuu angled the remaining empty chair toward the dark-haired woman and was still able to see both Natasha and the couple behind him. Gavin sank back against the credenza, and Raine's shoulder brushed his as she did the same. Neither one was inclined to shift their position, not when they had a good view of all the players.

Natasha wasted no time getting to the point. "You're here about River Drake."

Gavin gave Iliana credit—she didn't appear nervous about being in a room full of Kyn. She cocked her head. "I am, yes." She angled her legs, hooked a foot behind her ankle in that way women did, and leaned forward. "Can I assume she's one of yours?"

Natasha put her hands on the desk's edge near her hips, one nail absently tapping against the surface, and neatly sidestepped the question. "What did she do?"

Rather than rushing to answer, Iliana took a moment before she said, "I'm not sure she did anything. I'm more interested in who she was with."

"And who would that be?" Natasha didn't give an inch.

"Colin Guthrie." Iliana shared the name as if it should mean something.

"Bet that's the boyfriend," Raine's voice brushed against his mind.

"That's a sucker's bet." But it sounded familiar for some reason, so he asked, "Who is Colin Guthrie?"

Iliana twisted her hips in the chair so she could see Gavin, and a tiny grimace swept across her face. "Colin Guthrie is Senator Albert Guthrie's only child."

Now he remembered. He looked at Natasha and didn't bother to mask his distaste. "Isn't he one of the ones behind the registry?"

In the months since Mulcahy's death, the human government had been pushing hard for a way to track the Kyn, especially as it became more and more apparent that their time in the shadows was about to end. Although the majority of those in power knew nothing about the Kyn, those who did had designated a special committee to oversee the eventual introduction of the Kyn to society. One proposal, mandatory registration of the Kyn, was turning into a major point of contention. The Kyn who called the Eastern Seaboard home were currently involved in negotiations with the human decision-makers to ensure that when the Kyn came out, they did so on their terms, not one imposed by bigoted, frightened humans.

"Unfortunately, yes," Iliana admitted.

"He isn't as vocal as the others, but he's definitely in favor of it," Natasha added.

"He's scared." Iliana's tone made it clear she wasn't making excuses, simply stating a fact.

"No, he's just a bigot." Raine's anger resonated through their bond.

He got where she was coming from, but on an intellectual level, he also understood the humans' justified fear. He couldn't hunt the worst the Kyn had to offer and not admit there were reasons for humans to piss their pants, but humans produced equally monstrous beings that gave Kyn nightmares. The difference was, they just hid better among human society.

"Scared or not," Ryuu spoke up, "it doesn't excuse intolerance."

"No," Iliana said. "It doesn't."

"But you're not here for political reasons, are you, Iliana?" Natasha cut in.

The agent shook her head. "No, I'm not. The senator and his son have a somewhat strained relationship. However, when Colin failed to show up to a scheduled lunch with his father, the senator realized that his son was missing."

"He couldn't just not want to eat with dear old dad?" Raine drawled.

Iliana shook her head. "It was impressed upon myself

and Chief Osborn that Colin would not have missed this particular lunch appointment."

"And why is that?" Natasha asked.

"It seems he was planning on introducing his father to his new fiancée."

A moment of shock zinged through the room, but it was Natasha who repeated, "Fiancée?" She looked at Ryuu, who shook his head.

Iliana caught the movement. "What am I missing?"

Ryuu glanced at Natasha, who hitched her chin in a silent signal to share. He turned back to Iliana. "Colin's fiancée? You mean River Drake?"

Iliana gave a cautious nod.

Ryuu frowned. "The information we received indicated that River was on vacation touring the States. There was no indication from her family that she was engaged."

"Vacation?" Iliana frowned. "That's not what I was told."

"Obviously," Raine muttered.

Natasha gave her a quelling glare then turned back to Iliana. "I understand that Division tends to hold their cards close, but why don't you share why you think River was in town."

Iliana shifted in her seat and shot a look at Ryuu. Whatever she saw must have reassured her. "The senator's representative shared that Colin had met River during his student exchange. He and River were on the same research team supervised by a professor at Cambridge. Their relationship started there. River was in town to interview for an internship."

There was so much to explore in her explanation, but Gavin went with his gut. "Was the senator aware his son was involved with a Kyn?"

"No," she said. "Colin did not disclose that fact until recently."

He put two and two together. *"Shades of Romeo and Juliet,"* he sent to Raine, thinking about how River had switched her reservation after checking in.

"Yep," she was quick to respond. *"And I bet River didn't tell Daddy she was dating a human politician's son."*

He spoke out loud. "She's the reason the senator and his son were at odds."

"Unfortunately, yes," Iliana admitted. Color darkened her cheeks, and her spine stiffened. "She's also the reason the senator is convinced his son's disappearance is directly connected to the Kyn community."

Raine snorted. "Let me guess. Because he's an ass and we don't like him, we must have targeted his kid? Which would make River some Kyn version of Lolita?"

Iliana arched a brow, and with remarkable tact, she stated, "While I don't agree with the senator's logic, it's not outside the realm of possibility."

"He's an irritant, I'll admit," Natasha said. "But not one that earns such a Machiavellian approach."

"Nor do we waste time targeting the innocent." Raine's unspoken implication was clear. That kind of play belonged to the humans.

It earned a sharp glance from Iliana that was strangely colored by a flash of compassion or maybe pity—he couldn't tell which. She turned back to Natasha. "While I believe you, the fact remains that Colin is missing. And witnesses put him with River. Until I walked in here, I was hoping you could help me find her."

"What changed?" Natasha asked.

Iliana motioned toward him and Raine. "As soon as I saw those two, I figured River had to be missing as well."

She took them all in before returning to Natasha. "She is missing, isn't she?"

"She is," Natasha confirmed. "Her family reached out to us because she hasn't been in touch. They were under the impression that River was here on a simple vacation."

Iliana glanced at Ryuu, her brow furrowed, then turned to Natasha. "Vacation?" She shook her head. "I was told it was an interview for an internship."

"It was." Ryuu held up his tablet. When everyone looked at him, he grimaced and dropped it back to his thigh. "Sorry, didn't get a chance to share, but updated information came in this morning. It confirms she had an interview scheduled on the down-low because her family wasn't keen on her living overseas."

"Who was she interviewing with?" Raine asked.

"Hang on. I didn't get that far yet." Ryuu looked at his table and started to pull up the information. Across from him, Iliana shifted uncomfortably in her seat.

Gavin got a bad feeling.

When Ryuu looked up again, his eyes had gained an amber tint, his face was dark with accusation, and his voice rode the edge of a growl as it broke the tense silence. "A research arm within Biovita."

Silently, Gavin cursed. Raine went rigid at the mention of the biotech company that had spawned the human geneticist who'd developed a drug that killed shifters.

Clearly recognizing the danger, Iliana's voice was calm and her gaze steady as she talked to the enraged shifter across from her. "The lab is still under surveillance even though we found no evidence that anyone at the lab knew what Sutler was up to."

Before Ryuu could snap at the brave but misguided human, Gavin asked, "Who arranged the interview?"

Iliana cleared her throat carefully and never took her gaze off Ryuu. "A professor she was working with at Cambridge. He and the project head were roommates at one time."

"Name," Ryuu demanded.

"Sean Haines." When his attention turned to his tablet, Iliana's shoulders slumped for a moment before she regathered her composure. "I can send you what I have."

It was clearly a peace offering, but Ryuu was too focused on his prey to listen. "Fine."

Gavin shared a look with Natasha. "That's too close for comfort."

"I agree." The Demon Queen's attention stayed on Iliana, who was doing her best not to react, which was a reaction all on its own. Natasha's voice dropped to a dangerous purr. "Agent Krychek, was Colin a part of this internship as well?"

Looking resigned, she sighed. "Yes."

Natasha arched a brow. "And yet Division doesn't think the company warrants a closer look?"

"There has been nothing to indicate any involvement in his disappearance."

"*You have to be fucking kidding me,*" Raine seethed through their bond, although nothing showed on her face. "*This stinks to high hell.*"

"*I agree, but for now, we play the game.*" It was a warning, pure and simple. He hadn't missed the minute shifts in Iliana's posture that said more than words. "*Like Natasha said earlier, there's definitely something deeper happening here.*"

Natasha, unaware of their silent exchange, made a non-committal hum as she studied Iliana. "Then I hope Division isn't insulted when we conduct our own investigation."

The fine line of tension that held Iliana's shoulders rigid, eased just a touch as Natasha brought the meeting to a definite close. "You are the top of your profession for a reason, Ms. Bertoi," the agent said as she stood. She brushed a hand over her hip as if smoothing out a wrinkle. "Division has no say into who or what you can investigate. We are simply hoping to locate Ms. Drake to see if she has any information about Mr. Guthrie's whereabouts."

Gavin recognized the political tap dance Iliana so skillfully executed. It indicated that Division, or more likely Osborn, harbored his own concerns about Biovita's involvement, despite the senator's pressure to conclude otherwise.

Natasha straightened as well. "Taliesin will do its utmost to ensure Division's message is delivered."

"Thank you."

Natasha inclined her head.

Iliana turned to him and Raine as Ryuu rose from his chair. "If you need anything." She pulled a business card out of a pocket and handed it over. "Please let me know."

Gavin took the card with a nod.

The agent turned to Ryuu. "Will you walk me out?" It wasn't really a question.

For a long moment, they stared at each other. Gavin was certain the minute they were out of earshot, they would have a very heated conversation. Still, Ryuu's voice was painfully polite as he said, "Of course." Then he followed her to the door and carefully closed it behind them.

CHAPTER 15

RAINE stopped in the open doorway of GAVIN'S office and rapped her knuckles on the doorjamb. "Hey." When he looked up from his computer, she said, "We've got an appointment with a Dr. Anders, head of Biovita's Research Department, at three thirty this afternoon."

He sat back and rubbed his hands over his face, probably hoping to erase the signs of exhaustion and stress. "No pushback?"

When he dropped them, she didn't have the heart to tell him they were still there. She settled her shoulder against the doorframe and shook her head. "Chatty receptionist heard Taliesin and made some interesting assumptions."

"Like?"

"Like, I was an investor. Seems Dr. Anders has spent the day drumming up funding for his newest project. Lucky for us, they had a last-minute cancelation from another interested party, so she was quite excited to slip us in."

He leaned back, folded his hands behind his head, and closed his eyes. "Any idea what the project is?"

She gave a half shrug. "Not a clue." And she wasn't

overly concerned. She and Gavin just needed a few minutes of the good doctor's time, however they could get it. What did concern her was how stressed Gavin looked. "Did you eat lunch?"

"Yeah, at my desk." He opened one eye. "You?"

"Same." The urge to reassure the normally self-assured man in front of her made her antsy.

Clearly picking up on her discomfort, he gave her a faint grin. "I'm fine, Raine."

Her brows rose in silent disbelief.

He dropped his arms and sat back up. "I'll *be* fine."

That she could believe.

He reached for his mouse and dragged it across his desk. "You know those missing Kyn that Dawson thought he recognized?" He looked up from his monitor, and she nodded. "Ryuu was able to trace two of them to Portland."

Hmm, interesting. "Which ones?"

"David Schulz, a wizard out of Pensacola, and Astrid Howell, a shifter from Canada." He pushed up from the desk, snagged his phone, and headed toward her. "Want to go see what kind of dirt we can find?"

She straightened as he came in close and wrapped an arm around her waist. She curled her arms around his neck and stroked his nape under the band holding his hair back. "You know how much I love getting dirty with you."

Wicked heat lit his jade eyes, easing some of the newly acquired lines bracketing them, and his lips curved temptingly. She went up on tiptoe as he dipped his head. Their lips met, and they indulged in a brief, but heated kiss. When he raised his head, his gaze roamed her face, and the earlier worry crept back in. She cupped his jaw and brushed her thumb over his lower lip. "We will find her, Gavin."

He didn't say anything, simply pressed a kiss to her

thumb then pulled back, letting her go. His expression resumed its normal detached demeanor. "Let's go rattle some cages, shall we?"

Gavin pulled up to a Craftsman-style house situated in one of Portland's older neighborhoods. The address they followed to get here proclaimed that this was Luna House, but there was nothing special about the neatly put together gray-and-white home to set it apart from its neighbors or indicate a business of some sort resided here. According to the information Ryuu had dug up—and he'd dug deep— Luna House was a haven for Kyn looking to escape dangerous situations. Most situations fell under the personal domestic kind, a problem within their community, just as it was with the humans, but there were other dangers Kyn hid from.

The treelined sidewalks ran along the narrow streets, and the small patches of deep green were accompanied by carefully tended flowers in various colors. She followed Gavin up the cement walkway to the sitting porch, noting the two discreetly positioned cameras that followed their approach. Gavin pressed the button on the small intercom set next to the door. Raine studied the tasteful wrought-iron grills that decorated the windows. Whoever lived here was highly conscious about security.

"Yes?" a polite, but reserved woman's voice answered.

"Hello, my name's Gavin Durand. I'm with Taliesin Security. My partner and I were hoping to talk to you about one of your employees. Astrid Howell?"

Silence answered then came, "One moment, please."

They waited without speaking. Less than a minute

later, the door swung open to reveal a striking woman. She was tall, with a body that showed she took care of herself and could probably take care of anyone who dared to test her. Her hair had probably once been as dark as her arched brows but was now that eye-catching silver some women were lucky to call theirs. Her dark eyes were sharp with a hint of hardness as if she had not only seen some shit, but endured some as well. Her full lips were unsmiling, but she was unfailingly polite. "Have you found her?"

"No, ma'am, we haven't," Gavin answered.

The woman stood in the opening as if guarding the entrance. "She's been gone for months." There was a hint of accusation in her voice as if it was somehow their fault.

Gavin remained unruffled. "We're aware, Ms…"

"Caroline," the woman offered, her tone short.

"Caroline, if you prefer, we can speak out here," Raine offered, sensing that there would be no invite to enter.

Sure enough, the woman nodded and stepped out, pulling the door closed behind her. She stood in front of the door and folded her arms across her chest, some of her earlier tension easing. "Thank you."

"Of course," Raine said and because she understood that this was a haven of sorts, added, "We aren't here to cause trouble for you or your residents. We're just looking for whatever information you can share about Astrid."

Caroline drew in a breath and waved them toward the bench and two chairs positioned on the porch. "Please, have a seat." She waited until Gavin and Raine had settled on the bench, then she dragged one of the chairs around to face them, keeping her between them and the door.

They waited for her to get settled.

"*You start,*" Gavin urged Raine, probably noting the way

Caroline kept flicking small glances his way. Unlike the normal female reaction, this one was warier.

"Caroline, my name is Raine. We're hoping you can tell us about Astrid, who she was last seen with, what her plans were, that sort of thing."

"I can tell you that she didn't just up and run away like they tried to imply." There was a whip to Caroline's voice.

Raine cocked her head. "Who implied?"

"The police," she all but sneered.

Confused, Raine asked, "Wait, you went to the police?" That didn't make sense. Kyn rarely involved the mortal authorities in their business.

She shook her head. "No, they came here when her landlord was unable to find her to collect his rent." Her nose wrinkled, and her lip curled in disgust. "They stuck around long enough to confirm she wasn't here, but when I tried to explain she wasn't the type to disappear without notice, they brushed me off."

Not an unexpected response. "Did you reach out to Astrid's family when she went missing?"

"There wasn't family to reach out to," Caroline said. "Her mother had passed away when she was younger, and she was raised as a permanent ward until she reached her majority."

Okay, so no family, but Astrid is a shifter. "And Vidis, did you reach out to him?"

Caroline bit her lip, and her eyes slid away. "We don't advertise who's involved with Luna House for obvious reasons."

They kept their employees as hidden as their residents, which was understandable considering there was no telling what lines a pissed off Kyn would cross when intent on terrorizing their favorite victims.

"I did notify the Pack, but that was, like, three, four months ago, when I was getting nowhere. I don't know what happened with the information, and since I'm not a shifter..." The older woman gave an uncomfortable shrug.

"Magi?" Gavin asked.

Caroline's eyes went sharp and guarded. "Yes."

Raine ignored the other woman's sudden wariness and thought about the timing. *"Could've been when Vidis and Xander were handling all the rogue Bitten."*

"I bet it was. It would explain how Astrid's disappearance got downplayed." Out loud, he asked, "How long had she worked for you?"

"About a month." Caroline looked at the door, a frown creasing her forehead. When she turned back to them, her face was set in resolute lines. "You understand what and who we are? What we offer?"

Raine studied the woman, noting the tiny tells of someone with heightened situational awareness, the casual side glances that monitored her surroundings, the shift of position that would allow her to easily reach the door before they could stop her. That was easy enough when she saw it every day in the mirror. "We do."

A car drove by, and Caroline watched it as it passed. When it was gone, she said, "When we decide to bring someone onboard, it is an intensive process that includes a deep dive into their background and current life situation."

"Because you can't afford to hire someone who will be a danger to your tenants," Gavin said.

Caroline gave another nod. "Astrid's interview spanned two months. During that time, she proved herself to be dependable and forthright." There was an ache in her voice.

"She made an impression." Raine kept her voice low.

"She did," Caroline agreed. She paused as if considering

what she would say next. "There are many reasons someone will want to work with Luna House, and the majority of those arise from deeply personal experiences."

Raine read between the lines. "Astrid was a survivor."

"In every sense of the word," Caroline said. "Her father was a drunk who killed her mother, and she was determined to ensure other children wouldn't be left alone in similar situations. She would not walk out on this position or me."

Gavin stretched out one leg, his thigh brushing Raine's, as he laid one arm along the bench's back behind her. "Was there anything or anyone here that cause you or her concern prior to her disappearance?"

"No." Caroline's answer was decisive and quick.

"How about any of Astrid's friends?" Raine asked. "Did you know any of them?"

Caroline started to shake her head then frowned. "She was new to Portland, and I know she met a couple of people online, and they would meet up for drinks and dancing."

Gavin pulled out his phone, called up the photos of the other missing Kyn, and passed it to Raine to hand to Caroline. "Any of those look familiar?"

Caroline took her time going through the photos, stopping every now and then. "This one? No, not him. This one." Her tone became more confident. "I think she went out with him." She handed back the phone.

Raine glanced down at the screen, where a young man stared back. He could've been any good-looking college student, if you went for the clean-cut young conservative type.

But Caroline wasn't done. "I was over at her apartment, and he showed up, said he was hoping to catch her for coffee. She told him that she couldn't as we were working."

She held Raine's gaze. "She and I weren't planning on working."

Raine angled the phone's screen toward Gavin. "She was looking for a reason to blow him off."

Caroline nodded. "When I asked her about him, she said that they didn't click. She had been brushing him off, but he wasn't getting the hint."

Gavin took the phone. *"David Schulz."*

Good thing he was up next on their list then, especially since Caroline didn't recognize any of the other faces in the photos, including River's. But there were two Kyn they didn't have photos for. Even knowing it was a long shot, Raine asked, "Does Luna House ever work with the homeless community?"

"Not directly, no." Clearly puzzled but determined to provide whatever help she could for Astrid, Caroline said, "There are rare occasions when our residents may be out on the streets between leaving their homes and coming to us."

Unsurprised by the answer, Raine sighed.

"However..." Caroline's brow pinched as she looked out over the yard. "I can pull Astrid's application to verify, but I believe she was volunteering with one of the downtown shelters while she was going through the interview process." The older woman looked back at them; grief darkened her eyes. "Astrid once told me that she was a volunteer addict, which was why she decided to go turn that addiction into a career in social work."

Gavin sat up and leaned forward. "We'd appreciate any information you're willing to share."

"I'll go get that for you, then." Caroline pushed up from her chair and turned to the door.

Gavin and Raine rose as well.

With her hand on the knob, Caroline looked back, a

baleful light burning deep in her eyes. "I know what logic is telling me." Her voice was empty, her emotions ruthlessly held in check. "But promise me you'll bring her home and ensure this doesn't happen to anyone else ever again."

Vows were never lightly given in the Kyn world, so instead of answering aloud to something they couldn't guarantee, Gavin gave the Luna House's guardian a solemn half bow, and Raine dipped her head in acknowledgment.

CHAPTER 16

"Dude, David was a straight-up dick," drawled the too-skinny young man who lounged in the doorway of an older apartment. "He owes us, like, two months of rent." He scratched the back of his sunburnt neck, and Raine prayed his board shorts wouldn't drop with the movement.

"More like three," corrected his roommate, who was perched on a sofa arm just inside the apartment and pulling on a tank over his tanned chest. His head of dark curls popped out of the tank as he tugged it down. "He still owed us half of his security deposit, swore he'd pay it back when he got that job, then he ghosted."

"Ghosted?" Gavin asked.

"Bailed, disappeared. Got keep up old man."

A phantom hand slapped her ass, and she dropped her head to hide her grin.

David Schulz's last-known address wasn't that far away from Luna House, but you wouldn't know it to look at the apartment complex. Unlike the neat and tended yards of prettily painted bungalows, it was a tri-level cement box that catered more to those just starting out. A mix of TV chatter and stereo-enhanced bass lines mingled with the laughter of tenants sitting on beach chairs in front of open doors. Although it wasn't fancy, there was still a sense of community, likely due to the fact most tenants were young adults on carefully crafted budgets, dedicated to living their lives how they wanted. Bikes were padlocked to the metal railings, and cars that were older than the tenants were parked out front.

Raine and Gavin gathered plenty of looks on their way to the second-floor unit that David had listed as his. When they knocked, they found his justifiably angry roommates instead. Interestingly enough, both were human.

Gavin and Raine were leaning against the railing as they talked to Jake of the board shorts.

"Which job was that?" Gavin asked.

Jake looked back at dark-haired Tony. "What was it? Like a doctor's office or something? Answering phones or some shit?"

Tony shrugged his tatted shoulders. "No, that wasn't it. No way in hell he'd waste his time doing something like answering phones."

Jake snorted. "Yeah, because he was *so* much better than that." He rolled his eyes and shook his head. "He didn't seem to understand he wasn't going to be able to stroll in and get the job he wanted with no prior experience just because he could bullshit with the best of them."

Tony stood and waited on the other side of the door, bracing his arm against the frame. "I want to say it was some type of data analytics for a research company. Oxo-something, I think. He was all excited about it, kept saying how it was just the first step in getting in with the right people, even though it was the wrong company. That once he got his foot in the door, the rest would be a cakewalk. Idiot." The last was muttered with obvious disgust.

"What do you mean 'wrong company'?" The longer Raine listened to the two men share about David Schulz, the louder the warning bells sounded.

"Like he put in multiple applications, but the one he was counting on didn't come through," Tony said.

"That's because Biovita doesn't just take anyone," Jake added. "Their requirements are phenomenally stringent for interns, but they do top-notch work, which is why everyone wants in."

"Looks like we'll have another name to ask Dr. Anders about." Gavin's grim mental voice was at odds with his apparently casual façade. "So he didn't get into with Biovita?"

"Nope," Tony answered. "We were riding his ass about rent and utilities, so he pretty much had no choice but to take whatever offer he got."

"Onidyn." Jake snapped his fingers, his grin huge. "It was Onidyn Research. Remember? April said she worked there for a couple weeks, then got tired of the mansplaining, so she left."

"Yeah." Tony nodded. "Sounds like David would fit right in, then."

"No doubt," Jake agreed.

Gavin was typing out a text, presumably sending Ryuu the name of David's employer.

Raine decided to get the two back on track. "So David got the job with Onidyn, and then how long before he took off?"

Jake looked at Tony. "I don't know. A month, maybe?"

"Sounds about right," Tony said. "Once he started, he wasn't home much."

"Yeah, I think he was schmoozing up the other employees," Jake added. "Because he was barely here. Just long enough to crash and shower mainly."

"He was definitely trying to worm his way into that crowd." Tony pushed off the doorframe and twisted his spine. "Saw him a couple of times downtown with a bunch of other wannabe suits. I work over at the Tap Room. He came in once, and then when I was heading home, he was over at one of the other bars."

Gavin pulled up their photo array of missing Kyn and handed his phone to the two young men. "You recognize any of these faces?"

Jake took the phone, then he and Tony went through the photos.

Tony took the phone. "Yeah, this one." He handed it back to Gavin, River's face on the screen. "She came in with another guy. He had left the table, and David made his approach. She shot him down, polite like, but Cara, who waiting on the table, overheard and said it was a definite shutdown." He grimaced. "Serves David right. Not cool to hit on a woman who is obviously out with another man."

"Definite creeper move," Jake agreed with a shudder. "But then again, there was something just off about the guy. He always made my neck itch."

Tony sighed. "Your neck itched because you refuse to use sunscreen, jackass."

"Whatever," Jake muttered, but Raine didn't miss the unease in his eyes. "Still, I'm glad he's gone. Makes it easier to sleep at night."

The fact Tony didn't laugh that comment off said more than enough. Then again, most wizards tended to give people bad vibes, likely because they tended to play with dark things. "Did David leave any of his stuff behind?"

Jake rubbed the back of his neck and looked at his roommate, who straightened and folded his arms over his puffed-out chest. "Yeah," Tony admitted grudgingly. "But we took it to Second Chance before Ike moved in."

"There goes our opportunity for going through his stuff for clues about what he was up to," Raine groused. *"If any of it was decent, it'd be the first thing to go at a thrift store."*

"A long shot for sure, but one we might need to follow up on."

Raine figured he was being optimistic, but she didn't argue.

The boys braced as next to her Gavin pushed up from the railing. "How long ago was that?"

The two young men exchanged shrugs, and Jake answered, "Two, maybe two and a half, weeks ago."

Raine looked at Gavin, both of them acknowledging the duo hadn't waited long to dump David's stuff. They had the two young men list everything they could remember donating, and after a couple more questions that went nowhere, Raine and Gavin took their leave.

CHAPTER 17

THE BUILDING THAT HOUSED BIOVITA WAS TUCKED BACK BEHIND the Hillsboro Airport, although Raine thought calling the collection of airstrips an airport was a bit of a stretch. Still the two-story muted-yellow structure that backed into a tree-heavy creek was just as architecturally dull as its almost-twin structure on the south side of the parking lot. She pulled the SUV through the roundabout, past the front entrance that sported the dubious protection of curved metal slats arched over the entryway, and into the less crowded parking lot. She cut through the midsection and came back around to where she could pull through.

"Let's hold tight," Gavin said as she shut off the engine. "Xander and Axel finished at the hotel, and Ryuu was sending them our way. They should be pulling up soon."

"Sounds good to me." Actually, anything that put off being schmoozed by some lab rat worked for Raine.

When they left Taliesin, Gavin let Ryuu know they were heading out. Even that minimal check-in was annoying, but both she and Gavin had learned the hard way to take those few seconds to give someone a heads-up, especially when they were walking into trouble that threatened to erupt with a vengeance.

She turned in her seat so she could see Gavin. The lines of stress were still there and so was the block he'd instigated on their bond. His constant rejection, unintentional though it may be, was driving her crazy. Maybe it shouldn't have bothered her as much as it did. After spending months intrinsically bound, though, she found the distance hurt, especially since if their positions were reversed, he would be all up in her shit in a heartbeat. She hadn't pushed it only because it involved his mother, and the associated emotional landmines were daunting.

But they were partners, as he liked to remind her when she was struggling, both professionally and personally. Normally, he was trying to get her to share, but now that the roles were reversed, he'd backed away. That gave her insecurities and doubts plenty of space to play.

Did he not trust her to help shoulder his worries and fears?

Gods knew he'd held her steady more times than not, and she wanted a chance to return the favor, but part of her was scared to make that demand. Those hateful whispers twined around her heart, leaving behind painful cracks. She tried to figure how to share without sounding like a whiny brat.

He looked up from his phone and arched an eyebrow. "What?"

She pressed her lips together and took a deep breath. "I know this isn't the place or time, but we need to talk about you and your mom."

His face blanked momentarily, then a frown creased his forehead. He opened his mouth, only to shut it without answering.

The silence in the car turned uncomfortable. Her stomach pitched, and ice invaded her chest. Somehow, she kept her voice even because even a hint of accusation would lead to nothing good. It took more courage than she'd expected to keep talking, especially when she wanted to get out of the car and just leave. "I get that you need to work through things on your own, which is why you won't let me in, but even if I'm not the greatest at family relationships, I can still listen if you want to vent or if you just need to—"

The rest of what she was so awkwardly trying to convey was lost as he leaned over, caught her face in his hands, and kissed her. She curled her fingers around his wrists, to hold on as his end of the bond opened. A miasma of worry, guilt, anger, gratitude, and love filled their connection, though his kiss stayed gentle. Feeling him slide back into the holes he'd left had tears threatening. The vise on her heart eased for the first time since his mother had called.

He pulled back just far enough that they could see each other without going cross-eyed. He held her gaze without letting her go. Under her thumbs, his pulse pounded. "I'm sorry."

She managed a small shaky smile. "It's okay. I just…" She shrugged.

"It wasn't you, babe." His gaze saw too much. "I've been so caught up in my own head, I didn't realize I was holding back."

She bent her head until their foreheads met, and she closed her eyes. "Partners, remember?"

"I remember." He pulled back, and when she opened her eyes, he admitted, "This whole situation is fucking with my head."

"Understandable. But I'm here, and I can help you unfuck it."

That got her something close to his normal grin. "I'll take you up on that offer."

"Just not now," she qualified.

"Later, when we're done here."

She raised her brows. "Promise?"

"Promise." He pressed one more closed-mouth kiss to her lips and let her go.

She resettled in her seat. "Now that we've got—" She caught sight of a familiar truck approaching. "They're here."

Gavin twisted in his seat as they both watched the black mud-spattered truck park on the other side of the tree a few spaces away. They got out and waited under the tree. The man who stepped out of the driver's side waited at the hood for the eye-catching blonde, then the two headed toward Raine and Gavin.

"Axel, Xander," Gavin greeted when they reached him.

Axel raised his chin to indicate his hello, his rough-hewn features unreadable. The dark sunglasses hiding his eyes didn't help either. Nor did the lingering scars from the claws that had nearly claimed his life.

The two shifters stood in front of Raine and Gavin. The shimmer of energy surrounding them nipped at Raine. Axel's was especially strong because he and his wolf were still dealing with the fallout from nearly being trapped in the Side.

"Hey, you two," Xander said as she pushed up a pair of retro round-lens sunglasses into her spiky blond hair tipped in...

"Pink?" Raine asked. "Since when do you do pink?"

Xander wrinkled her nose. "Since Ryuu won our M&M bet."

"Do I want to know?"

"Don't ever bet on blue."

Raine shook her head. Xander and Ryuu regularly engaged in outrageous bets. The last one proved Ryuu's flair in the kitchen, which resulted in some cupcakes that tasted phenomenal despite their X-rated appearance.

Gavin turned to the silent man at Xander's side. "You doing okay?"

The question wasn't a simple inquiry, but a captain evaluating his soldier. Axel ran a hand through his thick dark-brown hair, which explained the hint of disarray in the short cut. His lips curved into a grim line. "Better. It helps having something to do. Sitting around drives me crazy."

"Fair enough," Gavin said. "Did you two find anything at the hotel?"

"Not much." Axel rolled his shoulders as if trying to get rid of the excess energy roiling around him. Something behind Gavin caught his attention, and Raine turned to see what it was.

A man had stepped out of the building and was standing near the front doors, his attention focused on the roundabout at the front of the complex. Clearly, he was waiting for someone.

"Ryuu was right," Xander said as all four kept an eye on the man at the entrance. "A shifter was there, but based on the scent trail, Axel and I agree it was left prior to what went down."

"So we're left with our rouge demon," Gavin said, exchanging a look with Raine.

"Which is going to be a bitch to track," Raine groused.

"Is Fahd available?" Xander asked as a dark sedan turned off the street and headed toward the roundabout.

The man at the entrance fussed with his clothes in a nervous tell.

After Natasha killed Jamie, Fahd was the lone Amanusa of the Wraiths. If he was available, that would give them an edge when trying to track down the demon.

Gavin shook his head. "He's on assignment. Otherwise I'd have already pulled him in."

"We were able to pin down Dani and Sam's last known location," Axel confirmed.

The dark sedan stopped in front of the anxious man, who moved forward, and tension slid down Raine's spine. That sixth sense that had saved her ass more times than she could count whispered a warning.

"Raine?" Gavin's voice joined the rising buzz in her head as a man stepped out of the sedan.

Sunlight glinted off the blond hair that topped the six-foot-plus frame of an immaculately dressed man. He stood in the open passenger door of the sedan and shook hands with the waiting man. Words were exchanged, then Mr. Anxious turned to the doors.

Recognition hit, triggering an old, entrenched fury. Every muscle locked in place. "Are you fucking kidding me?" she all but hissed.

The blond man looked around. When his sunglasses-covered gaze spotted the quartet in the parking lot, he stilled and stiffened.

"Is that—" Xander started.

"Yeah." Raine's voice was low and lethal. "Jonah fucking Talbot." Head of Talbot Foundation and her personal nemesis. If it were up to her, he and his father's legacy would be wiped out of existence.

"Raine." Gavin's voice was hard with warning.

"I'm good." She didn't take her gaze off Jonah.

Another heartbeat passed as Jonah continued to stare their way. The other man said something, and Jonah turned away to follow him inside.

Raine blinked and shoved back her emotional reaction. When it was safely stuffed away, she turned back to the group and repeated, "I'm good."

Gavin studied her for a moment then nodded. "Right."

Xander made a disbelieving snort. "Uh-huh, sure you are." When Raine turned and glared at her friend, the petite shifter didn't back down. "If you want to be believable you might want to get rid of the I-want-to-bathe-in-your-blood look you've got going on." Her smile was all teeth. "Not that I blame you, but still"—she waved a hand—"full daylight and all."

The last bit of murderous need sank back under Xander's dark and dry humor, and Raine managed a casual shrug. "Don't worry. I like this outfit. I don't want to stain it." She turned to Gavin. "You think he's one of the potential investors?"

"It's possible," he answered. "Talbot Foundation's research has taken a huge hit in the last year."

All four exchanged knowing looks since the Wraiths played a pivotal part in the impetus behind that hit.

"We need to know what he's up to," Raine said. "Find out if this mess is in any way connected."

"What is with humans and their science?" Xander groused.

Raine said, "It's the closest they can get to replicating magic."

"And they hate not being in control," Axel added. "If they can't own it, they'll make sure no one else can either." He turned to Gavin. "Does his presence change your plans?"

Raine didn't take offense at his implication, not when

she was too personally invested to maintain the emotional distance needed to evaluate the potential threat. Like Axel, she looked to Gavin as their captain to make the final call.

Instead of answering Axel's question, Gavin asked one of his own. "Were you and Xander planning on following up on Dani and Sam?"

The burly shifter folded his arms over his chest. "Yeah, they used a mobile health unit that's currently parked over at Fifty-Third."

Gavin looked at Raine. "Why don't you go with Xander and leave Dr. Anders to me and Axel."

It was more an order than a suggestion, but swapping partners made sense. If she ran into Jonah inside the lab, there was no guarantee things wouldn't disintegrate into violence. "Will do."

Gavin took in Axel's untucked button-down collared shirt and dark jeans. "You good with playing the money man for Taliesin?"

Axel's smile was sharp. "Of course. I'll just channel Vidis."

"Not sure that will be any safer," Raine shot back. The Northwest Alpha's hunting instinct was in no way diminished when he donned his role as Taliesin's chief financial officer.

Axel slid his sunglasses down, and his dark-brown eyes, lit with the feral light of his unsettled wolf, met hers. "I can promise no one will be left bleeding." His "Can you?" was left unspoken.

Before she could snap back, Xander bumped her shoulder. "Come on, let's leave them to brown-nose."

Raine gave in with a sigh. "Fine." She looked at Gavin. "Watch yourself."

"You too."

With that, Raine turned and led Xander to the SUV.

CHAPTER 18

"Gavin's mom hooked up with Westbrooke?" Xander drawled as Raine pulled away from Biovita.

"So it appears." Raine slid a sidelong glance at her friend. "Were you there when Vidis spoke to him?"

"I don't kiss and tell," Xander warned.

Raine fought back the urge to roll her eyes because her best friend had a tendency to overshare, normally after a copious amount of alcohol. But she let Xander have her delusion. "Don't want a blow-by-blow. Just your impressions on the man."

Xander took a minute, clearly gathering her thoughts. "A voice over a phone line isn't much to work with."

Raine drummed her fingers on the steering wheel. "I get that, but other than knowing he's on the Council and acts as a liaison with the human's European governments, I can't get a picture of who I'm dealing with."

Xander hitched a leg up into the seat, and despite the seat belt, she managed a position that let her see Raine. "Well, we know he's doing the dirty with Gavin's mom."

"Yeah, not sure that's helpful," Raine said drily.

"No, but I do find it interesting, considering Westbrooke's reach. Is she using him, or is it a true love match?"

Raine wasn't comfortable sharing Gavin's opinion that his mother wasn't capable of a true relationship. Besides, she worried his experience with the woman colored how he saw her and her choices. Instead, she went with the neutral, "In the end, does it really matter?"

"Maybe," Xander said. "If she decides to use that relationship to get to Gavin and by extension the Northwest, then that *maybe* becomes *yes*."

Stunned by the shifter's implication, Raine risked looking away from the road to glance at Xander. "Is that what you think? That Nyla faked her own kidnapping to get Gavin's attention?" She turned her attention back to the road and shook her head. "No way. First, Gavin barely has anything to do with her. She's tried repeatedly to reforge her connection with him. I've been there before when she called, and let me tell you, I did not envy her. Gavin was cold as ice. When she called this time, it was clear she expected him to blow her off, and when he agreed to see her, she was relieved, really relieved."

"And second?" Xander asked.

"Second, it may not be her that's trying to find a way into the Northwest."

Xander's laugh was soft. "Oh my god, he was right."

Not quite following, Raine frowned. "Who?"

"Warrick. He warned me you'd think Westbrooke was up to no good."

"Maybe he isn't," Raine argued. "Leo's name wasn't alone when we were trying to figure out who was gunning for Mulcahy and Natasha. Maybe Westbrooke's involved up to his eyebrows and is just using Drake's request to cover his ass." She warmed up to her theory. "What if Westbrooke's behind the missing Kyn and this is his way of not only removing Nyla but the Northwest from whatever diabolical plans the Council has?"

"I think you and I have become way too cynical," Xander said.

She might be right, but after all the betrayals and lies of the last year, Raine wasn't inclined to take anyone or anything at face value. "Is there such a thing?"

Instead of answering, Xander sighed. She was quiet for a moment then said, "My impression of Westbrooke was that he was genuinely worried about the missing Kyn, including his goddaughter and now Nyla. I can't speak for his initial call, but the one last night when he called Warrick for an update, it was definitely Westbrooke the man, not the councilman in charge."

"Why is he checking in with Vidis? Why isn't he calling Natasha? Or Darius?"

"Because Westbrooke wanted to let Warrick know he and Giles Drake will be arriving as soon as they could get the travel arrangements made."

Raine figured if Xander didn't sound happy about it, odds were that the Northwest Alpha wasn't happy either. "Bet that didn't go over well with Vidis."

"Nope." Xander popped the *P*. "My mate does not appreciate another shifter throwing their weight around in his territory."

Raine winced. The last time Vidis went head-to-head with another Alpha, it did not end well. "Should we prepare for another Chavez situation?"

A snicker escaped Xander. "Not quite. For one, Drake isn't a wolf."

Raine blinked. "Wait, seriously?"

"Drake isn't just a last name," Xander said.

Raine's brain put two and two together and screeched to a halt. "There's no way dragons still exist, Xander."

"You sure about that?"

Since Xander wasn't laughing, Raine wasn't sure whether her friend was fucking with her.

"Oh my gods." Amusement suffused Xander's voice as she let Raine off the hook. "Your face, Raine. Priceless."

Without taking her eyes off the road, Raine smacked her hand into Xander's shoulder "Bitch."

Still snickering, Xander said, "Honestly, take it with a grain of salt. Dragon shifter stories are rampant, but there's not much proof. Just the 'my grandmother's uncle's second cousin' saw one once' accounts."

"So, if Drake isn't a wolf or a dragon—"

"Ah, ah, I didn't say he wasn't. I just said there's lots of unfounded tales about them," Xander corrected. "However, if any of those bloodlines have survived, they wouldn't be inclined to advertise."

No, they wouldn't. Risking exposure, especially to humans, would be fatalistically detrimental to them. "I wonder if we can get him to shift and find out."

"I dare you to ask him," Xander said. "I want to make sure my marshmallows and chocolate are ready to go when you do."

The idea was tempting, but Raine let it go to focus on more important things. "How soon do you think Westbrooke and Drake will be here?"

Xander dropped her leg and twisted until she was once again sitting facing forward. "Given the sense of urgency I heard, I'm waiting for Natasha's call to come in and meet them."

If they wanted to hunt unhindered, they needed

something solid quick because once the two men showed, egos and politics would turn the whole situation into a tricky mess. "You think the mobile health unit is going to give us anything solid?"

"It's a hell of a long shot, but it will confirm the last time someone had eyes on Dani and Sam." Xander shook her head and rubbed the back of her neck. "They should've never been abandoned."

Raine got it—pack was all about family. "I'm not sure even if you had offered, these two would have taken you up on help."

Unfortunately, the Bitten saw themselves more like unwanted, embarrassing relatives people didn't admit to having. It left them unprotected and easy prey for those intent on harming the shifters. After the Motoki Pack lost one of its most-loved members to a drug that turned the highly controlled shifters into feral wolves intent on carnage, Xander had been hellbent on bringing the Bitten into the pack so they couldn't be used again.

"I know." Xander folded her arms and sighed, her resignation clear. "The Bitten don't trust easily, rightly so. Dani and Sam have been here for a while now, and every time we made an approach, they made the necessary noises just so we'd leave them alone."

No surprise there. It would be hard to believe that the creatures that turned you into a moon-driven monster, would now want to help you.

Raine turned off the main road and onto the one that led to the park. "I'm surprised Dani and Sam would make use of this mobile health unit."

Most Kyn avoided anything having to do with human medicine, especially since they didn't suffer from most human illnesses and mortal medicine was a crapshoot when used on the supernatural.

"Remember, Bitten are transformed humans. So it's a combination of old behaviors and a need for quick cash," Xander said. "They don't have our natural inclination to stay far away from humans and their needles."

That made sense, but it was also dangerous. "How big of a problem is it? Having Kyn donating blood and whatnot?" She made a left and saw the truck parked at the end of the parking lot. There wasn't a line waiting, but there were people scattered about. Some sat at nearby picnic tables. Others were sitting on the curb of the sidewalk. But they all watched as she pulled in.

"Good question. The Bitten tend not to stick around long, so there's really no way to tell, but we know Talbot's mad scientist got samples from both Kyn and Bitten, so some Kyn are willing to risk it."

"Which makes it easier for men like Talbot to target us." Raine shut off the engine and studied the comings and goings happening at the mobile health unit.

Xander unsnapped her seatbelt. "We've always been targeted by the humans, Raine." She reached for her door. "It's just that now their aim is better."

Raine and Xander stood on either side of the truck's rear opening as the harried woman in scrubs wrapped a blood pressure cuff around a scrawny, scratched arm of her patient. "Yeah, I know Dani and Sam, but I haven't seen either one lately."

"Do you remember the last time you saw them?" Xander asked.

The woman held up a finger, and the two Kyn waited as she tracked a pulse, waited for a beep, and made a note on her tablet. "All right, Jerry my man, you're doing better, but you need to take your meds on the regular." She unwrapped the cuff then tossed it onto the nearby counter, along with her tablet. She twisted on her stool and reached into a cabinet to pull down a bottle. She shook out a few tablets and handed them to her patient, along with a bottle of water. "Take these now. I'll get you some more to hold you until next week, okay?"

"Sure thing, Kel." The man took the pills and drank a third of the bottle while the nurse put together his prescription. When she handed them off, she added in more verbal directions, then he was scrambling out of the truck.

Kel's shoulders slumped, and she dragged her hands through her short hair. "Hopefully, he'll be back." She shook it off, straightened, and folded her arms, which were covered in brightly inked sleeves, as she eyed the other two women. "Tell me again why you two are asking about Dani and Sam?"

"We're looking into a series of disappearances, and their names turned up," Xander explained.

"Uh-huh." Kel sounded unconvinced. "Dani and Sam are good people." And clearly, she was protective of her patients. She waved a hand to indicate those milling around outside, waiting their turn. "Most of them are. They're just caught up in some really shitty circumstances. Just because they're displaced doesn't mean they're up to no good."

Raine didn't miss Kel's tone, and it made her like the nurse more. "We don't think Dani and Sam have anything to do with the missing, but we think they might have gotten caught up by whoever's behind it."

"Why? Those two are outside the age range that's normally targeted." When Raine and Xander didn't say anything, the nurse gave them a cynical eye. "You know, you're probably barking up the wrong tree. Most likely, they decided to move on. Lots do."

Xander shook her head, her voice firm. "Their friend doesn't think so."

Kel raised a brow. "You talking about Mike? Tall, lean, kind of nervous and twitchy?" When Xander nodded, Kel frowned. "Guess that explains it."

"Explains what?" Raine asked.

She looked out over the parking lot. "Why Mike hasn't been by for his script."

"So, the last time you saw Dani or Sam?" Xander pressed.

Kel scratched by her ear. "I come through here every couple of weeks. I don't remember seeing them last time, so at least that?"

It wasn't much, but it was something. Xander and Raine asked a couple more questions, but Kel didn't have much more to offer. They thanked her and walked away. As soon as it became clear they were leaving, Kel's patients crept back in.

As they walked away, an undeniable weight settled onto Raine. "Let's hang here for a few," she said quietly.

Xander nodded, and they headed toward a nearby tree with a wide trunk. She leaned back against the solid surface, her hands under her hips.

Raine stood at her side, leaning her shoulder against the rough bark, as she tried to pinpoint who was watching them. From behind her lenses, she studied the park and its occupants, not sure what she was looking for but not in a hurry to head back in.

It was interesting to note the clear delineation between those taking advantage of the mobile health unit and those out enjoying the day. A trio of joggers veered around an older man pulling a wagon filled with his belongings as a dog of indeterminate origins stayed close to his side, his gaze watchful as he protected his human. A few kids played near a woman who sat on a blanket and watched them and their belongings. There was a mix of bodies napping in the grass and taking advantage of the sunshine. The nearby benches were seeing some action, then there were those determined to get in their all-important exercise, oblivious to the world around them.

Just another lazy afternoon at the park, but that prickle of unease stuck with her.

"Three o'clock," Xander warned in a low voice.

From behind her dark lenses, Raine scanned the indicated area, and her gaze drifted over the parkgoers. She wasn't sure what it was, but something about the male dressed in cargo shorts and a T-shirt at a picnic table caught her attention. He was seemingly focused on his phone.

"Table?" she asked Xander.

Xander turned her face away as if looking back at the mobile health unit. "Yep. He's doing his best, but he keeps watching us."

Raine followed her lead and shifted her attention away, not willing to reveal that they were aware of the guy. "You're not exactly flying under the radar." *Understatement of the year.*

Xander's turned her head with its spiked white-blond hair tipped in pink toward her. "What? You don't like my outfit?" The petite blonde was dressed in chain-draped black cargo pants and biker boots. Her metallic purple tank revealed the lean muscled arms decorated with ink, and her sunglasses didn't do jack to hide the delicate tattoo that covered the claw marks on her face.

"It's definitely you," Raine said with a small smirk.

Xander shifted her weight, lifted her arm to tug her sunglasses down just low enough to peer over the top rim, and eyed Raine's outfit of black jeans, olive-green T-shirt, and heavy-soled boots. Her gaze deliberately touched on the dark, white-streaked hair pulled back in a braid, the ink that peeked out from under the short sleeves, and the leather cuffs around Raine's wrists. "Not all of us can get away with Laura Croft-Rogue crossover."

Raine coughed to cover her amused snort. "Please, I'd need a hell of a lot more cleavage to pull that off. Plus, I'd rather have Yelena's outfits."

Xander grinned and shoved her glasses back in place. "Yeah, those Black Widows are the shit."

They bumped fists, and Raine said, "He's on the move."

Sure enough, the guy at the table had stood up, shoved his phone in a pocket, and tugged his hat down. As he stepped over the bench, he snuck a glance their way. Between the hat and the sunglasses, it was hard to get a face, but he was definitely interested in the two of them.

Xander settled back against the tree as the guy angled away from the parking lot and moved deeper into the park. "Want to make a bet he's trying to circle behind us?"

"Sucker's bet," Raine said. "We need some cover."

Xander tipped her head toward the trail to their right. "That path should take us into the trees and out of sight of most."

"Wanna be bait or hunter?"

Xander pushed off the tree with a put-upon sigh and brushed her butt off with her hands. "Bait." She tugged on Raine's olive shirt. "You'll blend better."

Together, they crossed to the trail that wound deeper into the forested interior of the park. There was something to be said for the overly abundant greenery of Oregon. The persistent forests were one of the biggest reasons both Lycos and Fey called the Northwest home. Keeping their pace casual, they followed the path through the dappled shadows and into the quieter area of the park.

Once they were clear of other parkgoers, Raine let her magic seep free to touch the innate power the natural world offered. It was hard to describe the connection, but it allowed her to track their prey as he trailed them. Jarring notes of sweat rode the slight breeze that carried a mix of damp earth and growing things. The slight hitch of his breathing didn't blend with the chorus of birds and insects. Anticipatory tension filled the natural calm that Mother Nature never failed to provide. Little signs came together in a vivid picture.

When the path diverged, Xander went right, moving into the thicker growth that offered deeper shade. They were about a hundred fifty yards in when she flicked her fingers in a sign for Raine to break off.

Raine tugged the shadows close and slipped off the path. As she trailed Xander, she debated pulling out one of her blades then decided against it. Too easy to damage her target. She slowed. Hiding in plain sight wasn't easy, not even for a shifter, but she had the added bonus of being Fey. And here in this natural arena, that became a huge advantage because Mother Nature welcomed her, cloaking her in a power much older than any Kyn's.

Xander moved farther ahead, but she didn't get far

before their watcher appeared. Raine stilled and dropped into a crouch as an unsettling brush of active magic nipped at her. Recognition hit—wizard, armed and ready.

The trees shivered, and the breeze kicked in, blowing away the disconcerting sensation. Raine pulled her magic close into a dense sort of shield, sank deeper into the weave of the natural world, and barely breathed. As the man crept closer, recognition struck.

CHAPTER 19

The man moved past Raine's hiding spot without making a sound, and she realized he was actively holding a silencing spell. She waited until he was a few feet ahead, then relying on speed and surprise, she stepped out of her concealment.

She locked her arm around his neck and kicked the back of his knee, dropping him to the ground. His baseball cap flew off, revealing brown hair, and his hands rose to claw at her arm. She increased the pressure on his neck by tightening the chokehold and leaning back, keeping him off balance and more worried about breathing. Magic gathered around him like a suffocating cloud as Xander turned around and headed back.

"Don't, David." She let her claws slip free and sank the tips into his neck near his carotid. "It won't end well."

His magic dissipated, and he raised his hands, palms out.

She didn't loosen her hold. Wizards were notoriously slippery, and she didn't want this one getting away. She put her mouth near his ear, knowing Xander could hear every word she said. "You're a hard man to find."

"Fou... found me," he choked out, his throat working under her arm.

Smartass.

Xander shoved her sunglasses into her hair as she stopped and crouched in front of the man. She reached out, and the man jerked backward. Her hand hung in the air as Raine squeezed in warning, and he stilled. Xander plucked his sunglasses off, cocked her head, and studied his face. "If she lets you go, you going to cause problems?"

"Nnn... no."

As Xander continued to study him for a long moment, Raine, not at all reassured by David's answer, used her ability to manipulate magic and deftly coiled a barbed strand of her power around the wizard's fluctuating signature. It wouldn't be enough to disrupt any magic he threw her way, but it would give her a few seconds of warning necessary to get to her blades or use her claws.

Xander straightened. "I hope you're not lying." She nodded to Raine to let him go.

Raine waited until Xander stepped back to release David and added a slight shove between his shoulder blades.

He stumbled toward Xander, caught his balance, and spun around. His hands went to his throat as he tried to watch both women warily. "Who are you?" he croaked.

Neither answered, but Xander pulled out her phone, started texting, and said, "I'll give them a heads-up to meet us."

"Sounds good." Knowing Gavin, he would probably beat them to the office. Raine grabbed David's arm and yanked him forward. "Let's go."

He struggled against her hold and snapped, "Where are you taking me?"

Her leopard still lurked under her skin, so when she dug her nails in, they pierced his skin. Not deep, but enough to make her point.

He stilled and hissed in a pained breath. "Watch it."

Instead of easing up on her hold, she stepped into his space until their faces were inches apart. He wasn't more than a couple inches taller than her, so it wasn't hard to get in his face. In a voice cold and sharp enough to cut, she said, "Shut up and move."

His eyes widened, and cracks appeared in his mask of bravado, but he didn't back down. Instead, his voice was weirdly intent when he asked, "What are you?"

For an answer, Raine let her leopard prowl to the surface and peer out through her eyes.

He paled then stumbled alongside Raine as she started back down the path. His voice was tight when he repeated in a louder tone, "Where're you taking me?"

"Taliesin," Xander answered as she swept by them. Without looking back, she said, "As we mentioned earlier, there are some people who'd like to ask you a few questions."

Nerves oozed, and the wizard's voice took on a higher pitch. "About?"

Xander turned to face Raine and David as she continued to walk backward. "Well, we can start with your recent whereabouts or lack thereof."

How she managed not to fall on her ass, Raine didn't know.

Xander stopped in the middle of the path and waited until David got closer. Then she peered over the top of her sunglasses, and it was clear her wolf was looking through her eyes. "Maybe chat about mutual acquaintances."

David's gaze bounced between the two women, and he swallowed. "I don't understand."

Raine let her lips curl up in a derisive sneer. "Don't worry. You will."

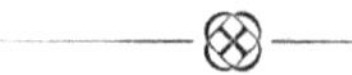

"Explain this to me again," Gavin demanded to the now-disheveled David who sat across from him in a small meeting room at Taliesin specifically warded to contain magical threats. It was a recent addition to the offices, one spurred by the disaster that had led to Mulcahy's death.

They were in hour three of their interview with the wizard, and it took every ounce of Raine's hard-won self-control not to shred the quivering mass of self-absorbed arrogance into bloody ribbons.

Ryuu, who was watching through a two-way mirror and monitoring the meeting's recording, had uncovered very interesting financial trails—from buried shell companies to the wizard, and mysterious deposits and anonymous donors to Biovita's Dr. Anders.

Then there was what Gavin and Axel learned about Dr. Anders and his newest research assistant hire, River Drake. Although River was scheduled to start her position in a couple of days, Dr. Anders was currently busy heading up a cutting-edge research team focused on switching human genes on and off. He called it the "accordion effect," but it was officially labeled as "gene silencing." No matter the label, it was uncomfortably close to the gene manipulation Raine had endured at the senior Talbot's hands. She couldn't escape the feeling that this latest research endeavor did not bode well for the Kyn as a whole. And that feeling only grew worse the longer they questioned David.

The rattled wizard fumbled with the nearly empty bottle of water as he downed the last of its contents. When he set the empty bottle back on the table, he kept his fingers wrapped around the plastic. "I told you, I was hired by Onidyn as a number cruncher."

"Your background is in genotyping." Gavin's voice was relentless. "How did you go from that to number crunching?"

David's lip curled. "Do you know how hard it is to get on a research team?" He leaned forward, his hand fisted on the table. "You run through all their hoops and kiss a ton of ass, and they still toss you aside for something new and shiny."

"Is that what happened when you applied to Biovita?"

A hint of superiority reemerged, and David's expression gained a mutinous edge. "Dr. Anders thinks just because he was on the team that founded the Xmas system, he's the end all be all of gene silencing, but the thing is Onidyn is already taking that research to the next level." He sat back and gave a nonchalant shrug. "I just decided to join the better team."

Gavin's brows raised as he pinned the recalcitrant man with a hard, disbelieving stare. "As a number cruncher."

David managed to hold Gavin's eyes for a few solid seconds before his gaze dropped, and he glared at the table.

"If numbers are your thing, explain the four sizable deposits to your account in the last two months," Raine demanded.

His gaze flicked to her and away. "I made some investments."

The urge to rip the truth from the stubborn ass was hard to ignore, but Raine maintained her lean against the wall. "Investments don't pay through shell companies."

David's lips thinned, and he folded his arms over his chest, clearly not willing to elaborate.

That was fine. Raine went back to an early line of questions, her voice icy cold. "Astrid Howell, River Drake. Where are they?"

His lips curled into a sneer, but it wavered just the tiniest bit as panic started to inch in. "I told you—I don't know anything about them or where they are." His gaze flicked to the pile of photos sitting face up on the table near Gavin and jerked his chin. "I also don't know anything about any of those people either."

Not buying his bullshit for even a second, she snapped, "Liar."

"I'm not lying!" he all but shouted. Then he jerked and slammed back in his chair. He dragged his hands through his no-longer-neat hair and pulled. "I told you. They were just a couple of rando chicks I tried to pick up." He tried to hold Raine's gaze but failed miserably. Instead, he appealed to Gavin. "I'm a guy. They're hot. It's a normal male-female thing, okay?"

Unimpressed with David's excuse, Gavin remained unmoved, his expression cruelly ruthless. "It's not normal for two women who don't know each other to run into you and then disappear. But those disappearances do make you the common factor, and you don't want to be the common factor, David."

"It's just a coincidence, man!" He rubbed his hands over his face and muttered a curse.

Raine finally pushed off the wall and stalked around the table. David watched her warily, his body stiffening with each step that brought her closer. By the time she stopped behind him, his tension was so thick, she could almost touch it. She leaned in, grabbed the armrests, and put her mouth next to his ear. His acrid scent of fear pleased both her and her leopard but made her nose wrinkle. "You keep lying, David, and we're going to have to get creative."

A shudder wracked his body as he tried to jerk away from her. The air around him prickled as he gathered his magic, an instinctive response to her implied threat.

She growled, and the animalistic sound filled the small room.

The quiver of power snuffed out, but David bolted out of his chair and backed into the far corner, trying to escape her. His eyes were wide, his pulse pounding visibly in his neck, and he fisted his shaking hands.

Gavin sat unmoved on the table's other side. "Let's revisit those deposits."

David started to shake his head, his gaze bouncing between Raine and Gavin. "I already told you—I made some investments."

"Yeah, that's not going to fly when we finish unraveling those shell companies." Raine hitched a hip on the table and folded her arms. "And that's going to happen a lot sooner than you think because Taliesin's got an entire unit devoted to digging that shit out. And right now, River Drake and Astrid Howell are Taliesin's main priorities." She cocked her head. "I don't know who you're protecting, but you might want to consider the fact that they aren't here, and we are."

For a long moment, David continued to watch them. Finally, his eyes closed, and he thumped his head against the wall behind him. "Godsdammit," he muttered as he slid slowly down the wall until he was sitting with his ass to the floor, knees bent, elbows braced, and his head in his hands. When he finally spoke, his voice was muffled. "It was just supposed to be some fast fucking cash."

"Who paid you?" Gavin asked.

David looked up, his face drawn, his eyes muddy with a combination of fear and resignation. "Don't have a name or face. Contact was all done online."

"That's not good enough," Raine warned.

He grimaced. "Look, I really don't have a clue on who's financing this. I found a posting from Onidyn Research. They were looking for data analysts and offered flexible schedules and a hell of a salary. I applied and got asked to come in for an interview."

"Where was the interview?"

He rubbed his knee. "One of those communal office spaces that have popped up lately. You know, the ones they rent out?"

"And you didn't find it suspicious that a research company would need a rentable office for interviews?"

"Not particularly," he shot back. "More and more, you either interview virtually or in some nearby location. Besides, Mr. Huxley explained the labs required high-level security to access, so they found it easier to conduct lower-level interviews locally."

That explained why Ryuu was having such a hard time finding a physical location for the labs.

"Do you know where Onidyn is?" Raine asked.

David shook his head. "Once I got hired, everything was done online."

"What exactly did you do for them?"

He swallowed hard, his gaze darting back and forth as his fear surged forward.

"David," Gavin called then waited until the younger man looked at him. "What did you do for Onidyn?"

"I swear, I don't know anything about the two chicks or anyone else," he babbled. "Mr. Huxley explained they were looking for volunteers to help with their testing. For each name I gave him, if they agreed to participate, I'd get a bonus. When the first deposit hit, I'd already given Huxley like five names." He looked at them both with a mix of guilt and trepidation. "I just assumed some of them agreed to be part of the testing process. I don't know anything about people disappearing."

Gavin sat back in his chair and narrowed his eyes. "You gave them River and Astrid's names?"

David managed a jerky nod.

"Why?"

His gaze dropped, and he licked his lips.

Seeing the nervous tell, Raine dug her fingernails into her palms so she wouldn't swipe out and slap him silly. "You were pissed because they turned you down."

Whatever he saw in her face had him shoving up to his feet and inching farther away, as he tried to dig his ass out of the hole he'd created. "It wasn't supposed to be anything mean, just an irritating call or two."

Raine straightened and took a step toward him.

He started to panic and raised his hands as if to ward her off. "How was I supposed to know they'd disappear?"

She went to reach for him to drag him back to the table, then a rift in the air opened behind him, releasing a wave of unsettling power into the room. Gavin's voice echoed in her skull as Raine lunged for a frozen, terrified David, barely getting her fingers around his wrist as a familiar horned figure wrapped lethal claws around the wizard and yanked him back through the magical tear.

Raine held tightly even as Gavin's shout followed her into hell.

CHAPTER 20
GAVIN

Looking back, Gavin wasn't sure what it was, but something made him leap from his seat and launch over the table as the tear between worlds opened behind Raine and David. He cleared the table and landed in a crouch as a monstrous form sank its claws into David. Gavin threw open the bond and reached for Raine, psychically and physically. His fingers brushed cloth as their minds touched, but it was too late. She was yanked backward into the Side, her mental touch turning static.

"Raine!"

Chaotic power generated by the Amanusa realm shoved him back, raking across his mind in a painful slash. He stumbled back, his spine smashing into a wall. The rift closed, and the door to the room slammed open.

"Gavin, are you okay?" Ryuu asked, his wolf dominant in the predatory light that set his eyes alight and tipped his fingers with claws.

"Get Natasha." His voice was rough with anger as his mind churned, but Gavin shoved off the wall and stalked to where the rift had appeared. He clung to Raine's presence, trying to reforge their connection, but the path was fragile, at best, as if one wrong move could snap it into nothing.

"Xander's on it," Ryuu said. "What in the hell was that?"

"That was the demon from the shipyard." Gavin reached for his magic and set his palm against the wall where the warding spell was anchored. Bolstered by his frustration and fear, power poured into the complex spells worked into the walls. Magic lit up under the influx. In the corner, just behind where the rift had opened, the wards flared into mangled life, tangled in a skein of nauseating yellow. He crouched in front of the mess and studied it, hoping to figure out how the demon had managed to breach the warded room.

"That's not right," Ryuu said, shock clear in his voice.

"No, it's fucking not," Gavin growled. Worry gnawed through his icy control and threatened to shake his tentative hold on Raine's flickering essence. Clearly, someone had tried to break the wards and, when that didn't work, decided to corrupt the magic binding it. The brute-force job was meant to force an opening, with nothing elegant or subtle about it.

The sound of running feet drew close then came to an abrupt stop. Someone sucked in a sharp breath.

"What happened?" Natasha's voice was rougher and deeper than normal.

Gavin twisted toward her without rising from his position. "A demon breached the wards and took Raine and that prick of a wizard into the Side."

Her head tilted back as she deliberately scented the air. He had no idea what she picked up, but a disconcerting flash of worry swept through Natasha's gaze before it shuttered into a steely ice. Her attention swept over the warped wards, and her lips tightened. She didn't waste time with any other questions, nor did she make Gavin request the obvious. The red ring in her eyes brightened into an unsettling flame, and an eerie shimmer erupted around her.

Ryuu inched back from the Demon Queen and positioned himself in front of Xander, clearly shielding his Alpha's mate as she hovered in the doorway.

A towering form wavered into existence, like a mirage with Natasha's petite human form a shadowed presence in its center.

Gavin tried not to stare, but a visceral compulsion wouldn't let him look away. He'd caught sight of Natasha's true form once before. It stood an intimidating eight-and-half-feet tall and was topped with ebony horns that curved with lethal intent. Fangs sat in a decidedly inhuman face illuminated by red eyes, and massive wings rose behind her. He forced his gaze away, knowing the longer he looked, the closer insanity crept. Amanusa had their own realm for a reason.

From behind him, Natasha's voice took on a bone-rattling depth, but Gavin couldn't make out the words. The warding magic shuddered then frayed into nothingness as an opening to the Side appeared, this one larger than the previous one. A painful jerk echoed down his bond with Raine, and he sank more of himself into it, determined to hold the connection. He was not about to lose her.

He straightened slowly and stared, trying to make sense of what lay beyond. His mind rebelled under the onslaught of a psyche-bending mix of twisted nightmares and horrific post-apocalyptic landscapes as a wave of black swept over his vision. Someone gripped his shirt and yanked him away from the warped reality with a sibilant hiss.

"Don't be an idiot, Gavin." Natasha pulled him back a little more. "Sit, wait."

He found his ass on the ground and blinked into Natasha's inhuman face. "Find her."

Something flickered behind her eyes, too quick to read. "That's the plan. You, stay here. Wait." He didn't want to, and she knew it because her grip tightened, the sharp tips of her claws scraping against his skin. "Don't, Gavin. I can't haul both of your asses out."

His bond with Raine trembled, and a sharp pain pierced his chest. He pushed his palm against the ache, gritted his teeth, and dug deep. "Go." The guttural demand was torn from him.

Without waiting, Natasha turned, stepped into the tear, and disappeared.

"Move," Xander hissed, and Gavin got the sense she shoved Ryuu out of the way. She came fully into the room, her energy barely contained.

It nipped along Gavin's skin, and he held up his hand to stop her. "Don't." It was a flat-out warning. He didn't want anyone near him right now. Not when he was so on edge. It was all he could do to hold on to Raine and not charge after Natasha into the looming hellscape.

He pushed to his feet and concentrated on his tenuous tie with Raine. *"Hold on."* He didn't know if she could hear him, wasn't sure it actually mattered. He couldn't not try. *"Natasha's coming, Raine. Just hold on."*

A faint quiver ran through their bond, and he swore he felt her just for a moment. The fleeting touch was enough to cement his determination, even if it was only hopeful wishing. He continued to murmur reassurances and sink his power into their bond, even as he counted his heartbeats and waited. Time passed, and he could hear

Ryuu and Xander talking, but he ignored them. He had one focus. Just one. Getting his other half back.

Time continued to stretch out with agonizing slowness as he raged an internal war. The mental fight was as draining as if it were physically happening. Slashes of pain scored across his mind, but with a strength of will honed by countless other battles, he set it aside and continued doggedly onward. The only acceptable outcome was bringing her back.

For a man used to taking action, being forced to wait on the sidelines was torture. The small part of his mind not centered on retrieving Raine had space to play on his buried fears and recently inflicted insecurities. The iron control over his magic that he'd fought so hard to regain began to melt under his rage, and the darker aspect he tried to cage clawed its way to the surface.

Two women, worlds apart, both held pieces of his heart, and he was struck useless, with no clear way to help either of them. As visions of Raine enduring gods only knew what, in a realm he couldn't cross, joined forces with haunting images of his recent nightmares about his mother, his unpredictable magic snapped the locks on his control, one by one. Anger, fear, terror, and frustration roiled into a looming storm that threatened to drag him away from the fragile anchors holding him together.

It wouldn't take much. *Just shift a line of power here, twist that one there, and...*

"Gavin, stop!"

He blinked and brought Ryuu's face into focus, his mind hazed by the lure of magic.

"Gavin!" This time, Ryuu's voice was a warning growl. "I don't know what you're doing, but you have to stop."

The shifter's razor-sharp demand broke through, and

Gavin released the lines of power he'd gathered unconsciously. The shimmer of magic slowly twining around the rift shuddered, then sank back to realign in its original position. Only then did he realize the shifter was between him and the rift, his eyes a burning amber, his lips curled back in a snarl, revealing long, sharp canines. Ryuu was doing his best to restrain him without inflicting actual harm.

Gavin backed away from his magic and ruthlessly tamped down temptation. There was no telling what it would do to Raine if he fucked around with the rift on this end. He sucked in air as he fought for control, his body rigid.

Ryuu watched him carefully. "You good now?"

Gavin managed a jerky nod.

Clearly not reassured, Ryuu waited a moment before he let the larger man go. "Can you—"

A wave of power burst from the rift. White agony edged Gavin's mind and vision as Ryuu spun around and dropped into a crouch, changing from man to wolf in a blur.

Deep in Gavin's soul, the bond he shared with Raine shuddered and threatened to shred. With strength born of desperation, Gavin sank everything he had into it, refusing to lose her. A heartbeat passed, then two, as the bond wavered ominously. Its threads thinned to gossamer strands. A void opened for a single, heart-stopping second, only to shatter when power screamed down the bond, turning those strands into crystalline brilliance.

Gavin leapt past Ryuu, ignoring the warning snap of the wolf's sharp teeth. Raine stumbled through the gap and all but fell into his arms. As he caught her, movement behind her formed into Natasha's demonic form, and his battered mind shivered under the visual onslaught. He dropped his gaze to the dark-haired woman in his arms and gathered her close.

Raine's face was ashen, but a bruise was coming up along one side, and a cut on her lower lip seeped a trickle of blood. But it was her eyes that sent ice careening through him. They were wide open and blank. The ring of gray that was normally closer to silver was almost white, matching the streaks in her hair gained from her last match with a supernatural heavyweight.

"Raine?" He kept his mental touch as careful as possible and tried not to acknowledge the fear huddled behind his concern.

Her presence brushed featherlight against his, but that was it. Before he could process the relief, something heavy hit the floor just behind her. In his arms, Raine flinched.

Her reaction scored his heart, and he tightened his hold as he curved over her protectively. He looked at the body behind her and into David's sightless eyes, his face contorted into a rictus of terror. Blood drenched his shirt from his nonexistent throat.

An invisible wind carrying painful burning bites, like tiny embers, whipped around him and pelted his skin. Gavin's gaze was drawn to the tear between worlds that hovered just beyond the now-dead wizard.

Inside something moved, something more than Natasha. As it drew closer, he realized that the Demon Queen was forcing another form toward the opening, backing it up step by reluctant step. It wasn't as large as her and was doing its best to fend off her attack. It wasn't working. The figure stumbled back as magic writhed around it, impeding its movements.

"Move, Gavin!"

He was already lifting Raine and moving away from the

opening before Natasha's order fully registered. The two wolves who were bookending him matched his retreat step for step until they were all standing on the far side of the room.

On the floor, in the space before the rift, a circle of power ignited, the symbols flaring into eye-searing life. Unseen lightning lashed through the Side, edging the flash of Natasha's claws as she struck out. The figure before her doubled over and flew through the tear. Its human veneer violently replaced its demonic form as it landed in the circle's center with a hair-raising snarl.

The pair of wolves at Gavin's side answered with bone-chilling growls as they stalked forward, staying clear of the circle's edge.

Natasha stepped through the Side's opening and resumed her human appearance. She brushed invisible dust from her shoulders and glanced at the two snarling, prowling wolves. "Back off." Deep and commanding, her voice drowned out all sound.

The wolves froze, and Gavin's ears rang in the abrupt, resulting silence.

The tear in the air behind Natasha winked out of existence, and the smell of sulfur and burning things faded. She grabbed a chair, dragged it around the edge of the circle, and sat, brushing her hand along her immaculate slacks. She looked at Gavin, her gaze back to normal, the lavender ringed with the thinnest rim of red. "Sit before you drop her."

Ignoring the order, he bit out, "What's wrong with Raine?"

Something flickered in Natasha's eyes. "I've told you before the Side doesn't play well with other Kyn."

He looked down at the unmoving woman in his arms.

"Raine, I need you to wake up." Again, there was that curious flutter, but she didn't respond. He looked back to Natasha.

She sighed, and her voice wasn't quite as hard as before. "Sit."

Clearly whatever was going on, Natasha wasn't going to share until she was good and ready. He looked around and spotted the other chair over to his left. He started toward it, only to bump up against a heavy, furred body. He looked down to find Xander staring at the trapped demon and snarling silently. He nudged her gently. "Xander, move."

She held her position between him and the demon writhing in the circle but looked at Ryuu. At some unseen signal, the other wolf padded around Gavin to the chair and used his head to shove it toward Gavin. Obviously, the two shifters were feeling a little overprotective.

As soon as the chair was within reach, Gavin hooked it with his foot and dragged it close. He sat, carefully cradling the silent woman in his arms against his chest.

"It's going to take her a bit to find her way," Natasha said.

He looked up and frowned, not quite following.

She explained, "Raine was able to get the true name of our friend here, but as you can imagine, it was well guarded. Unfortunately, we hit a bit of a snag."

"What kind of snag?"

Natasha's wince was tiny but there. "Demonic bloodlines can be a tad tricky to navigate, and this one belongs to the Blood of Iniquity. However, when I went to retrieve his name, that bloodline didn't react as expected. Raine tried to help, but mental and emotional manipulation is one of Iniquity's fortes."

Understanding hit, and with it came a mix of frustration and aggravation. *"Dammit, Raine."*

When the expected pithy response didn't come, he bit out, "And illusion? Is that one of their fortes as well?"

Natasha frowned and shook her head. "No, that belongs to the Blood of Secrets." She eyed their captive. "He shouldn't be able to wield dual bloodlines."

When she didn't elaborate, Gavin turned his attention to the figure struggling in the circle, his movements hampered by unseen bonds. He wondered what Raine had endured while helping the Demon Queen and, worse, what repercussions she would suffer. He reached for his magic as a familiar touch brushed against his mind and heart. When the world wavered and resettled, gnarled lines of power twisted around the figure in the circle. Thick links of black-streaked red held the figure in place, some of them severed, some of them disappearing, most likely into the Amanusa realm.

Relief crowded close and brought a spark of solace. *"Raine?"*

"Here." The answer was faint.

His eyes closed for a moment as he dropped his head over hers, and the uncomfortable grip of fear on his chest loosened. *"Come back."*

There was a pause, and he felt the sensation of claws sinking into the bond, not to shred but to anchor. *"Trying, don't let go."*

He endured the ache as those metaphysical claws dug deeper, and Raine fought her way back. *"I won't."*

His mind raced even as he sank more power into their connection, determined to make it as solid and unshakable as possible, as he continued to reassure Raine. He got the impression of a big cat carefully navigating a tenuous path, as bit by bit, her presence drew closer. A fragmented,

"Careful," whispered across his mind, followed by a monstrous figure that didn't belong to Natasha.

Heeding Raine's advice, he studied the trapped figure, taking in the bloodstained T-shirt and jeans. It was hard to tell if the blood belonged to him or to David. He met the disconcerting red gaze, bright with feral cunning, and felt a lethal coldness fill his veins.

The demon's lips curled back, and a vicious snarl emerged.

Gavin remained silent.

The demon turned toward Natasha and lunged, only to slam up against the circle's boundary. Magic flared as he struck out at the invisible barrier. Burn-like marks rose on his skin with each impact.

"Enough." Natasha's power flexed and flared along the magical chains, yanking the demon back to the center.

The demon's struggles slowed then finally stopped. He stood there, chest rising and falling, his hands opening and closing into fists, as he glared at the coolly composed woman facing him.

Natasha took her time studying him. "Harold Albert Dalterman."

The demon shuddered as his human form wavered, sharing glimpses of the monster.

Gavin looked away and managed to stifle his snort. *"A demon named Harold? Seriously?"*

"They can't all be Damion." Raine sounded stronger.

He rubbed his chin over the top of her head.

Natasha demanded, "Since you are not one of mine, I would like to know who invited you into my territory."

CHAPTER 21

Raine fought the urge to look behind her, where a nightmarish world howled. With one hand anchored on her tie to Gavin and her other buried in the ruff of the leopard padding along at her side, she continued to move forward. The leopard kept pace, its ears flat against its head while a constant stream of pissed-off rumbles fell from its snarling muzzle, but it, too, didn't look back.

"Yeah, I feel you," she whispered to her wilder half. She wasn't exactly happy about where they were either.

Thanks to Gavin's spurt of amusement at the demon's name, it was easier to fight the instinctive need to turn and face the menace behind them. But she knew better. Working on the magical plane was a bitch. She felt like she'd been struggling through a never-ending cesspool of vileness while dodging an overly handsy octopus armed with sharp objects and lethal intent. She wouldn't be surprised when she finally opened her eyes, to find her body battered and bruised.

And it wasn't just her body paying the price for her unexpected trip to the Side. Her brain felt like it was covered in varying cuts, some deeper than others. Being dragged into the Amanusa realm was the last damn thing she'd planned to do today, and she had no intentions of ever making a return trip. Her hindbrain babbled hysterically as nightmares of the world she was never meant to see grasped for purchase. The leopard froze, its paws flexing, claws slicing out to grip the path, and let loose another disgruntled snarl. Its head started to turn back.

Desperate not to lose her progress, she clutched its ruff and reached out to the man anchoring her. *"Gavin."*

"I'm here. Just a little more."

The anchoring thread thickened and brightened, luring her forward. Setting one foot in front of the other, she forged ahead, dragging her leopard with her. Around her, the tapestry of magic danced as if caught in a windstorm. She did her best to ignore it.

Distantly, she could hear the conversation happening in the room at Taliesin. Power rode through the threads around her like a lightning storm, adding a reddish hue to her surroundings. After seeing it in action, she recognized it as belonging to Natasha. Ahead, a pulsating door shimmered. Its surface was alternately slick and shiny, then dull and gray. Her connection to Gavin was tethered on the other side.

Harold's voice twisted through the air, tight with pain. "Don't know."

Raine could've told him it was stupid to deny Natasha anything, but it wasn't like he would listen. She dared a look at the knotted tangle surrounding the trapped demon. From this side, Natasha's spell was a daunting column of constantly shifting red fire streaked with black. Inside,

Harold writhed, shifting from human to demon and back as power wove around and through him.

"Explain." Natasha's icy command echoed around Raine, each repeat taking on a deeper, colder note.

She turned away from the storm of magic, and the straining demon held in its unforgiving grip. Frustration gnawed at her as she struggled to move forward against an invisible wind and away from the ongoing confrontation.

A high-pitched whine rose to ear-splitting levels, then Harold's voice broke through. "Hired job."

Raine reached the strangely disturbing door as power washed the world crimson. She held still and braced as an unearthly howl tore through the air, raking across her eardrums like nails. *It hurt so fucking bad.*

Frustrated and hurting, she cried out and hit the door with her shoulder, desperate to escape. Surprisingly, the door gave way, and she stumbled across the threshold. Harold's anguished cries chased her into the mortal realm. She kicked out a foot and kept the door from closing completely, knowing she would need access. With the way her head was pounding and as shaky as she felt, she wasn't sure she would have the strength or balls to reopen that door so soon. Around her, the world reset with a violent jerk as her leopard and the magical tempest disappeared.

The abrupt transition was so startling, she held still, afraid her mind was playing tricks on her. The steady beat under her ear drowned out the painful echoes of Harold's shrieks, and strong, solid bands held her close. She raised heavy arms and wrapped them around familiar broad shoulders, burying her face against Gavin's solid chest. Mentally, she maintained her precarious balance between worlds.

"Harold, you really don't want to piss me off." Natasha's voice was icily pragmatic.

Raine forced her aching eyes open then squinted when the fluorescent lights burned her retinas. She turned into Gavin and waited for her eyes to adjust before carefully turning her head. She found Natasha sitting on the other side of the circle, legs crossed, her red-tipped nails tapping against her knee.

Harold was in a heap on the floor, his muscles twitching involuntarily as blood seeped from his nose, mouth, and ears. The demon was definitely not having a good day. That made two of them.

Natasha's voice dropped to an inescapable depth. "Answer my question."

"Hired through the dark web." Harold's voice was muffled. "No names."

"Handle." Gavin's voice rumbled in his chest. "Get the handle the posting used. Ryuu can have our people track it."

Natasha eyed the demon, and when he remained silent, she sighed. She raised a hand then muttered something under her breath, and magic flared.

Deep inside, where she was still connected to the tapestry, Raine felt the shift of power, along with something else. A whisper of warning had her croaking out, "Stop."

Gavin's body jolted against hers.

Raine stayed focused on the Demon Queen. "Wait, Natasha." This time, her voice was stronger.

Natasha stilled, her gaze shifting to Raine. "I see you made it back."

"I took the long way around. Whatever you're planning on doing, hold off."

Natasha cocked her head to the side with a curiously disconcerting reptilian movement. "Why would I want to do that?"

"Because he wants you to keep going," Raine said as she split her attention between worlds. Through the partially opened doorway, the swirl of power twisted and turned in a dizzying dance, but it was hiding something.

"Is that so?" Natasha practically purred as she eyed their captive. "Interesting."

Raine gripped Gavin's shirt and closed her eyes. She leaned through the doorway and studied the magical landscape, trying to pinpoint what was bothering her. *"Something's off."*

Gavin didn't hesitate. *"Show me."*

With their bond unhampered, she shared what she was looking at and paid close attention to the thick lines winding around Harold. *"Amanusa threads are bumpy, knotted, but look at his."*

"Those tangles aren't natural."

"No, they aren't." Someone had fucked around with this demon's magic. Someone or something had changed it, not drastically, but enough that it was impacting the power currently keeping his ass in check.

Gavin's response was equally unhappy. *"I thought we were the only ones who could do that."*

"That's what I thought," she answered absently, her focus on the unusual pattern surrounding the demon. She nudged the lines, trying to get a sense of their weave. She sucked in a sharp breath.

"What?"

"Look." She delicately nudged the unnatural threads aside and revealed the dull glow of a spell.

Gavin's growl echoed on both planes. "Godsdammit, Natasha, I think he's hexed."

Natasha's spine snapped straight, her gaze dropping to Raine then rising back to Gavin. Her voice was grim. "Can you reverse it?"

He asked Raine, *"Can we?"*

Anxiety pricked at her as she studied what they unearthed. *"I'm not sure it's even a hex, Gavin."*

"Whatever it is, we have to get rid of it, if we want answers."

"And if it kills him?" She hated to ask because she knew Gavin was counting on Harold's answers to locate his mother.

Gavin's tone was grim when he asked, *"Can we get him to talk before it does?"*

"I don't know. At best, we might be able to reweave it, maybe buy us some time." But she wasn't keen about manipulating another's magic, especially when it was clear she wouldn't be the first to do so. So far, they'd been lucky, but luck had a way of running out at the worst times.

"Gavin?" Natasha interrupted their private conversation. "Can you reverse it?"

Gavin and Raine shared a look, and she didn't need their bond to understand the drive to get answers so they could find his mother was riding him hard. Harold was their only lead to Nyla. Raine's instincts screamed for caution, but she held Gavin's gaze and answered Natasha. "Maybe, but it might kill him."

Undaunted, Natasha said, "Fair enough."

Xander's low, unhappy rumble was echoed by Ryuu's. The Demon Queen ignored them both. "We don't have the luxury of discretion."

Before Raine could poke at Natasha's implied urgency, a dry, raspy chuckle drew everyone's attention to Harold. His red gaze darted from Natasha to Gavin and Raine, lit by a deep, dark light of vicious anticipation. "Go ahead, assholes. I dare you. At least I die knowing you'll be coming with me."

A wave of lethal intent washed from Gavin, and Raine shared it as she stared at the arrogant piece of filth and seriously considered gutting him. Pain was a wonderful motivator. Unfortunately, it tended to make people say what their tormentor wanted to hear. Too damn bad they needed what was in his head because killing him outright would take a lot less effort than what she and Gavin would endure manipulating the demon's magic.

Raine had a dangerous thought—maybe there was another way. Though she preferred not to remember, she recalled how she and Natasha were able to obtain Harold's name. It hadn't been pretty, and it proved the Demon Queen knew exactly what she and Gavin were capable of. She needed to tell Gavin—just not this minute.

She looked at Natasha. "Can you repeat what you did in the Side?"

Natasha's smile was slow and cruel. "I can, yes."

Harold's mocking arrogance faded, and fear crept in as his head darted between the two women. "No! No, you can't!"

Natasha looked down at the squirming demon at her feet. "Oh, but I can, dearest."

He continued to shake his head furiously, panic clearly taking over as he began to struggle against Natasha's bindings.

Natasha ignored him and studied Raine. "Are you sure you're up for this?"

She was not, but that wasn't an acceptable answer. "Yeah."

Gavin's arms tightened then relaxed as she sat up slowly. *"Raine."*

She patted his arm. *"Just stick with me."*

His sigh ruffled her hair.

Gavin helped her to her feet. Raine winced once or twice when her abused body protested. She held his arm for a moment, finding her balance. When she was steady, he moved to her back and set his hands on her hips. Together, they faced Natasha, with Harold between them, his vocal protests gaining strength and pitch.

Raine shoved open that mental door and stood poised on the threshold. She needed to warn Gavin. *"We're going to create the opening Natasha needs to tear through his mind."*

Gavin's skepticism was obvious. *"You're telling me she can't access his mind?"*

"Not without help." She shot him a look. *"Whatever they did to Harold and his magic locked her out. I was able to get her in the first time, but we barely got his name from him without scrambling his brains. This time..."* She shook her head. *"I'm not sure we'll be that lucky."*

She could feel Gavin studying her, but she kept her gaze on Harold's writhing form as her stomach pitched. What she was going to do was beyond cruel. It was also necessary, but that didn't ease the sting of her conscience.

"He's not going to survive this." Nothing in Gavin's tone revealed his opinion.

"No." She knew her response was brutally cold. *"He's not."* She met Natasha's gaze. *"Ready."*

Natasha didn't wait. Her other form wavered around her. She raised her hands and made a wiping motion.

Raine stepped through the doorway, Gavin at her side. *"Whatever you do, keep your gaze on Harold, not Natasha."*

"Is this like a Medusa thing?"

"More like Lot's wife."

Power raged through the landscape, and trapped in the center was Harold, his body engulfed in a web of flames. On the far side stood Natasha in all her demonic glory, and Raine's mind shivered as she averted her gaze.

"You'll have to work fast." Natasha's voice sounded as if she were standing at Raine's shoulder.

Raine took her at her word. She and Gavin moved as one toward the weave surrounding Harold. Thanks to their previous encounter, it didn't take Raine but a heartbeat or two to relocate where the tear had been clumsily mended. This time, since she wasn't teetering on the verge of insanity, she slipped easily among the threads. With Gavin's steadying presence, they undid the knots and reopened the route for Natasha. Harold's magic fought viciously. Lines of power whipped across Raine's skin like a living web intent on tearing skin from bone. She heard Gavin's pain-filled hiss and gritted her teeth against an echoing one.

"Go," she managed to get out.

Natasha's power swept past them. Raine shivered under the impact but didn't loosen her hold. Gavin bit off a curse but held on. With her path now cleared, Natasha faced Harold. Both were in their demonic forms. To fight the urge to stare, Raine concentrated on the anchoring threads thrashing against Natasha's influence, but she couldn't block it all out.

Natasha's talons curled around Harold's neck and held him aloft, apparently unaffected by his desperate clawing at her arm. "Now that I have your attention, Harold, let's try this again. Who sent you?"

Raine tuned out the choked denial and paid attention to the writhing threads. The spell she and Gavin had located earlier pulsed like some abnormal heartbeat. The threads coiled around it picked up the beat and wriggled as if alive. Raine sucked in a breath as she realized what she was seeing. *"Gavin!"*

"I see it." He sounded grim. *"Warn Natasha."*

"Natasha! Get to the point! We're going to lose him."

With a hair-raising snarl, Natasha snapped back, "Hold him as long as you can."

Raine wasn't sure that was an option. With each pulse of the spell, the strange knotted threads grew agitated and the unnatural knots in the lines started to loosen. Raine realized the threads bound Harold's human and Amanusa halves. She could hear Natasha press Harold for answers, but her concentration was locked on reweaving the unraveling lines. She and Gavin worked fast, but not fast enough. The magic holding Harold's two halves together disintegrated rapidly, leaving her and Gavin with nothing to work with.

Raine reached for her magic and sank it into the threads she held. Gavin did the same. Frustrated and anxious, Raine called out, "Natasha!"

For a moment, the thread held, and she thought they might have a chance, then a thunderous command filled the air. *"Göster bana!"*

Harold's agonized scream chased the echoes of Natasha's, and that thrice-damned spell imploded. The lines in Raine's hands burned, but she held on grimly, hoping it would give Natasha a chance. She blinked her vision clear of spots as a string of low-voiced curses came from Gavin. When she could see again, she knew they were screwed. The spell had decimated Harold's magic, leaving behind crumbling strands that faded into dull gray and drifted away like ash on wind as she watched.

"Natasha, back off now!"

"On three." Gavin counted down as the decaying magic crept closer and closer.

Raine prayed the Demon Queen was listening, and when Gavin said, "Three," she let go.

Harold's blood-curdling scream ricocheted through her skull. She hunched over and covered her ears, trying desperately to block out the sound. When it finally fell silent, Raine slowly lowered her hands and looked toward Harold and Natasha.

The Demon Queen, her human form intact, stood over a motionless form, her face a mask of pity and disgust. Raine stared at the contorted remains of Harold and felt empty.

Gavin moved up to her side. "Did you get it?"

Raine blinked, thinking he was talking to her, only to realize his question was directed at Natasha.

Natasha turned crimson eyes their way. "Yes."

CHAPTER 22

Raine was sprawled over Gavin's chest as they lay in the dark bedroom. The dappled moonlight played on the walls and ceiling in a mesmerizing dance. He was combing his fingers through her hair as she listened to the steady beat of his heart under her ear. It was a small oasis of peace in an otherwise-shitastic day. Tired as she was, she hadn't managed more than an hour or two of sleep before nightmares shoved her awake. Not of Harold's death, as gruesome and appalling as it was, but the haunting snapshots of her abrupt introduction to the Side. To combat the disturbing images, she picked through the information Natasha shared in the aftermath of Harold's lethal Q&A session.

Natasha had been able to retrieve workable bits and pieces while delving through Harold's fracturing mind. He had lied about answering an ad on the dark web. In fact, he'd been planted at the High Pointe Hotel as maintenance specifically to wait for Nyla's arrival. When Gavin heard that, he had been far from happy, and she couldn't blame him. That meant someone who was privy to his mother's agenda was also keen on betraying her.

Raine and Gavin had one name that rang that bell for them—Corwin Westbrooke. Natasha and Ryuu weren't as convinced. Well, Natasha wasn't, and Ryuu was staying out of the argument.

Westbrooke's name had initially popped up when Darius hit town after Mulcahy's death and the assassination attempt on Natasha. Ultimately, Leopold DiMarcco had proved to be the culprit, but still, Westbrooke's behavior seemed shady. Raine understood her deeply ingrained cynicism colored her view of the Kyn councilmembers, but that didn't mean it hadn't been earned. As for Gavin's inclination to point to Westbrooke, it didn't take a genius to understand that personal bias. Natasha was left to play devil's advocate when Raine and Gavin voiced their opinions.

She pointed out that Westbrooke was driving the investigation into Nyla's disappearance and that Westbrooke's goddaughter was also missing. Darius had also uncovered that Westbrooke had personally initiated and financed the search for the missing Kyn. Not only that, but Westbrooke had recently begun to position himself against Leo in Council matters. Westbrooke claimed Leo's decision to stay apart from the humans would not only endanger them as a whole, but cripple them financially, thereby reducing the Kyn's ability to play among the global powers. In that, Westbrooke was firmly on the Northwest Kyn's side, albeit with differing priorities.

However, for her and Gavin, that didn't mean jack squat. Just because Westbrooke could talk a good game didn't mean something deeper wasn't at play. Stories abounded about the Council, and gods alone knew just how deep those machinations went. Raine just knew she wanted nothing to do with any of them.

All that aside, the other snippets Natasha had pulled from Harold held much more promise. Although she wasn't able to get an actual name out of Harold before he imploded, she did confirm that Onidyn was a front to lure in unsuspecting Kyn. But for what purpose or by whom remained unknown. Raine had her own suspicions, though —ones she would only discuss with Gavin.

"That spell," she said, her voice quiet, "at the end with Harold, have you seen it before?"

The hand in her hair stilled for a moment then returned to its stroking. "That exact spell? No."

She caught a note in his voice. "But something similar?"

He sighed. "Yeah, but it was a long time ago and only once, so I could be wrong."

When he didn't say anything more, she prompted, "And?"

"And I was told at the time that magic was outlawed by the Council centuries ago." His fingers curled into her hair, his knuckles brushing the back of her neck.

She raised her head and looked into his night-shadowed face. "Who told you that?"

His gaze drifted over her face. The dimness softened the lines stress had carved into his face over the last couple of days. "My mother."

The answer didn't surprise her. Nyla was a renowned witch in her own right and wouldn't blink at sharing certain information with her only son, even if that information was frowned upon by others. Raine shifted so she could fold her arms over his chest and set her chin on the back of her hands as she watched him carefully. "What did it do? The original spell?"

He untangled his hand and brought it around to brush back the strands falling around her face. "It killed the descendants of a Kyn woman who had married and had children with a human."

Raine raised her eyebrows. "I'm guessing that wasn't a random hook-up type thing?"

Gavin's lips twitched. "No, like most black magic, injured pride played a huge part. The caster was a rejected suitor."

Rejected for a human—yeah, she could see how that would ruffle feathers. "Wow, talk about a sore loser."

Gavin folded an arm behind his head. "According to my mother, the wizard was hunted down and eliminated, and all his spells, including that one, were destroyed by the Council."

The cynic in her sneered. "Well, I'm guessing someone missed something somewhere."

"Maybe," he agreed. "Or..."

"Or," she repeated, easily following his thoughts. *Or someone on the Council decided the spell was too valuable to lose.* "So, the initial spell targeted a specific family."

"In a way, yes. There was much more to it, but at its core, it was tied to a unique bloodline."

"And any magic tied to blood is always that much more powerful." She turned the pieces over and over, trying to figure out how it all fit. "Natasha said Harold shouldn't have been as powerful as he was, that his bloodline wasn't about illusions, but doubt."

Gavin snorted. "I'm not so sure. He was damn good with an illusion."

"And he was even better with screwing with my emotions," she admitted reluctantly.

"What do you mean?"

She sighed. "The reason I can't sleep isn't just because of what I saw in the Side. It's that he decided to fuck with my head while I was in there."

"You weren't in that long."

"Long enough." She looked away and lay her head on her hands. It wasn't easy to admit the next part. "If it hadn't been for Natasha, I'm not sure I'd have found my way out."

She had been reeling under the initial onslaught of the reality of the Side when Harold clawed his way into her mind with frightening ease. He plucked out her insecurities and doubts then proceeded to play them like a maestro. It was only Natasha's unexpected appearance and initial attack that gave Raine an opening to regain her footing. When Harold's grip slipped long enough for her to realize what was happening, she fought back. Then between her and Natasha, they forced Harold to retreat into the waking world.

She turned to look back at Gavin. "So, to recap this mess, we've got a demon with a magical signature that's beyond weird, doing things he shouldn't be able to do, who kidnaps a powerful witch who happens to know a forbidden spell that targets bloodlines and is trying to track down missing Kyn of mixed blood."

Gavin's face was grim, but the fingers he stroked along her cheek were gentle. "We also have Jonah Talbot poking around a human lab that's learned how to turn on and off genetic code, while Natasha's trying to navigate the political pressure of exposing the Kyn to humans. Then there's our mystery player who knows things they shouldn't and betrayed my mother."

Raine grimaced. "Gods, what a mess."

On the nightstand, Gavin's phone buzzed. Raine sighed

and rolled off him so he could grab it. She lay on her side, head propped on a hand while he thumbed through the screen. When his body coiled then shoved up to sitting, she asked, "What?"

His eyes met hers, renewed determination burning bright in the depths. "Ryuu thinks he may have found a possible location for my mother."

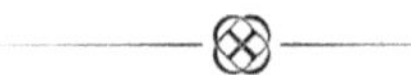

Dawn hovered on the horizon when Raine and Gavin strode past Taliesin's empty reception desk and down the hall to Ryuu's office. When they reached his office, it was clear Ryuu had never left. He sat in front of his computer, his T-shirt a wrinkled mess, his hair on end, and his bloodshot eyes ringed in dark circles.

"Hey." Raine held out the cup of coffee she and Gavin had stopped to pick up on their way in. "Here."

He looked up, and it took a moment for their presence to percolate. "Oh hey, that was fast."

"Not like we could sleep." She returned to the doorway, not wanting to risk the typical reaction computers tended to have around her. She leaned against the doorjamb and sipped her tea, while Gavin took the only empty seat in the room. "What did you find?"

"I did some digging using everything we had from Onidyn, Biovita, and the Talbot Foundation. I even pulled in the military since Cawley's name came up again. First, Onidyn is most definitely a front with some shady-as-hell military ties. It's held by a little-known global conglomerate buried under layers of red tape that are buried even deeper in the US Government's Office of Science and Technology. If we hadn't already run some of these searches before, I'm not sure we would've ever connected the dots, tenuous though they may be."

"How tenuous?" Gavin asked.

"It won't hold up under scrutiny," Ryuu answered.

Raine tapped a finger against her cup. "So, whatever is going on, someone really doesn't want it to come to light."

"Very powerful someones," Ryuu agreed, then catching her raised eyebrow, he explained, "There're too many players involved for it to just be one person."

"And all human?" Gavin asked.

"From what I can tell so far, yes," Ryuu said. "But that doesn't mean that there couldn't be Kyn involved."

That, unfortunately, was all too true. Still, Raine knew that until they had proof otherwise, they needed to proceed as if dealing with humans, which meant whatever happened could not be traced back to the Kyn. "You said you might have a possible location on Nyla?"

Ryuu nodded, shuffled through one of the piles on his desk, and pulled out what looked like a map. "I won't go into detail, but I found one address that I can link to Onidyn. It's the only thing I have on the company, as it appears to exist solely on paper." He handed the paper to Gavin. "It's a land parcel owned by the city, bordered by federal land, but leased to a subcontractor, and that subcontractor's name showed up in Onidyn's paperwork once. A year ago."

Gavin took the paper.

"Satellite imagery shows a couple of buildings on the lot, but I can't find any building plans or permits. Nothing to indicate why they're there or what that parcel is used for." Ryuu sat back and rubbed his hands over his face. "I know it's thin."

"Paper," Gavin said as Raine came up behind him to

look at what he held. It was a black-and-white image of two buildings half hidden by trees. The angle showed only the flat rooftops and a single dirt road.

Ryuu dropped his hands and looked at Gavin. "But it's the best I could find."

"You said it borders federal land?" Raine asked.

"Forest Service," Ryuu confirmed. "Out near Mount Hood."

Gavin pulled out his phone and stood, handing back the paper. "Send that to me."

Ryuu sat forward and danced his fingers over the keyboard. "Done."

Raine drained the last of her tea and tossed her cup into Ryuu's trash can.

His "Good luck and be careful" followed them out the door.

CHAPTER 23

Raine and Gavin stepped out of the elevator into the quiet lobby lit by early-morning sunlight. A shadow darkened one of the front glass doors before it was opened, and Xander ducked under the masculine arm holding the door wide and moved inside, coffee cup in hand. This morning, the blond shifter wore cargo pants, heavy-soled boots, and a black T-shirt with a cute orange fox and the words "look at all the fox I give"—her version of business casual. She shoved a pair of sunglasses up into her spiky hair, revealing the bruise of shadows under her eyes.

The man coming in behind her and staying protectively close could have been easily overlooked by anyone not paying attention. He stood roughly six feet, with brown hair and an average build. There wasn't much to set him apart except his dark eyes. Then, there was no escaping the wolf staring back—Warrick Vidis, the Northwest Head of the Lycan House and Xander's mate.

Xander caught sight of them and called out, "I thought Natasha sent you two home?"

"She did," Raine confirmed as she and Gavin slowed to a stop to meet the other couple. "But then Ryuu called us."

"He found something." It was a statement made in Vidis's pleasant baritone.

"That's the hope." Gavin rested his hand against the base of Raine's spine as he answered. "We won't know for certain until we check it out."

Xander and Vidis shared a look, the kind couples tended to when holding an entire conversation without words. In this case, as they were a bonded pair; words probably were exchanged, just not where anyone could hear. Vidis sighed, and Xander turned back to Raine and Gavin to ask, "Want some company?"

Sensing Gavin's hesitation, Raine used their connection to nudge him. *It wouldn't hurt.*

Much like the alpha, Gavin sighed, except his was limited to the rise and fall of his chest. He studied Xander. "You sure you're up for it?"

Xander lifted her coffee cup. "Once I finish this, I'm good for a few more hours."

Coffee, bags under her eyes, and Vidis hovering at her side. Raine took in the signs surrounding her best friend and asked, "Long night?"

Xander nodded as she finished her sip of java. "Natasha had me sitting on Talbot."

Gavin's body tensed, but his tone remained casual. "And?"

"And nothing," Xander said. "He spent his evening with his phone glued to his ear. Didn't stop burning the wires until about two and finally called it a night around three."

"Wonder who was on the other end?" Raine muttered.

Xander's grin was all kinds of wicked amusement, her wolf lurking in her amber eyes. "Me too, which is why I was going to ask Ryuu to see if he could get his hands on Talbot's phone records. I tried calling him first, but no answer. Since I wasn't sure if he was here or not, I decided to pull in the big bad wolf"—she bumped her hip into Vidis with a playful grin—"to help convince Ryuu's people to bow to my brilliance."

The alpha curled his arm around her waist and pulled her under his arm. "I think you overestimate my influence, pixie girl."

"Nah, I just like to watch while you snap and snarl," the little blonde shot back. "It's kind of hot."

Ruddy color crept under Vidis's skin, and Xander's laughter drowned out a barely there rumble. Vidis shook his head and turned back to Gavin and Raine, his face impassive. "Darius called Natasha last night. Westbrooke and Drake are on their way into Portland."

This time, it was Raine's turn to grimace. "Great. That's just what we need, more noses poking around."

Vidis looked at her. "He's a father worried about his daughter. Did you think he'd stay away?"

Raine held his gaze, refusing to back down on her opinion. "It's not Drake I'm worried about."

Vidis's dark eyes sparked with something close to humor. "Natasha and I will do what we can to keep Westbrooke out of your way, McCord." His humor faded, replaced by his normal somberness. "Unfortunately, I can guarantee he won't hold back for long."

And that was what she was afraid of. Once Westbrooke decided to interfere, things could get messy. *Speaking of which...* "Did anyone tell Drake his daughter was hooked up with the senator's son?"

Xander glanced at Vidis, who caught her look. He did a half-annoyed, half-frustrated head shake before answering.

"Not yet. We asked Darius to hold off until the two men get here."

Reading between the lines, Raine understood that Natasha and Vidis wanted as much information as possible before laying everything out to Drake and Westbrooke. It made sense. It was much easier to read people when they were sitting across from you than trying to do it over the phone.

"Hopefully, we'll have more to work with when they get here," Gavin said.

"That would be good," Vidis said.

"Right, then." Xander turned to Vidis. "You, go bug Ryuu." She got on tiptoe, pressed a quick kiss to his cheek, and dropped back down. "I'm going to go keep these two out of trouble."

Vidis turned to Gavin. "Call me if you need bail."

Gavin gave him a small grin.

Vidis turned to Xander, caught her frowning face between his hands, and dropped a kiss against her lips. "Take care of my mate."

"Same goes, alpha mine," she returned.

Vidis let her go, gave a nod to Gavin and Raine, and headed to the elevators. Xander watched him leave, and when the doors had closed behind him, she turned to the waiting couple. "So, what are we doing?"

"Road trip," Raine said as they all headed toward the doors.

Gavin added, "Got an address to check out."

"Fun." Xander shot back the rest of her coffee.

"Maybe." Gavin held open the door so Raine and Xander could pass through. "Maybe not. Depends on what we find."

Xander tossed the now empty cup into the bin just outside the entrance. "Or who."

"Or who," Raine agreed.

With traffic, it took them about an hour to make their way to the location Ryuu gave them. Conversation was sparse, and music played low as Xander napped in the back seat, while Gavin stared out the passenger window. As for Raine, she was doing her best not to get caught up in her head. There were too many unanswered questions that could send her spiraling down the rabbit hole, and her attention needed to stay focused on getting them to their destination in one piece.

The navigation system took them out past Gresham and over the Sandy River. Ryuu hadn't been lying about it being in the middle of nowhere. The forest huddled around the asphalt ribbon interrupted by the occasional turnoffs into private properties. The side roads were so few and far between as they got closer to their final stop, Raine slowed, keeping an eye out for an option. About a quarter mile out, she got lucky. There was a scenic turnoff on the wrong side of the road, but at least it had somewhere to park. She pulled in and took one of the end spots.

Not long after, Gavin, Raine, and Xander jogged across the historic roadway and slipped into the heavy foliage on the other side. It wasn't long before the woods swallowed them whole.

"All right," Gavin said as they stood under the dense canopy of leaves and huddled around his phone. A cool breeze swept around them, rustling the leaves. "According to this, we've got about a fifteen-minute hike until we hit this road."

"That's not a road." Raine studied the dirt tire tracks cutting through the dense overgrowth.

"But it's definitely in use," Xander said.

"How can you tell?" Gavin asked.

Xander looked up from the screen and tapped her nose. "Exhaust. It's faint but close."

Raine raised her head as her leopard padded close to the surface. She drew in a deep breath as the breeze flitted around them and caught the faint but bitter bite of spent fuel. If Xander hadn't mentioned it, she would've missed it. But there was something else out there, some hint that she couldn't decipher.

"What?" Gavin said.

Raine blinked and frowned. "I don't know, but there's something else."

"Friend or foe?" Xander asked quietly.

Raine shook her head, frustrated. "Can't tell."

Xander peered into the forest with focused intent. "Should we split up? Come at it from different directions?"

"No," Gavin said. "We don't know what or who we're facing. We're better off sticking together for now."

With that, they set off through the trees and heavy undergrowth. Gavin took the lead, using his phone as a compass. Their pace was steady, all three at ease in the forest. Raine heard it first and held up her fist to stop the others. All three froze in place. The faint rumble of an engine drew closer. The mechanical gurgle was similar to a motorcycle, but a change in pitch as the engine revved turned that guess to ATV.

All three Wraiths dropped into a crouch as the sound

got louder. They watched as a four-wheel all-terrain vehicle lumbered through the forest just ahead of them. The body was a dark forest green against the black metal frame, allowing it to blend into its surroundings. The driver's face was obscured by a helmet, but sunlight glinted off the oversized empty cage in the hauler behind it. Raine's nails dug into her palms as she watched the ATV turn and head away from where they were hiding.

All three waited as the engine's rumbles faded into quiet and the normal sounds of the woods resumed. Only then did they rise to their feet. They looked at each other but didn't say a word. There was no need. Instead, they stayed within the screen of the forest, picked up their pace, and followed the ATV's path.

The rumble of the engine led them farther into the woods, and after another five minutes of fast hiking, they hit the edge of an unexpected open space. Staying inside the shadow of the trees, they studied the small clearing that held the ATV, what appeared to be an equipment shed, and a smaller building that bore the markings of the US Forestry.

Xander touched Raine's shoulder and pointed to a tree just ahead. It took Raine a second to see it, but when she did, she raised her lip in a silent snarl. Cameras were concealed in the trees.

"Gavin, eyes in the sky."

Crouched just ahead of her, he slowly turned his head, stilling when he spotted the devices. *"Drop back."*

Raine caught Xander's eye and motioned her to retreat, then all three inched back into the thicker concealment of dense trees. When they were sure they were clear, they huddled together to plan their next move.

"We need to take the cameras out," Raine said. "What about that *Conspicio* spell? Cheveyo used it when we hit that lab, looking for you."

"We can't risk it," Gavin argued. "Magic and electronics don't mix. We use that, we short out the cameras. Those go down, we all but shout we're here."

"What about using the shadows to get inside?" Xander offered.

"Risky," Raine said. "We don't know the interior layout, which raises our chances of being spotted."

They all looked back to the larger of the two buildings. Shadow Walking was a rare skill for those with Fey blood somewhere in their ancestry, and while most of the twelve Wraiths had mastered the mental fortitude to travel the twisted alleyways that wound between worlds, not all Kyn could make the trip. Much like an unanticipated visit to the Side, it could take its toll, no matter how much Fey blood ran in their veins.

"Can't be all that complex," Gavin said as they studied it. "It's, what? Maybe fifteen hundred square feet? And we're looking at, what? Two, maybe three, people on site?"

"If that," Xander said. "I'm only picking up three strong scents, one faint. Nothing that says Kyn, though, so I'm thinking they're all human. Just a heads-up, someone in there likes to oil their gun."

Right, so they were going to Shadow Walk in, but that still left an even bigger obstacle. "And what if Nyla or River, or both, are in there?" Raine asked. "How do we get them out? If they're in bad shape and we drag them out through the Shadowed paths, they may not survive."

Grim lines darkened Gavin's face, but his tone was resolute. "Getting out will actually be easier."

"And why's that?" Raine asked.

"Because"—Gavin looked at Xander—"the big bad wolf is going to try and blow their house down. And while they're chasing her, we can take my mother and River out through the front door."

It was a stupid-simple plan of distract and divert, but between Xander's wolf and Gavin's illusion ability, it might just work.

Xander cocked her head. "You want me to guess when I should shake my tail?"

Gavin's hand disappeared into his pocket. "You can use this." He pulled his hand out and held it palm up, exposing a smooth aquamarine-colored stone. "It'll light up when we're ready to leave."

He motioned Raine closer. She closed the small distance between him, and he used a finger from his other hand to slide along the underside of the cord that held a small silver charm in the shape of a lynx at her neck. With the stone in one hand and Raine's charm in the other, he took a breath then whispered a spell. Magic pooled in the stone then stretched along their bond to wrap around the charm. The minute they were all connected, the stone began to glow as if lit from within.

Gavin let go of the charm, and the light in the stone winked out. "Touch it."

Raine reached up and caught the charm between her fingers.

"Think of Xander."

As soon as Raine brought the shifter's image to mind, the stone relit. She grinned and let go of the charm. The stone went dark. "Nice."

Gavin held the stone out to Xander, who took it. "Pretty. What kind of stone is this?"

"Not a stone," Gavin said. "It's an aquamarine crystal. They conduct magic better than stone."

With their communication in place, it was time to move.

CHAPTER 24

Raine stood next to Gavin on the far side of the building, where the trees crept close to the back wall and offered concealment from the security camera that rotated like clockwork. A battered picnic table sat all by its lonesome in a patch of grass a few feet from the metal exit door. They had taken the time to circle the building and study what they could of the layout. The encroaching forest provided plenty of shade and left sunlight hopscotching to find a way to penetrate the gloom.

There were few windows, each covered with security bars. Only this far side offered a glimpse inside, for all the good it did. The cracked window with the loose security grill looked into the back of what appeared to be a storage space. The two half-hidden basement wells nearly buried by the undergrowth were more promising, though. Strange, they were only on this side, but Raine wasn't going to question wonky construction, especially when it gave her hope they might finally catch a damn break.

And based on the eagerness seeping down the bond

from Gavin, she wasn't the only one. His voice curled through her mind. *"Ready?"*

She adjusted her hold on her favorite wrist blade, nodded, and opened the metaphysical door to the Shadowed paths. A silent, icy wind whipped around her, the frigid energy piercing her bones like shards of ice. Normally, there were architectural anchors she could use to navigate. This time, though, they were going in blind, so she kept her attention on Gavin's back as he led the way. She forced herself to ignore the distorted shapes writhing on the edge of her vision. He took the lead not only because his sense of direction when in-between worlds was much stronger than hers, but because she'd reluctantly admitted that her psyche was still bruised from its run-in with the Side.

Walking the Shadows was always a trial, and this time proved no different. The relentless energy and warped reality threatened to drag her into the darkness but anchored by her connection to Gavin and sheer stubbornness, she moved relentlessly forward. They followed the shadows down through the basement walls and into the basement itself.

Movement whispered at the edge of her vision, but she refused to look. Sharp, thorny fingers plucked at her clothes and hair, the phantom touch creepy as hell. Raine gritted her teeth and managed not to swipe out with her blade. A voice in her head chanted, "Don't look, don't look, don't look." That, of course, made it harder to ignore.

Ahead of her, Gavin stopped and looked back over his shoulder. His familiar presence threaded through her mind, its warmth chasing back her anxiety. *"You good?"*

She grimaced and glanced at his face but didn't look for

long because the shadows morphed his profile from familiar to disturbing. *"Yeah."*

He took her at her word and turned back. There was a shift in the surrounding energy as he opened the way between worlds, and they stepped back into reality. Her stomach pitched and rolled, and she sucked in a quiet breath then blew it out as her stomach settled. The tinge of ice that layered her skin melted into a thin film of clammy chill. She shrugged it off and muttered a nearly silent, *"Tachair."*

A small ball of light ignited and hovered near her shoulder. It shed just enough light to turn the near-black interior into a hodgepodge of discernible shapes.

Gavin had taken them to what appeared to be a supply closet filled with metal shelves lined with medical equipment. Raine's tension ratcheted up a notch. This did not bode well, but then again, humans' curiosity tended to make them poke and prod into things, live things with disastrous results. A sharp, lingering scent of disinfectant hovered in the air, and old nightmares crept closer. She shoved them back with years of hard-won experience. There was no room for her to indulge in a mental breakdown. They needed to get in, find out what was going on, then get the hell out.

Gavin moved up to the closed door, pressed one palm against the surface, and wrapped his other hand around the knob. Raine came up behind him, her ears straining to make out any indications of movement on the other side. Her leopard crept close, prowling just under her skin, adding its heightened sensitivity to hers. Air crept through the gaps that lined the doorframe. Minuscule shifts in its movements indicated the presence of someone else on the other side. A soft warning growl rumbled through her mind, followed by *"More than one."*

She shared that with Gavin. *"We need a distraction,"* she added.

They both arrived at the same conclusion within seconds. *"Xander,"* he said, but she was already reaching for her charm.

She didn't want her friend to blow it all in one shot, so she visualized a short burst of flashes, praying Xander could read between the lines. They waited in the tiny room, ears pressed against the door. Within a couple of minutes, the thin line of light under the door sputtered then steadied. A startled exclamation broke the quiet followed by the squeak of chair wheels rolling over the hard floor. Raine made out a muffled click, then a curious but not alarmed "What's going?"

Youthful excitement answered. "Dude, there's a freakin' wolf outside!"

"Bullshit!" came the rejoinder.

"No, seriously. You need to see this."

"I'm not supposed to leave."

A derisive snort answered. "Who's going to know? It's not like you're taking off. Just come up and check this out."

There was some muttering and more squeaky wheels, then someone went upstairs. A series of electronic beeps followed, then a door opened and closed, leaving behind a waiting stillness. She and Gavin exchanged a look. She raised a brow; he inclined his head and twisted the knob.

Slow and silent, he pushed open the door just enough to see out. Fluorescent light filled the opening. Raine waited behind Gavin as he peered out. He ducked back inside and looked at her. *"Cameras and two cages, but I can't see if anyone is inside them."*

"We need to blind them." She felt Gavin gather his magic.

Gavin sketched a symbol on the air, and the faint outline of a rune appeared, only to drift away a second later. Magic wafted out, and the glow simmering deep in Gavin's green eyes sparked then dimmed. He met her gaze. *"We've got maybe three minutes tops before the cameras go down."*

"Let's make it count."

Gavin opened the door, and they slipped inside the basement.

Even though she braced, the sight of what was clearly a lab still created a momentary hitch in Raine's step. She quickly recovered. *"Take the room on the other side. I'll get this one."* Thankfully, there were only two doors, each on opposite sides of the room. The middle was filled with a long lab table covered in electronic equipment, some of which appeared to be running, and a couple of rolling stools. Behind a half wall near the front edge of the room was a staircase angled up to the main floor.

Gavin rounded the table, and Raine went to the heavy door with a narrow window inside. She looked for an electronic keypad but found only the door and a solid lock. She peered through the window, and at first, she thought it was empty. When she changed her angle, though, she caught the edge of something lying just out of sight. She reached for the handle and found it locked. No surprise.

She turned away and looked around the room, searching for keys.

A muffled curse and a pulse of fury had her turning to Gavin. He was standing in front of the other door, his hands fisted and pressed against the glass.

"What?" She asked, even though she had a feeling she knew.

Sure enough, Gavin's furious voice swept through her mind. *"My mother's in there."*

"We need keys."

He continued to stare into the room, and bursts of volatile emotions battered Raine, too fast to be defined. *"Gavin,"* she called sharply.

Finally, he turned from the door. *"No, we don't."* He pulled out a knife, and magic ignited down the blade. He turned back to the door and shoved the knife's point into the lock. A concentrated burst of power decimated the lock. He pulled his knife from the lock and sheathed it. Then he stepped back and shifted his stance.

Raine realized he was planning to kick the door in. *"Gavin, stop! They'll hear."*

He shot her a glare filled with frustration and fury, but he heeded her caution. He stood there for a second, dragging in a deep breath as he fought for control, power coiling around him. Above them, indistinguishable voices were pitched with excitement. Hopefully, Xander was keeping them busy.

Gavin grabbed the handle, sent magic into the inert object, and gave it a vicious twist. The snap of metal sounded overly loud, but Raine was already turning to her door. She placed one hand, palm down, just to the side of the lock then jammed the point of her blade into the lock. She threaded her magic down its sharpened edge and forced it into the delicate components. Under her palm, a tremor ran through the door as the lock gave way. She twisted the knob and started to open the door, then a soft exclamation came from behind her.

She looked back to see the other door open. *"Gavin?"*

"Clear that room." His voice was tight, but the emotional storm behind it was worrying.

She cautiously opened the door, stepped over the threshold, and came to a stop. She'd thought she was prepared for anything. She was wrong.

The room, painted an unrelenting white, was clearly a cell. The unforgiving sterileness set her teeth on edge. The bed was a thin mattress spread over a metal shelf attached to the far wall at about thigh height. A crumpled olive-green blanket was wadded up in the middle, part of it spilling over the side to puddle on the floor, but there were no sheets or pillows. The floor was angled toward a drain in the center, likely to make cleaning it out a simple matter of hosing down the surfaces.

Old horrors crept closer, and Raine pushed them back as she swept a glance over the four plain walls. Strangely the room was devoid of cameras. Not a typical expectation for a lab holding cell unless this room was purely for containment purposes. Her gut knotted.

She started to turn away, then something moved in the shadows under the bed. She froze, hand on the door, and waited, barely daring to breathe. The hair on her arms rose as the sensation of being watched settled over her. She called out softly, "Hello?"

A heartbeat passed, then from the narrow space under the bed and behind the fall of the blanket, a hand appeared. Nails broken, long fingers marred by scrapes and cuts, curled around the blanket's edge, and pulled it aside. A shattered gaze stared back.

"River," Raine breathed through the unexpected shock of heartbreaking empathy.

Her bond with Gavin trembled under the avalanche of emotion, and he asked, *Is she okay?*

The girl jerked back into her hiding spot, the blanket rippling at her quick retreat.

"Damn them, Gavin." Raine dropped into a crouch, her heart in her mouth as her brain struggled to process the glimpse she'd caught of the young woman. The face was a sickly pale, the dark hair, dank, dull, and matted, but it was the eyes that reflected true horror. A feral madness glimmered in the depths, something beyond human, beyond Kyn. It was so alien, Raine had trouble defining it. *"Getting her out won't be easy."*

"Do what you need to." Gavin's voice was unrelenting. *"We don't have much time."*

She inched forward without coming out of her crouch. "Hey, River," she crooned. "We're here to take you home."

There was movement in the shadows, but River stayed out of sight.

Raine's heart pounded as memories pummeled her. The disorienting sense of reality from her time being trapped in a madman's lair returned with a vengeance. She knew all too well how hard it was to trust appearances. She held out her shaking hand and kept her voice soft and unhurried. "River, sweetheart, we need to get you out of here."

A sound slipped from under the bed, an unsettling cross between a growl and a cry.

"Come on, sweetheart," Raine urged softly as she inched closer, her hand steadying. "Let me help you get out of here."

"Can't." The one word was guttural, nearly incomprehensible.

Raine crept closer, almost within touching distance of the blanket. "You can't, what?"

The blanket rippled, and the battered hand appeared once more to grip the edge and hold it aside. River came into view once again. This time, Raine was close enough to make out a fading bruise that darkened the girl's face from temple to chin, the cut lips, and bloodshot eyes. "Chained."

River's vocabulary seemed to be limited to one-word answers, but it was clear enough to make Raine's blood boil. "Chained?"

River painfully crawled out from under the bed, dressed in stained beige scrubs. She'd obviously given her captors a hell of a fight because the markings on her face and hands were duplicated along both thin, needle-marked arms. Scrapes and bruises marred her collarbones exposed by the baggy top. She was much thinner than her picture, and the happy, excited light was now a dark, baleful glow that rode the edge of sanity.

Clear of the bed's frame, River went from hands and knees to her hip, then she slid her legs out from under the bed. Metal rattled across the hard floor as River adjusted her position so Raine could see the cuff locked around her ankle. The skin around the metal was torn and bleeding. The edges of the wounds carried an unhealthy black tinge. "It's anchored to the wall," the girl said. "I tried pulling it out, but..." She reached for the chain, her hands shaking.

Raine reached out to stop her, but when River violently flinched from the impending touch, Raine raised her hands. "Sorry."

River's head shake was jerky. "I can't... I don't..."

"Don't worry about it," Raine interrupted her. "You okay if I take a look at it?" She waited for River's nod then moved around so she could see how the cuff was attached. She kept her movements smooth and unthreatening, not wanting to trigger River any more than she already had. The cuff was a solid band of what looked like silver, which was poison for shifters, but was most likely silver mixed with a stronger alloy. Otherwise, River would be in much worse shape.

"There's no key," Raine said as tremors wracked River's emaciated frame. She glanced up. "How they'd get this on you?"

River gave a shaky shrug. "I don't know. Woke up, and it was there."

"I'm assuming you can't shift."

The girl shook her head.

Raine traced the cuff circling River's ankle. When she remained unaffected, she muttered, "Silver." She ran her hand along the links of the chain. Her skin itched and burned. Yep, the chain contained iron, not silver. *Sneaky-ass bastards.*

"Raine, we need to move out." Gavin's curt voice filled her head.

She wanted to ask about his mother, but River was her priority. Raine held her hands just a hair's breadth above the chain, looked at River, and said, "Close your eyes."

As soon as the girl's eyes fluttered closed, Raine sank a violet burst of phosphorescent white fire into the links. In a matter of moments, the unnatural flame seared through the links, severing the chain. Raine grabbed the blanket from the bed and wrapped it around the shivering young woman. "Can you stand?"

River clutched the blanket, and with Raine's help, she got to her feet. Together, they stumbled out of the cell.

CHAPTER 25

Raine kept her arm anchored around River's waist, feeling the press of the girl's ribs just above her arm. Gavin stood at the base of the stairs, a woman wrapped in a blanket similar to River's, held against his chest. Her face was obscured by a tangle of burnished copper, but a bruised and battered arm looped around his neck. An unforgiving fury lurked under the stark lines of Gavin's face and found an echo in Raine.

There would be no leaving this place unscathed.

"Signal Xander." Gavin's voice was harsh.

Raine brushed her fingers over the charm and sent a pulse of magic to signal the shifter outside.

Almost immediately, excited exclamations sounded from above. "Oh my god, did you see that?"

"No fucking way!"

"Grab the gun."

"Shit, we can't leave."

"Like anyone would know. Look, they're locked in their cages."

Nice to know Gavin's spell that looped the video feed was still holding.

"Three minutes—five max—then I'm heading back."

"Whatever."

The two men ran out of the building, the door slamming closed behind them. Raine hoped Xander watched her ass because it would suck to get River and Nyla out, only to have to go back and drag Xander to safety.

Gavin barely waited for the voices and footsteps to fade before he was heading up the stairs. Raine followed, with River leaning heavily against her. When Gavin reached the top, he murmured something to his mother, shifted his stance, then slammed his foot against the door. Wood cracked, and hinges protested, but the door flew open and smashed against the wall. Gavin blocked the door's return with his shoulder and strode into the main room.

Raine got River up the stairs and tried her hardest to block out the young woman's pained whimpers. Once inside the now-empty top floor, Raine stopped to give River a moment. Tremors wracked the battered woman's frame, and her breaths were coming out in short gasps. Raine took in the space. A rumpled cot was shoved into the far corner, and a duffel bag was tucked underneath it. Two scratched and dented desks sat facing each other in the center of the room, computer screens and keyboards on top. One desk held a neat pile of files with a couple of papers near a keyboard and a soda can on a coaster. The other desk held only the keyboard, mouse, and a dark screen.

A squeeze at Raine's waist had her looking at River. "You okay?"

She nodded and straightened painfully. "I'm good."

The previous haziness was gone, replaced by a grim light of determination, but her jittery edge told Raine the girl was hanging on by her fingertips. Tightening her hold, she led River to the door. Behind her, Gavin called her name. She had River lean against the wall by the door and turned back to Gavin. "What?"

"Find out what's in there." He jerked his chin at a narrow closet in the corner then crossed the floor to the exit.

"Got it." She looked at River. "Can you stay here for a second?"

River braced a hand on the wall and gave Raine a nod.

When Raine was sure River wouldn't drop to the floor, she left the young woman and headed to the closet. As she passed the second desk, she noticed the computer screen flicker. She ignored it and slid open the closet door. "Well, shit."

"What?"

She shifted so Gavin could see the rack of computer equipment that filled the space. "They're sending information somewhere else." Even if they took out this lab, they couldn't erase whatever information had already been sent elsewhere.

"We'll figure that out later," Gavin said as he stood near River. "For now, we take this place off the board."

"Agreed." She looked from River to Gavin. "Get them out while I take care of this."

Gavin nodded then moved closer to River. "Can you walk on your own?"

River raised her head and met his gaze. "I think so."

Gavin adjusted his hold on his mother, shifting her higher in his arms, and gave River his back. Over his shoulder, he said, "Grab hold."

The girl reached out and curled her hand around the edge of Gavin's belt.

"Ready?" he asked.

"Yeah," came the husky reply.

Raine left them to it and turned her attention to the rack of electronics. She brushed her fingers over the cool metal case on the top rack, and her magic speared the electronic guts. The magic surged through the top one then cascaded through all the delicate electronics below, leaving behind a shower of sparks and nose-curling smoke. Hearing a sharp pop behind her, she twisted to see the computer on the desk flicker to black.

Good enough.

She moved to the broken door and stood at the top of the stairs. She gathered her magic then sent it out to wash through the basement. Power licked like a relentless wave, lapping at the various electronic equipment and leaving shorted circuits and damaged boards in its wake. An electrical fire sparked near one of the bigger pieces of equipment, but Raine couldn't have cared less. It wasn't like they were going to leave this place standing.

She turned away from the nascent fires breaking out in the basement lab then stalked across the floor and out into the bright sunlit morning. She looked over to find Gavin standing at the edge of the forest. River stood next to him and, surprisingly, so did his mother. Despite his arm curled around her waist, she also had a hand pressed against the thick trunk of the tall tree. As Raine closed the distance between them, she felt the tug of magic, and her steps slowed. It took a second to realize that tug wasn't from Gavin, but Nyla. Raine fought back the urge to lower her mental protections and find out exactly what Nyla was up to.

Before she could give in, Gavin's voice filled her head. *"Wait."*

"What's she doing?" Not that she thought Nyla might betray them, but Raine wasn't exactly good with trusting the intent of others.

"Re-anchoring her magic." Something dark swam under his response. *"Whatever they did to her locked her away from accessing her powers. She's reestablishing her connection to her magic."*

Unlike wizards, most witches fueled their magic through Mother Nature, and for a powerful witch like Nyla, that was doubly true. Even as she watched, Raine could see the change in Nyla. She was no longer hunched over as if something deep inside pained her, but she still leaned against her son. Her eyes were closed, her face drawn, but the deep lines marring her face were easing.

River had her back pressed against the tree, but her gaze was darting around the clearing, like a wary animal. Something about the girl worried Raine.

A howl went up, and the hair along Raine's arms rose. She spun around, blade in hand and magic at the ready. "Go!" she urged Gavin. "I've got this."

With a muffled curse, Gavin reached for his mother and River.

Raine left him to it and turned toward the sounds of someone rushing their way. Two men broke through the forest and stumbled into the clearing. They rocked to a stunned halt.

For a breathless moment, everyone stilled. Then one of the men yelled, and the other lifted a weapon that looked like a gun. Raine's magic flared to life as she brought up a shield. It wouldn't stop the bullet, but it could shift the projectiles' trajectories. Her knife was already flying through the air, end over end, when the first shot sounded, but instead of the expected sharp crack, it was a harsh puff of air. The tranquilizer dart hit the magical shield, slowed, then dropped to the group just shy of her foot, as her knife sank into the shoulder of the man who'd shot the dart.

His pained yell was drowned out by a violent wash of power that knocked Raine off her feet and sent her sprawling on her ass. She shoved upright in time to see a stream of flames sweep over both men. Their screams echoed through the clearing, only to be snuffed out by an unearthly roar. She blinked as she tried to process the shimmering shape that prowled forward. A long neck, vast wings, muscled arms tipped in deadly claws, and a serpentine body wove through the air of the clearing, its shape flickering in and out of focus.

"What in the..." The rest of her words died in her throat, and her brain stuttered to a halt. *"Gavin, is that—"*

"A dragon," he confirmed.

She tore her gaze away from the mirage-like image of a mythical creature that shouldn't be there. She turned to see Nyla clutching Gavin's arm that was held out toward River, who was otherwise occupied. Magic, fierce and wild, danced around her and down the tether that locked the woman and the phantom dragon together. Her eyes were wide open and filled with an unearthly flame, her mouth twisted into a snarl, and her hands were curled into claws. She screamed, and the dragon's roar filled the air. The two burnt bodies crumbled, their cries finally silenced.

Raine winced and noted movement in the nearby underbrush. Catching a glimpse of fur, she realized Xander was creeping up behind River. The knots in Raine's guts warned her if Xander pounced on River, things would end very badly. She scrambled to her hands and knees, yelling, "Xander, hold!"

Thankfully, the shifter listened, but Raine's sudden

move and yell caught River's attention. The dragon turn in sync with the girl until both girl and dragon were looking right at her.

Raine's pulse spiked, but she slowly pushed back until she was sitting on her heels, her hands held out, palms forward. "River, can you hear me?"

The girl's head cocked, and so did the dragon's as it twisted and turned in the space between them. It was disconcerting to watch, but it was River, her voice a deep growl, that answered. "I hear you."

"I need you to rein it in for me." Keeping her voice calm was hard, especially since her leopard was coiled in a crouch and hissing just under her skin. Not to mention, Gavin's anxiety was snaking down the bond as well, taking her anxiety up to new levels.

When River didn't answer, Raine decided to risk dropping her barrier. She felt Gavin brace even as the clearing lit into eye-searing life. Magic danced around River and her dragon like a dervish, spinning and sparking with a power Raine had never witnessed before. The dance of it was beautiful but deadly. Raine didn't want to mess with River's power, not after it had clearly already been altered. Not wanting to make things worse and uncertain about her next move, she reached for Gavin. *"I don't know what to do."*

"I don't think there's anything we can do." His response was grim. *"I'm not sure, but anything we try will hurt both of them."*

Raine didn't want to kill the girl, but she also didn't want to end up as the main BBQ course. Even knowing they were racing a clock, she tried to figure out what she was seeing. It didn't take her long to understand rage was fueling River's reaction. That was an emotion Raine understood.

"Get your mom and Xander out of here."

"I'm not leaving without you."

"I don't plan on sticking around long, but I want you all out of the line of fire."

"Dammit, Raine."

"Go, please, Gavin. I need to focus on River."

"Don't get hurt." Gavin started to move his mother back into the forest and motioned Xander to follow.

Raine focused on River and kept her voice low. "I know you're pissed, River. You have every right to be, but I need you to come back."

The dragon and girl both screamed. The dragon whipped its head around and sent another stream of flames over the burnt remains. It licked at the far wall of the structure and began to eat up the wall.

"They're dead." Raine kept her tone bland. "Can't kill them any more than that."

The serpentine head turned toward her, and a world of rage, fear, and pain stared back. The emotion wasn't just the dragon's. There were two souls involved, both battered by a shared nightmare. "They hurt me."

Raine swallowed and fought back the empathy that threatened to choke her. "But you're still here, still standing. They aren't."

This time, it wasn't River, but the dragon that reacted. All the fury, pain, and fear escaped in a deafening roar that reverberated in Raine's bones. Fire washed over the building, lighting it up as if a switch had been flipped. Raine raised a hand to shield her face from the press of lethal heat and turned away, catching sight of River's rigid body. The young woman's spine bowed as she struggled to hold the creature in check. River was fighting her way back. Raine silently cheered her on because whatever River had endured hadn't broken her, which explained why Raine wasn't currently imitating a human shish kabob.

Unfortunately, she couldn't show River or her dragon any mercy because sympathy would be viewed as weakness. It was a truth she understood because that same feral turmoil lived in her when Mulcahy brought her out of the lab. So she kept her tone cold and channeled her uncle. "You can burn everything to ash, and it won't change a thing. Whatever they did, it's done. You have two choices, River. Deal with what they left you or become the monster they wanted."

She waited until she had River's attention, then hard though it was, she held that unearthly gaze with her own. "Choose your path, River."

For a long moment, the forest around them went silent as if the world were holding its breath, waiting for River to decide. The only noise was the mutterings of the fire devouring the building behind them. Raine kept her focus on River, not on the dragon coiling in the air around them, and saw the moment the young woman chose to stand back up. Those eerie flames burned white hot then began to die down. The dragon slowed its looping flight without losing focus on Raine. She ignored it, giving River the space to regain control on her own. The dragon began to fade until the flames in her eyes flickered out, leaving behind dazed, bloodshot brown eyes.

River pushed away from the tree and stumbled forward. Raine was there to catch her. As she held the girl, she whispered, "Good choice."

CHAPTER 26

Raine worked fast to dowse the last of the flames from River's temper tantrum, tapping into Mother Nature and utilizing the moisture in the surrounding air. Even aided by magic, it still took too damn long, but she didn't want to risk a forest fire. She made sure there was nothing left of the building or the two men. Before she had a breeze blow away the ashes, she retrieved her blade and tucked it away. She couldn't erase all signs of the fire or hide the remnants of the burned-out basement, but she managed to do enough to leave the humans uneasy when they came back to check on their men.

By the time she wrapped her arm around River's waist and started hiking back out to where they'd parked the SUV, exhaustion was creeping in. Gavin had touched base a couple of times and bolstered her magic on the more difficult parts of the clean-up. She'd learned his mother was coherent and upright, but not willing to discuss what had happened until they were somewhere safe. Since Raine really didn't want to be out here anymore, she was more than happy to beat feet back and haul ass. Questions swirled, but she held them back by concentrating on keeping River moving.

Sweat was a damp line down her spine when she and River broke through the forest and limped across the road to the SUV. Luckily the lot was empty except for her SUV. Gavin saw them coming and met them halfway. He swept up River and carried her the last bit. Xander, in full fur, stuck her head out the passenger window and whined.

Raine raised a hand. "I'm fine." She sat on the rear bumper, arms braced on her thighs as she tried to find her equilibrium. Hearing the door close, she straightened, pulling out her keys.

Gavin came around and took one look at her then at the keys dangling from her hand. "Don't even think about it." He snagged the keys and started for the driver's side. "I'm driving."

Not about to argue, she shuffled to the passenger side and hauled her butt into the seat. She was snapping the restraint in place when she twisted to see the two women behind her and Xander in the far back. "We can stop and get water and food, if you want."

Xander managed to shake her head and disappeared into the cargo area. River shivered and shook her head, but Nyla answered, "Can we get somewhere safe first?"

"We can do that," Raine said as Gavin opened the door and got behind the wheel. She waited until his door was closed before saying, "Head to Mulcahy's."

He put the keys in the ignition, turned the engine over, pulled out his phone, and handed it to her. "Call Cassandra. Tell her to meet us there."

"Got it." She took his phone and pulled up the healer's number. Thankfully, Cassandra didn't ask questions, simply agreed to meet them at Mulcahy's house.

"Your house, Raine," the older woman gently reminded her. "He left it to you. It's yours."

"Doesn't feel like it," she muttered, able to admit that much to the woman who'd helped put the damaged teen she once was back together.

"Time, child," Cassandra chided. "It takes time."

Raine hung up with Cassandra and scrolled through Gavin's phone. She found Natasha's number and called it. The call went to voicemail after two rings. Throttling back her frustration, Raine waited for the beep and left a brief message. "Located our lost items. Taking them into the old man's place." She hung up and dropped Gavin's phone into the center console.

Gavin shot her a side glance. "Your code-speaking skills need sharpening."

She lay her head against the headrest and closed her aching eyes. "Best I could come up with on short notice." When Natasha caught a whisper that the human government was determined to eavesdrop on Kyn business lines, she'd ordered all crucial information be shared cryptically. As being dodgy wasn't Raine's strong suit, finding the right phrasing in any given situation was a crapshoot. "Trust me, she'll figure it out."

The rest of the drive was made in silence laden with a nervy tension. By the time Gavin turned onto the private road to Mulcahy's house, Raine's headache was crossing into migraine territory.

An older compact was pulled off to the side and parked just outside the gate that locked the world away from Mulcahy's house. As they approached, the driver's-side door opened, and a small woman got out. White hair pulled back in a single thick braid fell down her back, and sunglasses sat on an ageless face that sported, of all things, a dusting of freckles instead of wrinkles.

Gavin slowed to a stop and powered down his window. "Cassandra, thank you for coming."

The older witch came up to his window, got up on tiptoe, and shoved her sunglasses back as she peered into the SUV, her head barely higher than the side mirror. It would have been funny considering how short she was, but Raine didn't feel like laughing. Cassandra's sharp blue eyes, which never missed a damn thing, swept over the two exhausted women in the back seat then drifted to Raine and back to Gavin. "Let's get them inside, shall we, dear?"

With that, she stepped back and returned to her car. Gavin shook his head, slid the window back up, hit a button on the visor above him, and put the car in gear. The gate rolled back, and Cassandra followed them up the rest of the drive to the circular courtyard.

Both Nyla and River demanded to walk into the house on their own, so Raine and Gavin played support, ensuring neither woman fell while slowly crossing the entryway and moving to the living room, where they collapsed on the U-shaped couch.

Xander padded after them and gave a short yip.

Raine waved her toward the stairs. "Upstairs, last door on the left."

With a soft huff, Xander prowled up the stairs to change.

Cassandra followed them inside, an oversized woven handbag on her shoulder. She closed the door then disappeared into the depths of the house as Raine and Gavin got Nyla and River settled. Clearly, Cassandra was familiar with Mulcahy's house because she returned carrying a breakfast tray that held a hand-carved bowl, unlit candles, bundles of herbs, a set of glass bottles, and a small blade.

When she saw that Nyla and River were each positioned on opposite sides of the couch, she smiled. "Perfect." She set her tray down on the cushion of the middle section then turned to Gavin and Raine. "While I get these ladies comfortable, I suggest ensuring the house wards are secure."

"I can help." Nyla's voice was raspy but clear.

"No," Gavin said with a sharp look at his mother. "You let Cassandra help you." He turned to Raine. "You set them. I'll reinforce."

Raine nodded because, though it might be overkill, they were better safe than sorry. She went to follow him, only to be brought up short when River caught her wrist and held on tightly. "Wait!"

Hearing the panic trembling under that one word, Raine turned back and dropped to a crouch so River wasn't straining to see her. "You're safe here. Cassandra won't hurt you."

The young woman shook her head in a short, jerky move, tremors wracking her thin frame. "I just don't want… I'm worried… what if…"

Realizing what River was struggling with, Raine covered the white knuckles of the hand locked around her wrist and squeezed the cold fingers. "You can do this."

River blinked rapidly. "It's still there." Her other hand curled into a fist and pressed against her chest. "I don't want to hurt anyone, but I'm… we're so…. angry." The last word came out on a hiss.

Witnessing River's struggle struck a deep chord with Raine, and memories of waking up to discover she shared her soul with another crowded close. She cleared her throat. "I can't promise that you won't hurt someone, not yet, but you made a choice. Keep making it."

River's gaze darted to Cassandra, who was murmuring to Nyla. "You trust her?"

Raine held the young woman's gaze. "With my life. Done it a few times, actually. If it helps put your mind at ease, Cassandra follows the Three-Fold law. She wouldn't betray you."

River took her time working through Raine's reassurance before she finally nodded and let her go.

Raine gave her a smile. "I'll be right back, okay?"

She waited for another nod before she got to her feet and joined Gavin. As soon as they were out of sight of the living room, Raine dropped the barrier that kept her magic at bay. As the psychic wall dropped, the ache in her head eased. She briefly considered that she might have overstrained her magical muscle, then nudged the concern aside as she touched the web of wards protecting the house and land it stood on. She and Gavin went into the library, where they would be safe from observant eyes.

Inside the library, they went to work. After rekeying the wards earlier, setting and reinforcing the massive protective network of spells was much easier. Having a visual map of the power grid helped immensely as well. Together, she and Gavin sank a hefty amount of power into the wards, reinforcing the protections already in place and tweaking others as the low-level hum of magic deepened in pitch. She was about to lock them down when Gavin stopped her.

"Wait."

"What?"

"I want to lock down access from the Shadows."

It took a second for her to understand. "You don't want a repeat of Harold's visit."

He arched a brow. "Do you?"

She shuddered. "Not particularly."

With skill born from countless hours of practice, she shifted their perception of the wards until it included the way points that would lead to the Shadowed paths. They wove a second, more-targeted level of wards that blocked the Shadows from infiltration. By the time they were done, Raine felt drained, emotionally, magically, and physically. Unfortunately, their busy morning was turning into a very long afternoon.

Gavin wasn't looking much better. There was a pale undertone to his skin and dark rings around his eyes, and the lines around his mouth had turned into furrows.

She slumped against the desk and rubbed her temples, where the ache had returned. "We need to get back out there."

"Kitchen first," Gavin said.

She followed him into the kitchen. A soft singsong murmur drifted from the living room, and a scent that made her think of a sun-filled meadow trickled down the hall. She filled glasses with cold water while Gavin rifled through the refrigerator behind her. Thinking of how thin River looked, Raine asked, "Do we have anything they can eat without upsetting their stomachs?"

"There's that stew we had the other night."

"Hopefully, it won't be too heavy for them."

"Better than nothing," he said. He brought out a container and portioned it out into a couple of bowls, which he then popped into the microwave.

While they waited for the stew to heat, Raine rinsed a couple of apples, sliced them up, and put them on a plate along with nuts. It wasn't much, but it was something. She pulled out a cookie sheet and set the glasses and hot bowls on top, leaving Gavin to bring in the fruit and nuts.

As she drew close, the press of Cassandra's power brushed against Raine, warm and comforting. It grew in strength as she got closer. Not wanting to interfere with Cassandra's healing, Raine stuck to the edge of the room and set the cookie sheet down on a long, narrow cabinet. She turned and leaned against it, waiting until Cassandra gave the go-ahead to approach.

Gavin had no such qualms—he set down what he held then went to his mother, who had her eyes closed as she sat propped up on the far side of the couch. At he got closer, her lashes rose, and she zeroed in on her son as he took a seat on the cushion near her feet and held out a glass of water.

"Here," he said, his voice gruff.

"Thank you."

Raine saw the moment Nyla's wariness turned to relief before a studied calmness veiled that momentary softness. She took the glass from Gavin, but he kept his hand under it, as it trembled. She wrapped both hands around the glass and took small sips.

Bruises, along with a collection of cuts and scrapes, marred her fair skin. The marks stood out in stark relief. Her auburn hair was tangled, her face pale, and her lips cracked, but overall, she appeared to be in fairly decent shape.

Unlike River.

Soft footfalls came down the stairs, and Xander stopped just outside the living room, tugging an oversized T-shirt down. She caught Raine's gaze and tilted her head toward the door. Raine got to her feet and met her friend.

"You got this?" Xander's question was soft so as not to disturb Cassandra and her patients.

"Yeah, you heading in?"

Xander nodded. "Vidis called."

Raine dug out her keys and handed them over. "Take my SUV. I'll pick it up later."

Xander took the keys. "I'll drop it off if you don't make it in."

Since Raine had no idea what the rest of the day would hold, she said, "Thanks."

With that, Xander slipped out, closing the door quietly behind her. Raine walked back to the living room.

"That's it, child." Cassandra's voice was soothing as she brushed a hand over River's head. "Hold your focus and breathe."

A lit candle sat near Cassandra's hip. In the bowl, a pile of stems and leaves smoldered, creating that sun-filled-meadow scent. Raine was relieved to see River's tremors had stopped. She lay on the couch in her stained scrubs, eyes closed, a faded wool blanket draped over her legs. Cassandra held River's battered hands, and Raine could all but touch the magic tethering the healer to the girl. Occasionally, River would flinch, and her eyes would dart behind her closed lids, but Cassandra continued to hum softly, apparently oblivious to the revealing reactions.

Raine continued to watch the healer, while Gavin and his mother conversed in low tones. Raine was so caught up in what Cassandra was doing with River that she failed to catch Gavin's conversation. It wasn't until Cassandra called her name for the second time that Raine realized she'd fallen into a daze.

"Sorry, Cassandra, I missed that." She rubbed her hands over her face in an attempt to wipe away the mental cobwebs.

"I need you to come here and help me with this." There

was no shift in Cassandra's soft, calm tone, but something about it brought Raine up on alert.

Raine took a seat near River's feet. "Tell me what you need."

Without letting go of River, Casandra turned to Raine and gave her a small smile. Magic swirled in tiny starbursts in her blue eyes. "There's a disconnect somewhere, and I need to find it."

CHAPTER 27

Raine let the world shift, and the magical tapestry unfurled in her mind's eye. Cassandra's power carried the glow of the moon on a summer night as it curled around River's angry oranges and fiery reds without touching. The young woman's magic was a mess. It took Raine a minute to figure out what Cassandra meant by a disconnect. Normally, when Raine viewed a Kyn through her unique lens, the colors were clear indicators of the blood that Kyn carried. In front of her now was a twisted, tangled mess of constantly shifting hues.

There were flashes of deep blues and greens, most likely inherited from her father's Lycos lines, but the thrashing, living tangles that shifted from the violent knotted colors of the Amanusa to the paler tones of the Fey were clearly the problem. Where the two dueling colors touched, a rough scar was left behind on the thread, turning River's overall weave into a chaotic mat instead of the living tapestry Raine was used to. She described to Cassandra what she saw.

The colors that belonged to the witch deepened in

response to an emotional trigger then resumed their normal tranquility. "Can you smooth out those patterns?"

Raine considered Cassandra's request while tension nibbled at her. As much as she wanted to help River, she wasn't sure this was the best way to go about it.

"You have to try." Gavin's voice interrupted her thoughts.

"I could cause more damage."

"I don't think so. Look closer. Look familiar?"

She did so and saw what she'd missed. Those rough patches were slowly fraying, the magic binding them together thinning as she watched. She'd seen something similar once before when Cheveyo was tangled with the Soul Stealer. River, however, was nowhere near as powerful as the head of the Northwest Magi. *If her magic continues to unravel—*

Raine cut off her dark thought before it could finish. Unwilling to add to River's existing stress and anxiety, she kept her curses silent. Then she told Gavin, *"I'm going to need your help."*

"I'm ready when you are."

She took him at his word, and together, they began to reweave River's magic. The fragile threads required delicate work, and she refused to rush. If she and Gavin couldn't fix this, they would lose River. Time slipped by, and Raine was prepared to shift the last few threads into place when she saw the emerging pattern and paused.

"What is it?" Cassandra's voice sounded far away.

Instead of answering her, Raine whispered to Gavin, *"Do you see it?"*

"Yeah." His answer was grim. *"But we don't have a choice."*

Gods, she didn't want to do this, but Gavin was right.

There was no other choice if she wanted River to survive. Sending up a silent apology the young woman would never hear, Raine wove the last of River's magic into place. "Now, Cassandra."

Cassandra's power swept over the construct, lightly brushing along the now-cohesive tapestry. Everywhere her magic touched, a small firefly of power sank into River's threads until the entire weave carried a low, simmering glow. No longer the earth tones of a typical shifter, River's magic now held a uniquely beautiful combination of colors that echoed all four Kyn bloodlines. The result resembled a living flame.

River sucked in a sharp breath and shuddered. The tapestry that made up her magic undulated with serpentine ease as her power reestablished itself. The movements continued for a long moment before they finally calmed and settled. Only then did Raine pull back, taking Gavin with her, and open her eyes.

River stared at her, eyes wide. In their depths was a glimmer of a slow-simmering flame. "What did you do?"

"I fixed what they broke." The earlier ache in Raine's skull was back, this time setting up shop in her temples and blurring her vision. She closed and rubbed her eyes, trying to ease both the pain and the blurred vision. When she blinked her eyes open, River had one hand fisted against her chest, and her gaze was focused inward.

Cassandra gave Raine a questioning look, but with no easy answer available, Raine gave a small shake of her head. Cassandra sighed softly and went back to healing River.

As the minutes ticked by, Raine split her attention between River and the soft murmur of conversation between Gavin and Nyla.

"I'll be fine," Nyla was saying. "I was pretty out of it that first day."

"Not a surprise since you were dragged through the Side."

"That was no typical demon, Gavin."

"No, he wasn't," he agreed.

Proving she didn't miss much, Nyla asked, "Was?"

"He's dead."

There was a pause. "Did you—"

"Natasha," he cut her off.

"I'm assuming she's the reason you found us?"

Instead of answering, Gavin asked, "Who on the Council knows about the *Exstripatio* spell?"

Cassandra's body gave a small jerk, and she turned from River and gave Raine a look. Something dangerous lurked in her gaze before she went back to working on River. Raine was unsettled by the disconcerting glimpse of ruthlessness from a woman who had only shown Raine endless patience and compassion.

"They're Council." There was a hint of impatience in Nyla's voice. "I'm sure most, if not all, know about the spell."

"But not all can cast it."

A frigid chill hit the room, so cold Raine's skin pebbled.

"Enough, Gavin, Nyla." The sharp reprimand came from Cassandra. She didn't bother to look at either of them but aimed a comforting smile at River. "That should ease enough of your aches and pains so you can rest." She carefully set the young woman's hand down.

River grasped the edge of the blanket and pulled it higher. "Thank you." Her voice was husky as she kept her head down and avoided meeting anyone's gaze.

Cassandra began gathering up her items. "Raine, I

know you have questions for her, but I want to request you keep them to a minimum for now."

Not about to disobey Cassandra, Raine murmured, "I'll do my best."

Cassandra straightened, the tray of items in her hands, as she asked River, "Think you can handle some water and soup?"

"Stew," Raine corrected, and River's eyes flicked to her. Raine shrugged. "Figured I'd better warn you it's a bit heftier than soup."

River stopped plucking at the blanket as her gaze darted between the two women. She licked her chapped lips. "If I take it slow, I should be okay."

Raine stood as River started to sit up. She waited through the winces and sharp inhales in case she was needed, but once River was settled in the corner of the couch, Raine went to grab a bowl of stew and a glass of water as Cassandra took her tray to the kitchen.

The silence between Gavin and Nyla was thick with tension, but neither broke it. It didn't help that the simmering emotion squeezing through Gavin's end of the bond made Raine's skin itch. Since healthy and productive family communication was beyond her, she had no idea how to comfort or help.

Instead, she decided to concentrate on getting what information she could from River. She handed over the glass first. "Start with this, and if it stays down, we'll move on to this." She lifted the bowl.

River curled both hands around the glass and took small sips.

Raine resumed her seat at the end of the couch and set the bowl next to her, keeping her hand on it so it wouldn't spill. She watched River drink and wondered where the hell she should start. She couldn't jump into what had happened to the girl while she was being held because that was the farthest thing from going easy. But if she heeded Cassandra's advice, she would have to start with either David and his stalker behavior or with River's involvement with Colin. Raine had no idea which was less emotionally taxing.

Before she could decide, River lowered her glass and spoke first. "Did you find Colin? Is that how you found me?"

"Who's Colin?"

Gavin murmured a quick explanation to his mother while Raine continued her conversation with River. "No, he's still missing." When River paled and the glass in her hands trembled, Raine gentled her tone. "Was he with you when you were taken?"

River's nod was jerky, but with a strength Raine was coming to expect from her, the young woman rallied. "Colin and I were out shopping when I got a call. It was a guy who claimed to be Dr. Anders's assistant. He said Dr. Anders wanted to meet with me one last time before the decision was made on the internship. I explained I was out, but he said Dr. Anders's time was limited, and if he sent a car, could I make the time? I agreed, but when I hung up, Colin said he was going with me. Said he wasn't comfortable with me going alone. The driver met us outside the shop we were at, and I remember getting in and heading out toward Biovita, then..." She shook her head and quickly smothered a flash of remembered fear. "Nothing. When I woke up, I was cuffed to a bed, my head hurt, and things didn't make sense."

That note in her voice found an echo in Raine's memories, igniting a surge of sympathy.

"This assistant," Gavin said, fracturing the moment. "What was his name?"

River held out her glass to Raine, who took it and set it aside. "I don't know." River rubbed at her head, her frown deepening. "I'm not sure, but I don't think he ever said."

Raine wasn't surprised. She handed over the bowl of stew and warned, "Small bites."

River balanced the bowl against her chest and took a careful spoonful. Raine let her eat as she added River's story to what David had admitted about giving up River's and Astrid's names to Onidyn. An arranged driver indicated someone had gone to a lot of trouble to get their hands on River without leaving a trail. The fact that Colin was with her meant someone was either thrilled beyond belief or sweating bullets right about now.

Raine looked at Gavin. "Ryuu needs to get Iliana to press the senator because I'm betting he's left some important information out."

"Senator?" Nyla finally spoke up.

"Senator Albert Guthrie," Gavin answered. "Colin's father." He turned to Raine, his voice grim. "You think a ransom request was made?"

"They targeted River because of David," Raine explained. "More importantly, they kept her alive."

"That asshole!" River hissed. "That's how they knew I was Kyn."

Raine nodded. "Yeah, David the dick didn't like being rejected, so he gave your name up to Onidyn's research team."

"They wanted Kyn test subjects." The young woman's voice was bitter. "But Colin's not Kyn. He's human, and they weren't expecting him."

"I'm sure they weren't," Raine said. "But now that they

have him, once they figure out who he is, they're going to scramble to cover their asses."

"And setting it up as if they planned on kidnapping a senator's son all along would be the best ruse to hide their real intentions," Gavin finished.

"But no ransom was demanded from Giles," Nyla said.

"That's because they had no idea she was Giles's daughter." Gavin pulled out his phone, and his fingers flew over the screen, hopefully texting Ryuu. "They thought she was just another Kyn that they could snag, and no one would come looking." He looked up from his phone and shot a dark look at his mother. "Of course, if someone had informed us that there were missing Kyn, we could have stepped in."

Color rose under Nyla's skin, but Raine didn't think it had anything to do with embarrassment and everything to do with temper.

"Don't you think you have enough on your plate, Gavin?" The gentle rebuke came from Cassandra, who had returned without being noticed and now stood at the entry to the living room, a steaming cup of tea in her hand.

"I think I'm getting damn tired of being blindsided," he groused, his voice holding the tone of an old argument.

When his gaze collided with his mother's and held, Raine knew he wasn't talking about his position as the Captain of the Wraiths. This was not the time or place for Gavin and his mom to battle it out, though. *"Gavin, babe, not now."*

He stood up abruptly and started to pace, one hand dragging through his hair, tearing it free from the tie that held it back. As much as Raine wanted to wrap her arms around him and take him away from this, she couldn't.

Whatever was between him and his mother, he had to set it aside until later.

"How many others?" The question was asked in a small voice.

Raine reluctantly turned away from Gavin and toward River, but Nyla answered, "At least ten, possibly more."

"Counting Dani and Sam, we're at twelve" Raine corrected.

"Who's Dani and Sam?" Nyla asked.

"Friends of Mike, your contact," Gavin answered.

"You met with Mike?"

"Didn't have anything else to work with, so yes, we met with Mike."

Deciding to step in, Raine asked both women, "Did either of you see any others?"

The two shared a look, then Nyla shook her head.

River said, "No."

So there had to be more than one holding location. She looked at Gavin. "We need to get into Onidyn."

"We need to find it first," he said.

Before they could discuss it further, a vibration ran through the wards. Raine shot to her feet. "Someone's here."

Gavin jerked to a stop and turned to the front door. "Probably Natasha."

That made sense. The Demon Queen knew where they were headed, and she was the only one who would dare tangle with Mulcahy's wards.

Power hit the first ring of protection and was repelled.

Gavin's grin was all teeth. "I think she's knocking."

The next burst was harder.

"And she's impatient," Raine muttered as she skirted

the couch and passed by Cassandra, who simply raised an eyebrow.

She reached the front door with Gavin on her heels. When she went to pull it open, he stopped her by pressing his palm against the door and holding it in place. He leaned in until his mouth was near her ear. "Play nice."

Raine tilted her head and brushed her lips against his stubbled jaw. "Only if she does." She bumped him back and opened the door.

CHAPTER 28
GAVIN

GAVIN FOLLOWED RAINE OUT THE FRONT DOOR AS THE LUXURY silver sedan came to a stop. The driver's door opened, and Darius unfolded from behind the wheel, garbed in his typical all black. The demon wizard skirted around the hood to open the passenger door for Natasha, and when the petite blonde stepped out, the back two passenger doors opened. The man who emerged from the rear passenger side carried an air of intensity that was hard to miss. His gray-streaked brown hair was cut short on the side but longer on top. His olive skin carried a permanent tan that highlighted the neat silver beard. He didn't look around, but under dark brows, his deep-set eyes zeroed in on Gavin and Raine. He closed the door and came up a step behind Natasha.

But it was the man rounding the sedan's trunk who put Gavin on edge. Tall and lean, his dark hair was streaked with silver. Dressed in tailored slacks and a shirt, it was clear he was used to wielding power, both financial and personal. His eyes were covered by a pair of dark lenses, but they didn't do shit to hide the fact the man was unnaturally focused on Raine.

Gavin's hackles rose, and he slipped around Raine and took up a position just in front of her.

"What the hell, Gavin?"

Raine's irritation would normally trigger amusement, but not this time. Ignoring Raine's not-so-delicate nudge in his kidney as the four guests moved toward them, he reached back to capture her fist in his hand. "Something's off."

She relaxed her fist then wiggled it until she could thread her fingers through his.

"Gavin, Raine," Natasha greeted as she walked toward them, the three men trailing behind her.

"Natasha." Gavin's gaze met the cold blue eyes of the man behind her. "Abazi." His attention swept over the two grim-looking men then dropped to the Demon Queen. "I was unaware you were bringing guests."

"You have my daughter," the bearded one said, his tone short, but his voice carried a singsong cadence Gavin would have pegged as Spanish, not Greek, if he hadn't known better.

"Giles Drake." He inclined his head to the older man. "Welcome." His gaze went to the man standing at Drake's side. "You are?"

Despite Gavin's curt tone, the man smiled slowly. "Corwin Westbrooke."

He felt Raine stiffen, and her grip on his hand tightened, whether in warning or shock, he wasn't sure. He squeezed back as he studied the man his mother had decided to align herself with. This wasn't a man a woman would find easy to manipulate, and Gavin wondered if his mother had recognized that fact yet. Though, knowing her, she would find the challenge… how had she once put it? Exhilarating.

"Corwin, what a lovely surprise." Cassandra's voice cut through the tense greetings.

Gavin turned to the side, forcing Raine to do the same, and Cassandra bustled past them and straight to Westbrooke. The taller man's smile went from polite to gentle and welcoming as he bent and accepted the smaller woman's hug.

"Cassandra, looking lovely as ever." There was a hint of the British Isles in his voice.

The older witch's smile gained a teasing edge. "And you would flirt with the devil herself if you could."

Westbrooke chuckled.

Cassandra looped her arm around his and started to lead him through the small group toward the house. "It seems we have much to discuss." As she drew even with Giles Drake, she reached out and patted his arm. "Your daughter is a strong one."

The other man visibly swallowed as a slight tremor swept through his taunt frame. "Yes, she is." His voice sounded choked, but he was quick to regather his composure. His gaze went back to Gavin, flicked to Raine, and returned. "If we could?"

"Of course." Raine gave Gavin's hand a tug, and he stepped back to her side. She didn't let go as she ushered their visitors inside. "She's inside to the right."

He felt her shift the wards to allow their visitors entrance, but he wasn't as trusting. It didn't take him much to activate a few warning snares in the wards just in case someone decided to start something. Raine flicked him a glance but said nothing.

Giles moved through the door, not appearing to rush, but not wasting time either. Cassandra and Westbrooke followed. Natasha and Darius waited for the other men to move inside before they stepped close to Raine and Gavin.

Natasha asked in a low voice, "How are they?"

"My mother will be fine," Gavin answered. "The girl..."

"Will also be fine," Raine finished, her tone resolute. Although her expression gave nothing away, Gavin could feel how close her nightmares crowded. Raine was connecting with River on a worrisome level, but he had to trust that Raine would navigate this latest development with the same inner fortitude that had kept her standing for years.

Natasha studied them, then with startling perceptiveness, she said, "Be careful, Raine."

A hint of affronted temper darkened Raine's face for a moment before steel replaced it, but her only response was an acknowledging head tilt.

The sound of excited voices drifted to them, and Gavin motioned for Darius and Natasha to enter. "After you."

He and Raine followed the couple into the living room, where River was wrapped in her father's arms, her face hidden against his chest, her body shuddering. The man's eyes were closed, his lips pressed to the top of his daughter's head, and it was clear the two were close.

Movement drew Gavin's eye to where his mother stood in Westbrooke's arms, and although he'd known they shared a relationship, seeing it was still a shock. It was difficult to witness for a myriad of reasons, one of which came down to the very painful history he shared with his mother. The other was because of the man holding her. The hard edge of Westbrooke's expression had eased as his hands gently drifted along her back in a soothing stroke.

But it was the unmistakable depth of emotion on his mother's face that gripped Gavin's guts in a cruel hand. The last time he'd seen anything close to that was before his father went missing. After their differing version of retribution had torn them apart, the mother he'd known had disappeared and been replaced by a coldly indifferent businesswoman.

Now, it was like stepping back in time, watching her cup Westbrooke's face as she told him something in a voice too low to hear. What hurt was that it was Westbrooke, not his father, the emotion was directed toward. Westbrooke nodded then dropped a kiss on Nyla's forehead. The tension that strung his mother's frame tight eased, and she curled into him, her cheek pressed against his chest, her eyes closed. The unexpected serenity that settled over her face twisted the painful claws in Gavin's gut, and he struggled with a riot of emotions he'd thought long lost to childhood.

"Gavin."

He blinked and turned to look at Raine. She reached up and captured his face in her hands, breaking the strange spell. Her gaze searching his, she asked softly, "You okay?"

He stared into the unusual silver eyes and into the heart of the woman who was his other half, and the dark hold of the past loosened. There was no judgment, no recriminations, just a silent offering of unconditional support for whatever he should need. Instead of answering, he pulled her close and buried his face in her neck. Within the safety of their shared connection, he made a difficult admission. *"Just trying to process the fact that my mother has a heart."*

Raine's arms tightened. They both knew it was more than that, but she followed his lead. *"It seems whatever is happening with them is more than politics."*

Gavin just held on as he tried to grapple with old resentments through the lens of an adult. *"I just wish it wasn't Westbrooke that made it beat."* The admission was rough and left unsaid the real seed of his anger.

But Raine, being Raine, knew him better than anyone and proved that. *"I can't speak to her relationship with your father, but what you don't see because you don't want to is that that heart includes you."*

Her words burrowed through old hurts and found an echo in a newly formed realization that his mother was just as human as the next person. Something about seeing her with Westbrooke had finally given him a glimpse of Nyla the woman, instead of Nyla his mother. He may never fully understand her motivations, but it wasn't as black-and-white as he'd thought.

Cassandra clapped her hands and gained everyone's attention. "We have two women who need to rest and much to discuss, so as much as I enjoy the reunions, may I suggest you all take a seat so Nyla and River can share their stories?"

Heeding Cassandra's gentle orders, everyone found seats and sat in nearby chairs positioned closer to the sofa. When they were all settled, the older woman turned to Raine. "Do you mind if I make myself at home in your kitchen? I'll get drinks for everyone."

"Mi casa es su casa, Cassandra," Raine said as she followed Gavin over to the loveseat sitting off to the side.

Cassandra disappeared down the hall.

Darius, who had taken a seat on the floor near where Natasha sat on the edge of a coffee table, turned to River, who was tucked into her father's side on the couch. "Do you want to start?"

The girl began to talk. Her story took some time, and his

mother, sitting close to Westbrooke opposite River and her father, filled in blanks where she could. When the two women were done, simmering fury clouded the air, and it didn't belong to just the female sitting stiffly by his side. No, this time, it was shared by all the Kyn in the room.

The humans were once again experimenting on Kyn and had, in fact, experimented on her. River's memories of the first week or so were unclear, hazed by the drugs the humans had given her. She remembered getting into the car that had taken her and Colin to Dr. Anders, then nothing. Whatever had been used to knock them out kept her off-kilter and unable to access her magic. Once separated from Colin, she had been strapped to a medical bed by what appeared to be a military medical team. They'd then proceeded to pump River full of a variety of concoctions. Some of the drugs had triggered violent seizures and debilitating pain. Others had twisted her perception of reality and left her reeling. Her voice roughened as she described what she endured at the humans' hands and how the different drugs had torn at her magic, reshaping it into something she couldn't control and didn't recognize. They had weaponized her blood until it hurt just to exist. When her voice faltered, Nyla picked up the conversation, giving River a reprieve.

The older woman's story started before she landed in Portland. Once she started retracing River's trail, she'd realized that River's disappearance was similar to the missing European Kyn. Most of those taken were young adult Kyn whose family bloodlines were either Lycos or Magi, and each had recently interviewed for research internships with various organizations. Each of those organizations had buried ties with a global conglomerate known as the Mendalian Group.

When Nyla discovered that the Mendalian Group had ties to the Portland area, she had reached out through her network of contacts for more information and gotten Mike's name. She was warned that it could be a shot in the dark, but she was willing to risk it. However, before she could make her meeting, Harold the demon had snatched her up and dumped her in the same lab where River was being held.

Her trip through the Side had not done her any favors, nor had whatever Harold had initially injected her with to keep her disoriented and confused for the first day. Luckily, she had been left alone during the second day and was uncertain why, but she'd spent it trying to get past whatever it was they'd given her that wouldn't allow her to tap into her power.

She'd known the Northwest Kyn were looking for her not just because of who her son was, but because the man in charge of the lab had gotten a phone call that left him furiously shouting orders as he stormed out of the lab.

Gavin asked her to describe the man in charge, and when she did, a frigid fury crawled through him. He looked at Natasha and growled, "That sure as shit sounds like General Cawley."

"He wasn't alone," River said before Natasha could respond. "There was another man, younger, but definite corporate type. He came in once and stood off to the side when they…" River shuddered, then she cobbled together her composure and raised her chin. "He was blond, tall." She eyed Gavin. "Maybe your height or close to it."

Raine leaned forward. "Did you hear a name?"

River's brow furrowed as she thought. "Yeah, but it was hard to make out. Joseph? John?"

Raine's hands fisted, and her voice was tight. "Jonah?"

River held her gaze and managed a jerky nod. "Could be it."

Feral rage filtered down the bond, and the snarling scream of a pissed-off leopard echoed through his skull, but the only outward signs of Raine's reaction were a muscle that jumped in her locked jaw and her nails that dug into his thigh as she held on.

He managed not to flinch under the wash of Raine's toxic mix of rage, guilt, and pain. He knew she was struggling. She'd had a chance to take out Jonah Talbot and chosen not to because there was no definite proof that he'd continued his father's atrocities. He covered her hand with his, and when she turned her head to look at him, he found himself staring at her leopard. She didn't say anything, most likely because she couldn't, but he held that disconcerting gaze with his, breathing for both of them until she could lock it down. It didn't take long, a breath or three, before she lowered her lashes, and her painful grip eased.

River, unaware of Raine's violent reaction, continued the story. Her voice faltered when she haltingly admitted to her worried father that whatever the humans had done had unchained the dragon thought lost to their bloodline. The young woman trembled as she faced her father. "I couldn't hold her back. She was so angry... is still so very angry."

Giles paled at the revelation, but his shock was quickly replaced by lethal protectiveness. He pulled River close. "It's okay, sunshine. We'll get through this."

River's voice hitched. "How? She just wants to burn the world, and so do I." The last half of her confession came out choked.

Giles closed his eyes, his face twisted with fury and pain, as he held his daughter close. When he opened his eyes, it was clear that while the physical form of the dragon had been denied to him, the soul of the fire-breathing predator was alive and well. He turned that alien gaze on Westbrooke, Natasha, and Darius. What may have been meant as a command carried the weight of a vow. "It ends. Tonight."

CHAPTER 29

"Drake," Westbrooke started, breaking the tension.

"No, Corwin," Drake cut him off, the storm of emotions twisted his features into a menacing mask. "Your word. This is finished."

Raine was in full agreement with Drake, and while Westbrooke studied him for a long, strained moment, she started formulating plans on how best to go about achieving that end whether or not the councilman agreed. As far as she was concerned, eliminating General Matthew Cawley and Jonah Talbot and their continued interference with the Kyn was a no-brainer. She penciled their names onto her mental list and added Onidyn and its insidious research.

Gavin clearly caught her thoughts and squeezed her hand that was still on his thigh. *"And if Natasha doesn't agree?"*

"What's that saying?" she shot back, forcing her hand to relax under his. *"Better to ask forgiveness than permission."*

In a deceptively casual move, he brought her hand up

and gave her fingers a punishing nip. *"Last time you tried that, you almost got caught."*

The reprimand made her shiver, even though they were surrounded by others. She curled her fingers around his and leaned into him. *"Only because it was you tracking me."*

It had taken Raine years to hunt down and kill those who held her captive, experimented on her, and killed her mother. Those long, patient years had honed her predatory nature and enabled her to excel at being a Wraith. No one would ever have connected the series of deaths linked to Jonah Talbot's father and his research team if Jonah hadn't requested Taliesin's help investigating a cluster of recent deaths tied to his company.

Mulcahy had brought in Gavin, and by extension Raine. When Gavin dug deep into the deaths related to Aaron and Jonah Talbot, both past and present, Raine had finally come clean about her involvement. She admitted to Gavin that she was behind the earlier cluster of apparent accidents so that Gavin could uncover the *who* and *why* behind the recent deaths.

"You understand"—Westbrooke's hard voice broke into Raine's ruminating—"that once this is done, things will be set in motion."

Things? What things?

Drake's lip curled into a sneer. "I'm aware, but, truly, I don't give a damn." Something dark and hungry swept over the older man's face. Under his tailored shirt, the muscles in his arms coiled as he held River close, clearly not about to let her leave his side. "It's time."

Westbrooke held his gaze, something unspoken passing between them. A muscle in his jaw jumped, then Nyla broke the two men's staring contest. She pressed her hand to his chest, and when he dropped his gaze to her, she angled her head in some kind of signal. Westbrooke sighed. He turned to Darius and Natasha, who had remained silently watchful throughout the conversation. "And where do you and yours stand in this?"

The slight ring of red around Natasha's irises burned, adding an unearthly glow to her already-unusual eyes. Not exactly a good sign of things to come, but her voice was calm and cool. "The Northwest has never hidden their position from the Council."

A flicker of arrogance drifted through Westbrooke's expression. "I'm not the Council. I'm only a small part of the whole."

Natasha made a tsking sound. "Modesty does not become you, Councilman Westbrooke."

A surprised burst of laughter escaped the man, and he shook his head. "You are as amusing as your mother."

That earned him a grimace as Natasha shuddered. "Gods, I hope not."

Westbrooke looked at Darius, who sat silently at Natasha's feet. "You should be aware that Zayn and I have recently shared some enlightening conversations."

Perfectly composed and unruffled as tended to be his way, Darius said, "I've heard."

Westbrooke nodded. "Then you understand. If I make this move now, we may lose whatever edge we had."

"Perhaps," Darius said. "Perhaps not, but this"—he looked at the young woman standing with her father then back to Westbrooke—"cannot go unanswered."

Westbrooke's gaze dropped to Nyla, and he brushed his thumb over her bruised cheek, his voice filled with quiet menace. "No, it can't." He raised his head, took his time studying the gathered faces, and stopped on Giles Drake. "Change is inevitable."

Whatever Drake saw in Westbrooke's face caused him to flinch, a tell he quickly masked. "I'm not like you, Corwin. I've already lost too much."

Something flickered in Westbrooke's face as his gaze swept over the room. When his clear blue-green gaze set off by an unusual ring of black snagged on her, Raine recognized something—an old, entrenched grief honed by guilt. It was there and gone, almost before she grasped it.

What the hell was that about?

Westbrooke shook his head. His voice was rough as he admitted, "So have I, old friend."

Nyla shifted the conversation as she leaned a little more into Westbrooke and asked Natasha, "Have your people been able to pin down any other locations tied to Onidyn?"

"When I last checked," Natasha answered, "they had significantly narrowed down the possibilities."

Nyla frowned. "What about the senator's son? Any word on his whereabouts?"

Tucked into her father, River jerked and whispered, "Colin?" with equal parts fear and hope.

Natasha spared the young woman a momentary glance of sympathy. "If he's alive, it's highly likely he'll be there."

"Based on what River shared, we should presume the boy's been used as a guinea pig." Darius directed his comment to Westbrooke, but no one missed River's pained whimper.

A grim darkness drifted across Westbrooke's face. "I'm aware."

Darius, his arm braced on an upraised knee, didn't back down. "His father's reaction could be problematic."

For the first time, Westbrooke revealed the coldly, ruthless tactician within. "Then we will have to ensure the senator knows who the true monsters are." His gaze went to Natasha. "It might be best to give Thaddeus a heads-up so he can put his people in play because the American Kyn are about to step out of the shadows and into the spotlight."

Raine felt both trepidation and an illicit thrill at Westbrooke's pronouncement.

With her cool composure, Natasha asked, "And the Council?"

"Are not your worry."

Natasha's spine went rigid with offended arrogance.

Before the gathering storm of wrath could break free, the councilman added, "Peace, Natasha. That is not a judgment of you or yours."

Clearly unappeased by his admission, she was curt. "Isn't it?"

"Not in the slightest." The curve of Westbrooke's lips held no amusement, just predatory anticipation. "Your focus should remain here, on this battle. Leave the Council to me. I promise they will not intervene. Soon they will be occupied with a much more difficult choice."

The air around Natasha shivered, and for a moment, Raine thought she caught a glimpse of ebony horns rising above the blonde's head, but when she blinked, the image was gone.

"That sounds... promising," Natasha practically purred.

Corwin inclined his head. "Then let loose your hounds, my dear, and wish them good hunting."

CHAPTER 30

It was hours later and inching past midnight when Raine left Gavin sleeping in their bed and made her way to the kitchen. For the first time since Mulcahy's death, the big house was filled. River and Nyla had retreated to separate guest rooms to rest under Cassandra's watchful eye while the rest of the group discussed their next steps.

Natasha and Westbrooke had disappeared during the discussions, presumably to talk to Thaddeus, the head of the Eastern Amanusa contingent. Thanks to Mulcahy's glimpses of the future and his impeccable instinct, the demon contingent of the Eastern Kyn were not only well entrenched in the humans' political playground, but critically positioned to ensure the Kyn's exposure to the masses would not end in genocide, on either side.

When Natasha returned, she asked Raine and Gavin to keep her updated on their plans since she and Darius had a few more things to attend to. Darius added a request to be included in the final stage of the hunt. Only when he got their agreement, did he and Natasha take their leave.

With no sign of Westbrooke or Drake, Raine and Gavin

had continued to work with Ryuu on winnowing the list of locations belonging to Onidyn. It took time, but eventually, they narrowed it down to three options. They were waiting on a few more pieces of information before instigating a simultaneous infiltration of the sites. Westbrooke had stopped by briefly and listened quietly to their plans before adding suggestions of his own. After some additional tweaks, she and Gavin had incorporated those ideas before asking Ryuu and his team to confirm Nyla's information—that Talbot Foundation, Biovita, and Onidyn were tied to Mendalian Group. When that confirmation arrived, Westbrooke had already gone to the room he was sharing with Nyla. Raine and Gavin nailed down the final details before they called it quits for the night.

Raine couldn't find it in herself to be surprised by the revelation that there was a dedicated group of humans that spanned the globe unified on wiping out the Kyn. It made a sick sort of sense. History proved how much mortals hated not being able to claim what they considered the top spot of the evolutionary ladder. Instead of recognizing that the Kyn, like any other culture, had its pros and cons, all the mortals could see was the perceived power the supernaturals held. They were blind to the price each Kyn bloodline paid to wield those abilities.

What Raine had always struggled with was the involvement of Kyn who used those like the Mendalian Group to further their own agenda in holding or taking power. The prime example was Leopold DiMarcco, one of the oldest Kyn sitting on the Council and Westbrooke's intended target.

If Westbrooke were being honest—and Raine knew that last bit was highly sarcastic, considering who she was thinking about—she wished him luck because he was going to need it.

Going up against Leo was beyond dangerous, which was why Natasha had skirted a direct confrontation the last time Leo had interfered with the Northwest Kyn. Not much daunted the Demon Queen, but that Kyn, as old as he was, made her think twice. Even Raine, who really, really craved Leo's blood on her blade for his part in Mulcahy's death, understood Natasha's caution. To some extent, she even agreed with it.

Raine rubbed at the dull ache in her temples as she padded down the hall. All of that and more had swirled through her head, leaving her unable to sleep. Since she didn't want to keep Gavin up, she finally stopped trying and slipped out of bed with the intention of making a cup of tea. She just needed a moment to process the last few days. River's face flashed in her mind's eye, and this time, her sigh was deeper. That was a whole other can of worms that was about to spill over with disastrous results.

She'd swung by to check on the young woman around eight or nine—she couldn't remember, but it was late enough that night had pressed against the windows. Giles Drake had taken advantage of Raine's presence to leave his daughter while he went to get them something to eat. While he was gone, Raine had asked River how she was doing. The young woman had tried to assure her she was fine, but Raine knew better. She recognized the cauldron of emotions burning deep in River's eyes, the caustic mix of rage, guilt, shame, and disgust. Raine had endured that same internal chaos.

"It doesn't make you a monster, River." When the girl paled and blinked at her, Raine continued, sharing an unexpectedly brutal moment of honesty. "That rage you feel, it's justified. You just need to channel it correctly."

"It's not me." River's voice was low but fierce. "It's the dragon."

"No, it isn't." Raine knew her voice was harsh, but River needed to understand this key element if she were to survive her ordeal and not become a target Raine would later have to hunt. "There is no difference between you and the dragon."

"I'm not a shifter," the girl argued even as fear flashed in her hazel eyes. Somewhere deep, she already knew what was coming.

"You are now." There was no mercy in Raine's voice. "Whatever they did, whatever they unlocked inside of you, it was already there. Dormant, but there. Now it's up to you to master it moving forward." She held that angry gaze. "And I'm not just talking about the dragon."

River's hand fisted against the blanket, and she remained stubbornly mute.

Hearing the approaching footsteps of River's father, Raine made one final offer. "When you're ready, I'm here." She turned to leave and was at the door when the sound of her name had her turning back.

"Why are you doing this?"

Raine debated how honest to be, but River had survived, and that deserved respect, so she laid it out. "You made a choice, River, one I want you to keep making because I don't want to hunt you."

River licked her lips nervously. "Is that what will happen? You'll try to kill me?"

"Only if you give me no other choice."

River's chin raised imperiously, and defiance hardened her voice. "I'm not a monster."

Not missing the implied challenge, Raine stifled her relief and agreed, "No, you're not." She held River's gaze with her own, and for the first time in her life, the truth her uncle, Gavin, and even Natasha had tried to make her understand finally penetrated. She shared that knowledge with the younger woman. "You're Kyn."

Even now, hours later, Raine was still reeling from that bit of self-realization. For years, she'd struggled with accepting the unique abilities that bloomed after her time in the labs. Even worse, she'd struggled to accept that she was far from what others considered "normal" for Kyn, never quite grasping that there was no "normal." She didn't want River to drown in the same dark waters, and if that meant taking on the responsibilities of keeping the girl's head on straight, so be it.

She stepped into the kitchen and noted that someone had left the light above the stove lit, so she didn't bother turning on any others. Instead, she moved around and started the kettle for tea. She was waiting for it to whistle when movement at the entryway caught her attention.

"You're up late," Corwin Westbrooke said as he wandered into the space. "Can't sleep?"

Raine shrugged. "Got a lot on my mind."

"Seems to be a common occurrence tonight." He pulled a chair out from the table and settled in, his gaze strangely intense as he studied her.

It was a little disconcerting, but then again, the man himself was a bit disconcerting. Deciding it was best to be polite, she offered, "Would you like a cup of tea?"

"Please," he said.

She turned to pull down another cup and could feel the weight of his gaze on her back. She set the cup net to hers and turned. "Why are you staring at me?"

Westbrooke blinked, his smile strangely wistful. "I should apologize, but I can't help it."

When he didn't say anything else, Raine quirked an eyebrow in silent inquiry. "Dare I ask why?"

The older man shook his head and proceeded to upend Raine's world. "You share your mother's beauty, but it's the strength of spirit you share with your father that brings me joy."

Shock left Raine numb, and she barely got the question out. "How do you know my father?"

Painful emotions tore through Westbrooke's face and turned his nearly translucent eyes stormy. "He was my son."

CHAPTER 31

WESTBROOKE's words echoed through her head until they blurred into a roar of white noise. Her mouth moved without conscious thought. "Repeat that."

"I see Ryan kept his vow," Westbrooke muttered as he rubbed a spot just above his eye.

Raine let that little bomb detonate as well and decided she would tackle that one next. "My father—"

"Was my son," Westbrooke finished as he flattened his hands against the table's top and watched her carefully. "Yes."

The single admission churned a whirlwind of questions, and she latched on to the first one. "He's dead?" Even as she asked, she knew the answer. She had always known the answer. That old grief reappeared, tinged with cold rage.

"Murdered, just before you were born."

"So you knew." It came out like an accusation.

"About you and your mother?"

She nodded.

He grimaced. "Not until years later." Those unusual

eyes homed in on her. "Finn did a hellishly good job of hiding the two of you."

"Finn?" It came out soft, so soft, she didn't think he'd heard because he kept talking.

"He even went so far as to use one of the minor family names when he and Catriona wed."

The shrill whistle of the teapot interrupted his story, and moving on autopilot, Raine turned and poured the two cups of tea. Westbrooke didn't say a word as she worked, but the rasp of the metal spoon against the ceramic mug broke the silence. Raine set the spoon aside and noted the fine tremor of her hand. She fisted it, blew out a long, quiet breath, and flexed her fingers. After she inhaled and exhaled a couple more times, the tremor was gone. She picked up the mugs and took them to the table where her... grandfather sat.

As she crossed the floor, she risked a glance at the magic that surrounded him. Something tight in her eased as she picked up the strong weave of Fey and Magi. There were a couple of shrouded threads, but she didn't have time to investigate further, nor did she want to get caught peeking. When she was seated across from him, she held his gaze. "Start with the bit about Mulcahy."

Westbrooke cradled the mug. "To understand that, you need context."

"So give me the context."

His lips twitched. "Finn was an only child. My wife, his mother, had a difficult time carrying him to term. More so considering the era. So Finn grew up indulged."

"Spoiled, you mean," Raine said before blowing across her tea.

Westbrooke shook his head. "No, indulged, as in neither of us had the heart to curb his curiosity. He wasn't one to accept things at face value, and he took a certain amount of pride in not following the crowd. Although he was born into wealth and status, he preferred to earn both on his own merits. He forged friendships that spanned bloodlines and economic statuses, even as he questioned the status quo."

Raine wasn't stupid; the picture Westbrooke was painting was easy to picture. "You mean you and the Council."

Westbrooke sipped his tea, and when he set the mug back down, he made minute adjustments until it sat just so. "Yes." He looked up and held her gaze with unflinching candor. "Finn and I had many conversations about the future of the Kyn. The Council wanted to preserve our bloodlines, our magic, but Finn argued that doing so would sign our extinction. At the time, I thought he was a foolish, headstrong child who failed to grasp how determined the mortals were on eliminating those they considered a threat." There was a shift behind his eyes as something ominous crept closer. "I lived through the Burning Times and the endless hunts by fanatical humans, but Finn was dazzled by their latest fad of enlightenment." He said the last word with a sneer. "He couldn't accept the reality that it was already too late. Emboldened by their hypocritical religions, mortals had turned us into the stuff of nightmares."

"That's because some of us are," she pointed out.

He lifted his cup and tipped it toward her. "True, but some became that due to what they endured. So who's the real nightmare in this?"

It was a circular argument that no one could win. She knew because she had it often with her uncle. "Get back to who killed my father and why."

"Definitely Finn's child." He sat back and drummed his fingers against the table. "Long, very convoluted story, short—Finn and I had a falling out over his rising disillusionment with the Council's edicts. Our arguments got more and more heated, as we no longer had my mate to play mediator. It got worse when I moved into the Council seat."

The use of the word mate caught Raine's attention but before she could pursue it, Westbrooke turned down an even more intriguing path.

"I should've remembered how much Finn loved his history, how deeply he believed in not repeating past mistakes."

"What mistakes?" It was out before she could think twice.

Westbrooke studied her for a long moment. "I forget how young you are." The typical condescending tone of an older Kyn was missing. Instead, he seemed to be reminding himself of the fact. "The magic that defines us has not always looked as it does now. If the stories are to be believed, each house—Fey, Magi, Lycos, and Amanusa— was birthed from a shared, chaotic, wild root. As with any growing thing, unexpected offshoots would occur, and when those unusual powers came to light, it was not unknown for that particular magic to either be forcibly grafted into an existing bloodline or excised completely."

"Bred into compliancy or killed. Lovely choices." Raine didn't hide the bitterness in her voice.

Westbrooke rubbed his thumb over the edge of his mug. "As I explained to Finn, it was not one I condoned."

Raine put two and two together. "But you didn't actively stop the Council from doing it, did you?"

Arrogance bled into his face, but something worked

behind it, pushing it aside for a wearied cynicism. "Early on, no," he admitted unexpectedly. "I was the newcomer, my influence negligent at the time. Not that Finn accepted that excuse. Instead, our arguments deepened. Eventually, I'd understand his position and change mine, but it was too late—my son had made a decision of his own. He changed his name and left for America without saying a word."

She didn't miss his regret and felt a pang of sympathy for a father who'd lost his son. "How long did it take you to find him again?"

"Too long, because when Finn decided to do something, he tended to do it right." His unmistakable pride was mixed with grief.

"You found him after he was killed," she guessed.

"Yes." Westbrooke's face hardened. "Finn had come back, presumably to investigate a threat aimed at his wife and unborn child. Instead of eliminating it, he was killed. I wouldn't have ever known if someone hadn't slipped up. I spent the handful of years retracing the trail to who set the trap in motion and verifying the participants. Once I was sure of their guilt, I began to pick them off one by one until they were all dead."

When Westbrooke fell silent, Raine demanded, "Who was it?"

He held her gaze, his indomitable will a baleful light. "That's a story for another time."

Raine felt her temper flare, but before she could snap out a response, he continued, "No, Raine, you have a game to win here. I don't want you on the board of mine. Not yet. I may have failed my son, but I won't fail you or River, or any of the others who should be allowed to grow to their full potential without interference. My pieces are nearly in place, and the final moves are coming. When I'm done, I swear to you, I'll share it all."

Raine studied his face and wanted to push, but steely resolution stared back. There was no doubt that Corwin Westbrooke was in a league of his own when it came to intrigue and secrets. That was why he held his seat on the Council. Half-formed ideas teased her, but she could wait and watch to see if any would solidify. "Your word that you'll tell me who was behind my father's death."

"When I'm finished."

She shook her head. "No, before you make your final play, you tell me. I've lost too many, and they've taken too many secrets to the grave to trust the Fates that you'll survive. With my luck, you'll get your ass kicked, then whoever you went after will come hunting me. I want to know who to look out for."

Instead of being offended, Westbrooke grinned, years fading from his face. "My word you'll have a name before my vengeance is sated."

"Your word," she repeated because Kyn never made vows lightly.

For a moment, they sat in shared silence, then Raine broke it. "You didn't answer my question." When Westbrooke raised a brow, she reminded him, "Mulcahy knew about you."

"I think he had his suspicions, but it was only when Council's split over revealing ourselves to the humans began to widen, that he and I realized the connection we shared."

"My mother," she said.

"And you. Initially, we both agreed that keeping Finn's name away from you or her was in our best interests. Unfortunately, the recent shift in internal attitudes made it even more imperative that certain minds on the Council remain blind to your acquired skills. I plan on ensuring it stays that way."

It shouldn't have surprised her that Westbrooke was aware of Mulcahy's intentions. Not if he'd worked as closely as he said he had with her uncle. Mulcahy would use whoever he could, do whatever he could to ensure her safety. It wasn't a truth she understood or accepted until after his death. That was when she began to understand what motivated his apparent distance from her. Not blame for her mother's death, as she'd always thought, but Mulcahy's way of protecting her and her unusual magic from the Council's avaricious eye.

Now, it seemed another powerful player wanted to do the same. Torn between annoyance at that presumed arrogance and the more mature acceptance of the protective logic driving such decisions, Raine decided to leave Westbrooke to it. If he wanted to keep her out of whatever game he was playing with the powers that be, so be it. He was right—she and Gavin had enough here at home to deal with, specifically cutting off one of the heads of the Mendalian Group.

Thinking of the man who shared her bed, she flicked a glance at her grandfather... and changed the subject. "How deep is Nyla in this?"

"More than her son would probably like. But not as deep as me."

Raine held his gaze with hers. "Does she know?"

"About you?"

Raine tightened her hold on her mug and nodded. The fact he only mentioned her and not Gavin gave her hope that Gavin's secret was still safe.

"No."

Relief coursed through her.

"But she's worried about her son."

Not about to touch that with a ten-foot pole, Raine lifted her mug and sipped her tea.

Correctly reading her silence, Westbrooke sighed. "Considering my track record with my own child, I'm not one to cast stones, but if I could ask a favor of you."

Raine looked at him and waited.

"Perhaps, he could make time to speak to her before we leave."

"I can't make any promises."

"Understood." He stood up with his cup in hand, looked at her for a long moment, then said softly, "I wish Finn had a chance to see you. He'd be so proud of the woman I see." Before she could respond, he wished her a good night and left.

She sat there for a long time, trying to sort out the mix of emotions clamoring inside her. She'd always thought having the answer to the question of her father would change things, but strangely, it hadn't.

Not really.

It was nice to know her father hadn't been a dick, far from it, but everything that was her—her insecurities, her fears, the nightmares that haunted her, the stubbornness— was all still there.

It also didn't change how she perceived Westbrooke. She didn't fully trust him, couldn't really because he was still a stranger. Maybe that would change. Maybe it wouldn't. Either way, one constant remained unchanged— she wouldn't be a pawn in Council games.

Not even for blood.

CHAPTER 32

RAINE SAT IN THE PASSENGER SEAT, SEETHING SILENTLY, AS DARIUS steered a dark sedan through the winding and picturesque streets of the Southwest Hills neighborhood. Under her skin, her leopard snarled and paced, its tail twitching in irritation. Her hands were curled into bloodless fists, her nails biting into her palms, as she struggled to keep her temper leashed.

Raine, Gavin, Xander, and surprisingly, Darius, had split into pairs. Their plan was to hit the top two locations Ryuu had pinpointed in the early morning hours. It helped that Axel had eliminated the third address some time before dawn. Darius and Raine had hit the jackpot and infiltrated Onidyn's lab, but that bright spot went dark when they discovered who that lab held: a nearly feral Dani, a barely alive Astrid, a very dead Sam, and a newly Bitten Colin.

It took both Gavin and Darius to keep Raine from wiping out all the lab's personnel, and they almost didn't succeed. Gavin got drawn in when Raine's reaction ricocheted through their bond like a lightning storm. Luckily, he managed to break through her rage long enough for Darius to stop her from tearing out the throat of the technician who had been passing the time by tormenting a vacant-eyed Astrid, who had pulled deep into herself in an effort to escape her hellish, new reality.

While Darius got the technician to talk, Gavin channeled Raine's furious energy into making emergency repairs on Astrid's magic. Whatever they had injected the young woman with had mangled the threads between her and her wolf until they were almost unrecognizable.

As for Darius, he used his time with the technician wisely. Funny thing, but when the man realized he was literally staring death in its face, he all but pissed himself as every dirty little secret came spilling out of his mouth.

Raine didn't care how Darius achieved such spectacular results. She just enjoyed the results—like the fact that one Dr. Anders was expected to arrive after lunch for updated test results. Once Darius sent the tech to his well-deserved, eternally flamed-filled end, they turned their attention to the three survivors.

After Raine carefully guided Astrid's bruised and needle-marked arms into a lab coat that was no longer needed by its owner and sat her down out of the way, she approached Dani. The one-eyed shifter was more of a challenge, and Raine had to use her ability to manipulate the older Bitten's magic to force her back into her human shape. Unlike Astrid's, the threads that bound Dani to her animal were bent, not broken. Once in human form, Dani's temperament eased from nearly feral into something closer to rational. The older woman's hands shook as she pulled on a pair of scrubs that Darius had found somewhere.

Then it was Colin's turn. The young man looked nothing like his photo. Unlike Astrid and Dani, who had been locked into medical rooms, he was held in a reinforced cage. Even worse, he shared the space with Sam's mangled corpse. Crouched in the far-back corner, his body covered in deep bites and scratches in various stages of healing, Colin stared at Raine with a wild, inhuman light burning in his eyes. There was no missing his intent—the minute she opened the door, he would attack. Not keen on adding to the kid's nightmare, Raine wrestled with how to get him out without hurting him.

The solution turned out to be Dani. The older woman all but shoved Raine aside, threw open the door, and stepped inside. She caught Colin as he leapt at her, teeth bared and hands clawed. Despite her looks and her impaired vision, Dani managed to take Colin to the floor and held him down until he submitted. Then she flicked a dismissive glance over Raine, stalked out of the cage, and snapped at Colin to "Hurry it the hell up." Surprisingly, Colin did just that.

Raine left Darius to lead the three survivors to the car then channeled her unbridled fury into annihilating the lab. By the time she was done, only ashes remained. Too damn bad it hadn't done shit to cool the anger boiling through her veins. As Darius drove them back to Mulcahy's house, Raine updated Gavin, who was making his way toward them. They agreed to meet at a nearby big-box store, where they would send Dani, Astrid, and Colin with Gavin and Xander back to the house, where Cassandra waited.

That decision hadn't come about without an argument. Gavin wanted to go with her and Darius to confront Dr. Anders. Raine pointed out that Xander couldn't drive and handle the badly damaged trio by herself. Reluctantly, Gavin gave in but insisted she keep their bond open, just in case.

Now, she and Darius were minutes away from the lavish home that belonged to one Dr. Anders.

"There." She leaned forward as a white two-story house with green shutters and an expansive veranda complete with a charming pair of rocking chairs came into view. Luckily, unlike some of its neighbors, it wasn't locked behind a gate. Instead, a pretty but useless white-railing fence separated the yard from the sidewalk.

Darius went a little farther, just beyond the curve of the street, before he pulled into a spot outside another home. This one set way back, the entrance at the top of a set of steep stairs that disappeared into the trees. He turned off the engine, and they got out. She waited for him to round the car before she started to walk back. A few moments later, she felt the familiar brush of magic at play and shot Darius a quizzical look.

"Cameras," he explained. "Nearly everyone has one nowadays."

"And having them all go on the fritz at the same time isn't going to raise questions?"

"Oh, they're still recording, just not us."

She quashed a flash of envy at the accuracy of his spell work, but then again, his skills were more akin to Gavin's, elegant and precise, versus hers, which tended toward blunt and brutal. As they got closer to Anders's place, she studied the area around the house. On the drive over, she and Darius had agreed to forgo a direct approach. Instead, they were going to do what Kyn did best—strike from the shadows. However, that required scoping out an approach that wouldn't lead anyone to suspect the couple strolling down the sidewalk. Thankfully, it was mid-morning, and most people were either out on errands or inside and occupied, leaving the streets quiet.

Thanks to the forest that grew between properties in this area, the space between Anders's house and his neighbor to the west was thick with trees and wild growth. Darius hopped the low fence, and Raine followed. They slipped into the cool depths of the trees. A couple hundred yards in, the green space curled around the back edge of the house. From within the concealment of the trees, she and Darius studied their options. This neighborhood was basically built into the hillside.

"I can go in there." She pointed out the back of what appeared to be the garage. It sat lower than the main house and was tucked under the protection of the nearby trees. "You take care of any surveillance, and I'll get you in the back door."

"I can hold the cameras, but not long."

"I won't need more than a couple minutes, tops." She slipped away and made her way to the garage. She found her spot near an old-growth tanoak tree whose trunk put it somewhere near the century mark. She crouched and set her palm against the moss-covered surface. The steady thrum of the surrounding nature tickled her palm like soft sunlight. She lowered her mental shield, reached for the door between worlds, and stepped onto the Shadowed paths.

Icy wind tore at her, but the hard core of anger that craved vengeance kept her warm and focused, shoving aside the typical distraction of the warped visuals. She didn't waste any time making her way into the house. Once inside, she paused and waited in the place between worlds as she listened.

A slightly garbled voice came from the front of the house. Based on the cadence, it sounded like Anders was talking to someone on the phone. Good, he was busy and not paying any attention. She took the step that brought her out of the Shadows and quickly crossed to the French doors that overlooked the backyard. She flicked the flimsy lock as Darius climbed the short set of stairs to the deck. She kept one ear on the drone of Anders's voice and one hand on the handle. When Darius dipped his chin, she opened the door.

He slipped inside and shut the door silently behind him.

She tilted her head toward where Anders was still talking. Darius took the lead, and Raine followed. Just outside what was clearly an office, they stopped to listen.

"Once you get the committee's approval, I'll be able to move on to the next stage of research." A chair squeaked. "Well, if that's the case, we'll need more test subjects." Another pause. "I understand, but I made that very clear to him yesterday, and he assured me it wouldn't be an issue." The pause this time was a bit longer. "Good, I'm glad to hear it. Look, I need to go. I'm running a little late this morning, and I still need to send in a report to the general before I go in." A chuckle sounded. "Oh, trust me, I get it." This time, the pause was short. "Yes, that works for me. Say around seven? I should have the data for you by then, so we can discuss the next stage." Papers rustled. "No, of course, I understand. Yes, I have your address here. Good, then I'll see you tonight, Jonah." Another protest from the chair was followed by Anders's sigh.

At Talbot's name, Raine met Darius's dark gaze and wondered if hers looked equally hard. She had no idea what was running through the demon's mind, but she knew what was in hers. A vow. Jonah Talbot was finished. No matter what Natasha or Westbrooke said, Jonah's days were numbered; she would make sure of it.

She crouched and freed her blade from its sheath in her

boot. When she straightened, Darius was sketching a symbol in the air. Not about to be taken unawares, Raine let her vision shift and watched as his magic flared to life. Ebony strands swiftly expanded like a web, and as it spread from Darius and covered the room beyond, those black strands took on a deep-ruby glow. Once the spell was in place, Darius stepped into the doorway, with Raine right behind him.

Anders shot to his feet, his chair scraping backward as he gasped in shock. "Who are you? How'd you get in here?" His voice cracked with belligerence and fear.

"Sit down." The command in Darius's voice was unmistakable, especially when reinforced by his magic. Two thick ribbons whipped around Anders and slammed him back into his chair.

Unfortunately, Anders was blind to the magic at Darius's command. As his body was yanked by what appeared to be an invisible force, his eyes widened with panic. Anders struggled uselessly against Darius's hold. He broke out in a sweat as his skin grayed.

"Enough." Darius tightened his hold on the human.

Anders's struggles stopped, mainly because magic was coiled around him like a snake, not allowing him to move. As Darius crossed to a chair positioned off to the side and took a seat, Raine approached the doctor from the other side. Anders's eyes darted between her and Darius. Raine made sure the doctor got an eyeful of her blade as she deliberately moved to stand behind him.

Darius rested his elbows on the chair's arms and pressed the tips of his fingers together as he considered the trussed-up human. "Dr. Anders, it's come to our attention that your research has violated Section 4B of the Agreement of 1946."

Dr. Anders swallowed and croaked, "I was assured my research would fall outside the restrictions of the government's treaty with the Kyn."

"By who?"

Anders's breathing grew choppy as he struggled against his invisible bonds and shook his head frantically. What he didn't do was answer.

Darius arched a brow. "I have no issues with forcing you to answer," he warned with silky menace as the air around him gained the slightest shimmer. "In fact, I'd enjoy doing so, so please, continue to play mute."

Icy trepidation crept over Raine's skin. Darius was up to something, something Anders would not like. Her lips curved with dark, anticipatory joy. *This should get interesting.*

Sure enough, a rough scream erupted from the man in the chair as his body bowed in agony. His face was a twisted mask of torment, but the white film that crept over his eyes as the minutes stretched on unsettled Raine. Darius was definitely not someone she ever wanted to fuck with. She held her position, knife at the ready, and waited, wondering if Darius was planning on scaring the good doctor to death.

Just when she was sure Anders would keel over, Darius sighed, and his magic withdrew just enough to release the human.

Anders slumped in his chair, his skin waxy, his breathing erratic. His voice cracked as he babbled. "It's not my fault! The general arranged it. Said it was an approved contract through the Department of Defense. That they'd had such an arrangement in place years ago with the Talbot Foundation and were reestablishing the previous study."

Like tiny snapshots, pieces fell into place. The current experiments Jonah and General Cawley were conducting were based on the nightmares Raine endured at Aaron Talbot's hands. Red fogged her vision.

Darius cocked his head, his voice cool and detached. "And you have proof of this?"

Anders nodded frantically. "Ye... yes."

Raine leaned in so she could hiss in his ear. "Where?"

Despite the magical restraints, his body jerked so violently, it shoved the chair a few inches to the left as he tried to see her. "Wha... who... whe..."

She grabbed his hair, yanked his head back, and set her blade against his throat.

"Careful," Darius murmured. "We can't be obvious."

She pulled the edge back so she wouldn't accidentally slice his throat. "Where is the proof?"

"Safe... safety deposit box." Tears leaked from Anders's eyes. "First and Polk, Union Bank."

Raine raised her gaze to Darius, who studied the now-sobbing man. Raine could feel his power as it nipped at her skin, but even more, she could see multiple threads sink into Anders's skin until they colored the human's veins an inky black. Despite Raine's hold on his scalp, Anders stared in horrified fascination as the black lines crawled up his arms. His mouth opened in a soundless scream that never escaped. Raine looked at Darius, who dipped his chin. She pulled her blade back as those unsettling veins of ink continued to crawl up Anders's neck. She shoved his head forward and stepped back.

Darius took his time rising from his chair and rounding the desk. When he got to Anders, he simply brushed his finger against the petrified doctor's temple. Anders began to seize, and moments later, he went limp, his eyes empty. Then he tilted over in his chair, toppling to the floor as the black slowly faded away.

CHAPTER 33

RAINE SAT IN HER SUV IN THE PARKING LOT OF UNION BANK, HER fingers absently drumming on the steering wheel as she watched the glass doors and waited for Gavin. Once Anders was dead, she and Darius had searched the office and found the safety deposit key tucked into the top desk drawer. Darius had remembered to snag the doctor's photo ID since it would be needed to access the box. With the lab destroyed, no one would be expecting Anders until his meeting with Jonah Talbot tonight. That gave the Kyn a head start of a few hours. Hopefully, that would be enough to let them take the lead in Cawley and Talbot's twisted game.

They searched the house for anything else that could link Anders to Talbot or Cawley and came up empty. Since technology and Raine weren't friends, she put a call into Ryuu, who directed Darius through a series of steps that granted Ryuu access to the laptop on Anders's desk. Once Ryuu got what he needed so he could search through the laptop, Darius and Raine left Anders's body where it had fallen. Darius assured Raine that it would appear as if he'd died of natural causes. They left the house undisturbed and made the return trip to Mulcahy's, where they picked up Gavin.

A brief argument ensued when Raine and Darius discussed who would accompany Gavin to the bank. It ended with a call from Natasha, asking for Darius to meet her and Westbrooke at Senator Guthrie's office. They wanted to let the man know his son was alive and find out just how tangled the senator was with the Mendalian Group before they returned Colin.

If they returned Colin.

Raine knew, better than most, that Colin's life as he knew it was over, and it remained to be seen what his new reality would look like. As far as she was concerned, the kid was better off sticking with them until they could be assured his father wouldn't lock him down in a lab somewhere else.

The door to the bank opened. Sunlight bounced off the glass as a figure strolled across the parking lot. An older, nervous man with neatly styled brown hair and curved shoulders strode to the rideshare waiting at the curb. To anyone watching, Dr. Anders was alive and well as he left Union Bank to head back to his office at Biovita.

I gave the rideshare time to pull out before I put the SUV into gear and followed. This Dr. Anders was about to be dropped off at a nearby university.

The plan was actually simple. Gavin, using his illusion ability, would pose as Anders and retrieve the items in the safety deposit box. So far, it appeared to be working. The true test would come later once the real Anders's body was discovered, and his steps were retraced. By then, though, it would be too late. If the information contained on those drives was what she thought it was, it would give the Kyn the ammunition they needed to derail whatever plans the Mendalian Group set in motion on American soil.

Fifteen minutes later, Gavin—as Anders—got out of the rideshare in a university parking lot. He pulled out his phone as the car left and appeared to be reading a text. She parked in a nearby spot and waited for Gavin to join her. He gave it a minute or two then headed over. Once he was in the passenger seat, she pulled out and headed to Taliesin.

"What did you get?"

"Two flash drives." Magic swept through the car like a faint breeze. Dr. Anders's profile wavered and faded, replaced by Gavin's familiar features. "We'll need to open them on an isolated laptop just in case. I've already given Ryuu a heads-up, so we'll hand these over once we're at the office."

"How long do you think it will take him?"

Gavin shrugged. "Depends if the drives are encrypted or not." He paused, and she could feel him watching her. "Now that we have a minute, tell me what happened between you and Westbrooke last night."

She kept her attention on the road. "Nothing."

"Raine." He loaded her name with an unspoken warning.

"Gavin," she shot back.

He didn't say anything for a long moment.

"Baby, talk to me." That soft entreaty accompanied by both love and acceptance, made emotion boil out of nowhere, pressing hot against her eyes and tightening her throat.

"Not fair, Gavin."

"Told you before, you're mine. I don't play fair."

That earned a watery chuckle, and she used her

shoulder to wipe at her cheek. "Westbrooke knew my father."

"And?"

"And..." Her voice wobbled, then steadied. "He was Westbrooke's son."

"Shit." As quiet as it was, that word still said it all.

"Yeah."

For a long moment, the car was quiet, both of them lost in their heads, but Raine held tightly to their connection. Gavin hadn't shut down. Instead, a constant pulse of comfort remained.

Finally, he asked, "Did Mulcahy know?"

"Eventually." She then haltingly shared the rest of the conversation.

When she was done, Gavin let out a low whistle of disbelief. "Damn."

It was easy enough to follow his thoughts. "Yeah. And now with River, Astrid, Colin, and likely Dani, we aren't going to be able to keep what we can do quiet much longer." As they were at a red light, she risked a glance at him. "We can't not help them, Gavin."

"I never thought we wouldn't," he said. "I just didn't want to advertise our abilities, not with the Council breathing down our necks."

The light turned green. "Well, if we can trust what Westbrooke said, that concern might not be as immediate as we thought. He made a point to tell me he was going to continue to protect me by not acknowledging our family connection. Said it was safer for me that way."

"He's right."

"But?"

"But can we trust Westbrooke?"

She grimaced. "Do we have a choice?"

"Not yet." He paused. "So now what?"

"Now? Now, I'm finally going to do what my uncle asked."

Gavin snorted with amusement. "He'd be laughing his ass off if he could hear you."

Her lips curved. "No doubt, but he was right. The new generation of the Kyn needs to be strong enough to survive not just the Council, but everything else that will be thrown at them."

"Agreed," he said. "This Mendalian Group is a concern."

"It is, but since Natasha loves screwing with the humans, we can let her and Thaddeus tackle the politics of it all."

"And in the meantime?"

She turned into Taliesin's lot, parked, and turned off the engine. Only then did she twist in her seat so she could see Gavin. "In the meantime, I have a few loose ends to tie up."

She held his gaze, refusing to hide her intentions. It wouldn't do any good anyway, considering how closely they were linked. She had a vow to keep.

Gavin's gaze drifted over her face for a long moment before he spoke. "You realize Natasha will take them both down."

"Financially and professionally. But that's not enough, Gavin, and you know it. If they aren't stopped, they'll just come back like the cockroaches they are. I'm not willing to sacrifice any other Kyn to keep the humans happy."

He wrapped a hand around the back of her neck and pulled her close. "Be fuckin' smart," he growled. "Or I'm going to be pissed." Then his mouth took hers in a kiss filled with frustration, love, worry, and need.

She gave as good as she got, her tongue dancing with his as she bunched his shirt in her fists and held him close.

When he finally let her up for air, she stared into his stormy green eyes. "I will."

Decrypting the information on the drives took Ryuu three hours, and when he was done, it was clear to even the blindest person that Jonah Talbot of the Talbot Foundation and General Matthew Cawley were behind a well-funded, highly illegal research targeting Kyn genetics for use in enhancing humans. That was a direct violation of the Kyn's treaty with the US Government. Not only had Anders kept an exhaustive paper trail, but there were also video and voice recordings. Dr. Anders had been serious about covering his ass.

By the time Gavin and Raine had plowed through everything, it was well past nine at night. Natasha, Darius, and Westbrooke had eventually joined them as they worked in the conference room, reading through endless email chains, lab reports, and financial spreadsheets. They created a list of names tied through money and deeds that enabled Talbot and Cawley to operate without oversight. Raine didn't recognize many, but Natasha, Darius, and Westbrooke clearly did.

Untangling the threads of conspiracy had been the easy part.

The recordings, though, would haunt Raine. During the taped conversations, two men who considered the Kyn less than human discussed how to harvest what they needed from live specimens or joked about the lethal results of a test. The humans were determined to replicate the Kyn's abilities, and failing that, they would be happy to just wipe them out of existence. The video recordings of horrific experiments tore at Raine's heart and soul, reigniting old nightmares even as it solidified her determination to make Talbot and Cawley pay.

And Raine wasn't the only one feeling the burn of retribution. As they gathered everything up to store until needed, Raine couldn't help but notice that Westbrooke had aged years in the last couple of hours. Natasha's expression was so cold, it was subarctic. The air of menace bleeding from Darius was almost choking in its intensity. None of the Kyn were unaffected, and the fury that filled the room had a life of its own.

"They have to pay, Natasha." Raine's voice was guttural as she handed the last of the paper files to the head of Taliesin.

The Demon Queen met her gaze, the ruthless predator evident in the dark light in her eyes. "They will."

"Your word."

The blonde inclined her head. "My word. If the humans refused to honor the Agreement, then when we step out of the shadows, it will be war." She turned to Westbrooke and handed him the flash drives. "You take this back. You make them understand the American Kyn will not stand by while we are being hunted. We are not prey."

He took what she offered and gave her an old-world bow. "I'll deliver your message."

Darius brushed his hand along Natasha's spine. "I'll take Westbrooke back to Mulcahy's then come get you."

Natasha nodded.

His dark gaze went to Gavin. "You'll stay."

Gavin nodded.

Raine, Natasha, and Gavin watched Darius and Westbrooke leave. Only when the soft ding of the elevator faded did Raine speak. "Why give him the drives? We need those."

"No, we don't," Natasha said, her voice weary. "Ryuu downloaded the originals of everything. What's on those drives are copies only." She drew in a big breath. "Giles Drake called me earlier. He won't be leaving with Nyla and Westbrooke tomorrow."

Raine wasn't surprised. "River?"

"Says she wants to stay here." Natasha's lips curved just the tiniest bit. "With you, strangely enough."

Raine acknowledged the burst of relief that replaced some of the worry she had been carrying. She hadn't wanted the young woman to leave just yet. Not when she was still trying to find her feet. "Unlike you, some people like me, Natasha."

"I can't imagine why. When he gets back, send Darius to my office. I have a few calls to make." She started for the door, stopped, and turned back, her gaze landing on Gavin. "Your mother asked if you could take her and Westbrooke to the airport tomorrow afternoon."

"Not a problem," Gavin said, but Raine felt the flash of apprehension and relief through their connection.

She waited until Natasha strolled out of the room before turning to Gavin. "Spill."

He didn't pretend not to understand. "I was hoping to get a chance to talk to my mother before she left."

"You could make her breakfast and spend the morning with her."

"I guess."

Raine eyed her man. "Gavin, she loves you. If you make the offer, she'll be all over it."

He rubbed the back of his neck. "I've just spent so long being pissed at her, it's hard not to stay that way."

Raine walked over to him, wrapped her arms around his waist, and lay her head against his chest. "Try. She's your mom. You might not heal everything, but at least make it so you two can talk."

His arms tightened around her. "I'll try."

"Good." She squeezed and closed her eyes, breathing him in.

His mouth brushed against her hair. "You okay, babe?"

"I will be," she answered honestly. She *would* be all right. With Gavin's support, she could take on the task of helping those like River, Colin, and Astrid. Somehow, the two of them would figure out how to nudge this newer generation into accepting who and what they were. They were Kyn, no matter how unique their magic. In fact, she would use her own skills to watch the backs of those like Natasha, Cheveyo, and Warrick as they led the Northwest Kyn into the harsh light of the mortal world.

Not just because that was what her uncle would've wanted, but because that was what she wanted. She and Gavin couldn't spend their lives hiding. They were Wraiths. They were Kyn. And together, they were unbreakable.

CHAPTER 34
THREE MONTHS LATER

"I'm so sorry for your loss, Erica," Jonah said into the phone as he pinched the bridge of his nose and tried to ignore the near-constant ache in his temples. "The general was a good man."

"He was a monster," said the woman on the other end of the line, her voice devoid of emotion. "I'm glad he's gone. Don't ever call me again."

The dial tone echoed in his ear.

"Goddammit," he muttered as he threw his phone down on his desk. *Could shit get any more fucked?*

The damn Kyn had destroyed everything, and it was that fucking pansy-assed doctor's fault. Those recordings that were shown in the closed session of the military's official inquiry could have only come from him.

He was willing to bet good money that Anders's death wasn't from an aneurysm like the medical examiner claimed. Somehow, someway, that bitch Bertoi had him taken out. If he had to guess, that bastard Durand was behind it because McCord would have left a mess.

Based on the records his father kept, she had very little control of the monster they'd created. Not that it mattered. She was the first success simply because she'd survived. Everything after her had just improved on their final objective. And they had been so close, so fucking close, to finally cracking the code to harnessing the powers of the Kyn.

Frustrated fury had him slamming his fist against the desk. The half-filled glass of whisky jumped and splashed a little. He swiped at the drops.

The inquiry had been bad enough. He could've recovered, but then his businesses had started to tank, with money disappearing like rats on a sinking ship. He was still trying to plug the holes. He'd even reached out to his connection with Mendalian Group, but the fucker had disconnected his line and wouldn't take his call.

Asshole! Leaving me swinging!

He shoved away from his desk and paced his office, dragging his hand through his hair. He should have left town when it all started, but no, Cawley had convinced him they were covered, that they had the government's backing.

Turned out that was bullshit too. A few weeks ago, when the politicians kept dragging their feet, the Kyn had decided to raise the stakes. Videos were leaked to social media, and now he didn't dare step out of his house, or the horde of reporters and protestors would swarm.

Fucking spin doctors. All of sudden, he and Cawley were the monsters. Cawley couldn't hack it; the stress had landed his ass in a hospital with a stroke a week ago. He'd never woken up, and they'd finally pulled the plug earlier today. Now it was just Jonah stuck in the role of scapegoat.

It was all bullshit, all the moral outrage about the Kyn

being treated inhumanly. *Please, they're monsters, not humans.* Once the Kyn showed their true colors, he would sit back and laugh his ass off as the humans screamed for protection.

A flicker of movement caught his eye, but when he spun around, no one was there. *Great, now I'm seeing shit. Damn, I need a break.*

He stalked back to his desk, snagged his whisky, and downed it in one gulp. He left the glass on his desk and went back to pacing. His mind spun in endless circles of fury and a fear he refused to admit.

There had to be a way out of this. Maybe he could get out of the country, start over somewhere else. He rubbed his hand against his hip, trying to eliminate the irritating itch spreading across his palm.

He would need to access the money he had tucked away where the government couldn't touch it. Maybe he would pay his overseas friend a visit first, just show up on the bastard's doorstep. *Bet that wouldn't go over well.*

His laugh sounded slightly manic. His hand started to burn. He stopped and shook it out, trying to see if he had been bitten by something. But his vision wavered, and he caught himself against the desk, thinking maybe he should cut back on the whisky.

He shook his head, and the world took a sickening lurch.

"Something wrong, Jonah?"

He spun around at the soft question and narrowed his eyes at the dark-haired woman sitting in his chair behind his desk. "How'd you get in?"

"Trade secret."

He was caught in the glow of her silver eyes and tried to

brace himself against the desk as his legs went out from underneath him. A faint flutter of panic tried to rise, but a wave of agony drowned it as if his blood were boiling in his veins. He tried to talk, but only an agonized groan escaped.

He blinked and found himself staring up at the ceiling of his office. He couldn't move, couldn't scream, and the pain was getting worse. A soft, chilling feminine laugh rattled through his brain.

Then she was crouched next to him, her arms braced on her knees as she watched him writhe on the floor. "Hurts, doesn't it?" Her tone was conversational. "Don't worry, give it another minute, and it won't matter."

He tried to reach for her, but the fire eating him from the inside out grew into an inferno. His screams were silent as his body shut down bit by bit as she continued to watch with a small smile.

"You know that magic you wanted so bad?" She didn't wait for a response, not that he could give one. "I figured it was time you tried it out yourself. Unfortunately, this little spell just gives you a taste of your own medicine, and once it's done with you, so am I." She leaned in until all he could see were her glowing eyes. "Enjoy your time in hell, Jonah. Your dad's waiting for you."

Another wave hit, dragged him under, and held him tightly in the inky arms of death.

If you're not ready to leave the shadows, sign up for my newsletter for your free copy of TANGLED IN SHADOWS, a short story collection from the Kyn at **https://www.sub scribepage.com/jami-gray-kyn.**

If you've left the shadows behind, but want to enjoy more of Jami's fantasy worlds, then check out IGNITION POINT and join the Arcane Families in this fast-paced urban fantasy series. Now available at your favorite book seller!

KYN APPENDIX

GLOSSARY

Amanusas:
One of four Kyn races, delight in chaos, half-demon and half-human or Kyn. Six bloodlines—War, Earth, Secrets, Enticement, Death and Inequity—referred to as 'Blood of'. For example: Natasha is Blood of Secrets.

Amá:
Navajo for "mother".

Ape':
Shoshonee for "father".

awéé':
Navajo for "baby".

ayóo-aniínishní:
Navajo for "I love you".

Baide':
Shoshonee for "daughter".

Between:

The second realm between the mortal and magical worlds, accessible by the Kyn.

Bitten:

Humans transformed to shifters through vicious attack. Magic needs human to be on brink of death to complete conversion. They are lower in the pack's structure as the control of wolf is tenuous at best. Tend not to live long.

Biovita:

A biotech lab in Hillsboro, OR where Brant Sutler, a human geneticist worked creating drug to turn Kyn wolves feral.

Blood ward:

A magical construct based on a castor's blood to defend or protect a place or person.

Bonded:

Rare metaphysical tie between Kyn, generally shifters, that connects two individuals at soul level. A step above mated. Partners generally don't survive the passing of the other.

Born:

Kyn Shifters who are born, some are Pure Bloods—rare few bloodlines.

Bound:

An Amanusa, caught in a casted circle by a summoner who uses all their names, to enslave—body and soul—to do the summoner's bidding. If a name is missed, they become half-Bound.

Chindis:

Vengeful spirits of the dead, raised by witches, however can be done by anyone with the ability, controlled by their summoner. Torment victims and rip them apart psychically. Generally are spirits of those who died violently or before their time. Once vengeance is taken, they'll rest.

Cinar International:

European based corporation.

The Council:

The ruling eleven members of the Kyn, chosen from around the world and headquartered in Turkey.

Division:

Preternatural Crimes Division, a group of talented and/or psychic humans who work for US Government and assist the Kyn on supernatural crimes.

Feral:

Wolves whose animal nature has taken control. Tend to attack humans and those closest to them. Nothing of the thinking man is left behind.

Fey:

One of four Kyn races, Sidhe descendants.

Kyn:

The entire preternatural community, composed of all four houses: Fey, Lycos, Amanusa, and Magi.

Lycos/Shifters:

One of four Kyn races, shape shifters, generally predator animals.

Magi:

One of four Kyn races, made of witches and wizards.

Mated:

Emotional bond created when two shifters commit.

Mavericks:

Lone wolves who have chosen to leave packs and roam on own. Can be Born or Bitten.

Mirroring:

Ability to send part of yourself into another by merging two magics, can add strength, but only as passenger. Empathic magic, deep level merger gives access to individual's mind/heart. Witches can mirror.

Pinnanku tease em puinnuhi:

Shoshonee for "See you again next time."

Sarielian Order:

The ultimate group of Wraiths, made of nine of the most dangerous Kyn of the world.

Shadowed Paths:

The walkways in Between, used when Shadow Walking.

Shadow Walking:

Ability to travel in the realm that exists between the waking world and the magical one.

Side:

A realm accessible to the Amanusa, not easily borne by other Kyn, completely unbearable by humans. A third plane of existence.

Sisna:

Sanskrit demon slur, lewd version of tailed demon or phallus-worshipper.

sitsi':

Navajo term for daughter.

Soul Stealer:

Nomâhtsé' héõo' Adanta - Eater of Souls, a psychic being created by black magic from the remains of a soul, tied to summoner. Gains strength eating the souls of others.

Taliesin Security:

The public security company housing the Northwest Kyn.

Tachair:

Gaelic word for "light", Raine uses it for light spell.

Three-fold Law:

Witches follow concept: What you do, will come back to you three-fold.

Tracker:

Shifters who are outside Pack hierarchy, their duty is to hunt/execute rogue shifters and threats (internal/external) to Pack.

Witches:

Practitioners of natural magic/white magic who follow the Three Fold law.

Wizards:

Practitioners of spells, potions, tend toward dark magic, use science and rituals.

Wraiths:

Twelve member highly skilled collection of North American Kyn who serve as the ultimate police for the Kyn and human monsters. They are not publicly acknowledged, basis of Boogieman stories for Kyn, even human not sure if they exist.

Yázhí:

Navajo equivalent of "little one".

88 Ivories:

Music/dance club in downtown Portland

CAST OF KYN

NORTHWEST KYN

Ryan Mulcahy (d.)
Former Head of Fey House,
Captain of the Wraiths,
Chief Executive Officer (CEO) of Taliesin

Natasha Bertoi
Head of Amanusa House,
Current Chief Executive Officer (CEO) of Taliesin

Warrick Vidis
Head of Lycos House,
Chief Financial Officer (CFO) of Taliesin

Cheveyo
Head of Magi House,
Chief Information Officer (CIO) of Taliesin

Carys Iver
Current Head of Fey House, Chief Legal Council for Taliesin

NORTHWEST WRAITHS

Raine McCord
Gavin Durand
Xander Cade
Jamie Ryder
Axel Kayser
Niall
Gideon
Dorian
Chayton
Fahd
Kevin Sullivan
Killian

SOUTHWEST KYN

Rio Castle
Head of Amanusa House

Tala Whiteriver
Head of Magi House

Tomás Chavez
Head of Lycos House

KYN COUNCIL SO FAR...

Leopold DiMarcco

Zayn Aimeric

Corwin Westbrooke

Malachi

Antonia

SARIELIAN ORDER SO FAR...

Darius Abazi

Arcane Transporter

***Go back to the beginning with Rory and Zev in this thrilling
urban fantasy series!***

***Meet Rory Costas, Arcane Transporter, and strap in for a
spellbinding ride through the Arcane world, where powerful
magical families make the mafia look like choirboys and
connections are everything.***

GRAVE CARGO

*When a questionable, but lucrative delivery job takes an unexpected
turn, will Rory survive the collision or crash and burn?*

RISKY GOODS

*A dead mage, a missing friend, and an unpredictable alliance merge
into a volatile package sending Rory careening through the Arcane
elite's deadly secrets.*

LETHAL CONTENTS

*A failed assassination, a kidnapped ally, and a treasonous scheme pit
Rory and Zev against a devious enemy determined to watch Arcane
society crash and burn.*

COLLSION COURSE

A last-minute Guild delivery, a cursed treasure, and a nefarious revenge scheme sets Rory on a collision course with one of Arcane's most wanted mages.

BLIND SPOT

A council contract, an obscure relic, and a lethal vendetta blindside Rory with dodgy ramifications and pitch her into a slippery tailspin.

TERMINAL DRIFT

Seething Family hostilities, a stunning classic car, and a last-minute trip to Sin City send Rory barreling towards a pivotal crossroad that will either put her in the driver's seat or hurtle her into oblivion.

About the Author

"This story is an emotional roller coaster, from betrayal, anger, fear, love..." —InD'tale Magazine

Jami Gray is the coffee addicted, music junkie, Queen Nerd of her personal Geek Squad, Alpha Mom of the Fur Minxes, who writes to soothe the voices crammed in her head. Her series combine high-stakes urban fantasy and edgy paranormal romantic suspense into books you don't want to put down. Buckle up and get ready for a wild ride through the fascinating worlds of the Arcane, the Kyn, the PSY-IV Teams, and the Collapse.

Come visit Jami's website at **https://www.jamigray.com** and stay up to date on what kind of trouble she's getting into and when you can expect to join in.

amazon.com/author/jamigray

instagram.com/jamigrayauthor

facebook.com/JamiGrayWriter

threads.com/@jamigrayauthor

goodreads.com/JamiGray

bookbub.com/authors/jami-gray

9 781948 884631